First paperback edition 2025

Anuci Press edition 2025
www.anuci-press.com

Main Cover Design by
http://elderlemondesign.net
Interior Cover Art by Kristina Osborn
Edited by Gabby Denise Mohammed
http://gceditorial.wordpress.com/about/Brenna
http://www.bookmarteneditorial.com

ISBN 979-8-9919612-7-1 (paperback)
ISBN 979-8-9919612-8-8 (eBook)

For my past self,
who thought I could never make it through my initial diagnoses.

The Exchange
&
Other Calamities

By
Mallory McCartney

The Exchange & Other Calamities Playlist

Kryptonite- Three Doors Down
Hungry Eyes- Eric Carmen
Fifty Mission Cap- Tragically Hip
One- Metallica
Style- Taylor Swift
Bodies- Drowning Pool
Dog Days are Over- Florence and the Machine
Strangers- City and Colour
Season of the Witch- Donovan
Goner- Twenty-one pilots
Hometown- Twenty-one pilots
Your Needs, My Needs- Noah Kahan
It Doesn't Matter Why- Silversun Pickups
Never Going Back Again- Fleetwood Mac

Author's Note

Dear reader,

Thank you for picking up my book; my collection of dark imaginations and fears that inspired my first horror short story collection. In public school, I watched *It* for the first time, though it wasn't until 2017 when I really sank my teeth into the horror genre and fell in love with it.

But since I was a kid who was *literally terrified* of the dark and things that go *bump* in the night, you may be thinking, *well how the hell did we get here?*

Like most turning points in life, it started with a journey.

In any other media format, this would be the moment to *cue flashback.*

It was early 2019. I was twenty-seven, I just started working in a career I loved, and I was writing part-time on the side. My loving husband and I were building the life we wanted and working on goals—professional and personal. We had three dachshunds, who we love to this day. Life was good. I remember it was New Year's Day, and I woke up not being able to breathe. We rushed to the hospital, and hours later I was diagnosed with pneumonia—not abnormal when living with chronic asthma, but shitty, nonetheless. I got antibiotics and was sent home for a week of rest.

Fast forward a couple of days. My memory now as I look back gets spots of blackout, and I don't know if it's my body's protective response to the trauma. I remember falling into bed, into blackness. Not gently falling asleep, not wanting to fall asleep at two in the afternoon, but getting dragged into a void against my will. It yawned open and closed its maws over me.

That was the beginning of my loss of control when it comes to my body and what my life looked like.

When I woke up to Matt, who had gotten home from work and found me like this, I said, "Something is really wrong."

And something was *very* wrong.

I had mono on top of the pneumonia.

Who the actual fuck gets mono at twenty-seven? That was my first thought. The second was listening to the doctor explain it would be a slow recovery, and my spleen was inflamed. I would be on bedrest.

Months passed.

Things got a lot worse.

Looking back now, going on six years later, I was naive in my hope that—through the endless appointments, seeing multiple doctors and specialists—even if my health felt complicated, I would receive answers promptly.

I didn't.

And it all started with a tick bite. I had been hiking in the summer of 2018 and remember the bite, but no tick was attached. I didn't seek medical attention; I didn't *know* that I should have.

Chronic Lyme disease, fibromyalgia, and chronic fatigue presented the monster.

I blacked out for almost a full year. I lost my long-term memory, I had paralysis in the form of bells palsy, and *every day* I lived under the constant fire of pain. Imagine your worst hangover combined with the flu. Every. Day.

My fight isn't one I look back on fondly, but I am proud that I made it through to where I am today. There were days I didn't think I would. Though my days aren't easy now, they are mine. And I have a better understanding of *how* to live with these diseases. I'm slowly taking back pieces of myself that were stolen from me. But even as I work on this collection in my edits and rewrites, allowing to channel and really face what I feel into my writing from the past six years into the genre that almost seems to go hand in hand with chronic illness, I just got slammed with news.

It's February 2024, and for the past year I have been having symptoms including heart problems, weird and intense face rashes, and swollen joints. I thought I was well acquainted with pain, but this . . . it's like barbed wire in between every joint, like being devoured from the inside out. My reality doesn't make sense to me right now. My core doctor is fantastic—which is rare, honestly—but I have to start over weaving through specialists again. Even though I was dismissed two years ago from specialists because I was "too young." What does that even mean? Disease doesn't give a damn about age. They think this festering illness inside me is an autoimmune disease, in which I got into a specialist clinic but then was told because one line on my bloodwork was negative its not anything they treat. I was then told I couldn't be helped because they didn't know what *it* is. It could be an intense symptom of fibromyalgia, or something else. And the follow ups? Nonexistent. I am now navigating advocating for myself in holistic medicine, because I don't want to ignore the weird symptoms, the flagged bloodwork; I don't want to just shrug it off and have it negatively impact my quality of life. It's been six years and I have been ripped back to square one, in a brutal fight with myself. It's a year later and I just got some answers after pushing for an MRI all of last year. I have a tear in my ACL and rotator cuff with no idea how that happened, and a whole lot of complicated tendinosis and bursitis surrounding the rips. I'm now starting a long rehab journey and trying to narrow down the cause with another specialist.

There are millions of people with similar stories to mine.

If you are reading this now and have gone through this—any medical trauma—I know nothing I can say will even begin to touch the grief and void that you are demanded to go through even though every fiber in your body screams for just a slice of normalcy. But do know that I stand with you, in strength, in remorse, in the unfairness of it all. I see you. And I don't really know right now what will happen, but in this moment, this beautifully sunny Tuesday on the cusp of spring, writing makes sense to me.

And I am furious. So be warned, this isn't a book about a young woman falling ill and getting the help and diagnosis easily. This isn't a story about how staying positive and working hard, showing up for myself in every possible way healed me. This isn't a story about how this terrible thing happened, yet it didn't become a part of me.

This is a story that was born from a terrible thing happening to me. This is a story born from the fact that I went from living a normal life, to not being able to work at all, becoming disabled from the chronic illnesses I live with. A story born from the fact I have to come to peace with chronic meaning I will never heal, I will always be symptomatic, and the best I can hope for is the symptoms to be less than the day before. This is a story born from the grief that I was failed by the medical system (like so many). This is a story born from rage, isolation, pain. This is a book that encompasses, and I hope shows, through metaphor and the written word, the reality of living chronically ill is messy, hard, life altering, grief laden, unfair, and it completely devours the life you had before.

To the friends I thought were true, that had my back and were in my life until I couldn't explain what was going on, or I couldn't go out to get drinks anymore, I *really* hope someone you know reads this; or even better, that you do.

I want invisible disabilities and chronic illness to be talked about more. The responses of:

"It's all in your head."

"You would feel better if you only lost weight."

"Have you tried yoga?"

"It can't be really that bad."

"You are so lucky you are at home all day and you don't have to work."

"If only you were more positive, you would feel better. Other people have it worse."

The list goes on. These need to be a thing of the past. Words are powerful, as well as the weight they can bear. But while we are here, I want to take a second to thank the two doctors out of six years that didn't gaslight me. They listened, and they tried to help. One figured out my chronic Lyme diagnosis even though it was really complicated and hard, but he saved my life in 2019. I couldn't see a light at that time, and he found me in the darkness and pulled me back from that edge.

So even though this is fiction, it is also my story with my truths in it. Writing has saved me in more ways than one. It helps me by allowing me to pour my experiences, reactions, feelings, loneliness and symptoms into my characters. It helps me try to make sense of what is happening. So just know the themes in this work will reflect that, in every story.

And being an artist, having my romantic notions of my life cruelly ripped away from me at twenty-seven, I found a muse I never wanted, but it's *my* muse, nonetheless.

The pain. The anger. The darkness.

I understood and felt that horror, truly for the first time in my life.

My fury was my pen, allowing me to find my voice writing horror. It allowed me to be creative in a genre I felt so connected to, because every day I was presented with a monster that has no cure. Unless you're living with a chronic illness yourself, or you are with someone who does, its hard to understand, a lot of people struggle to understand because they cannot physically see it. Not even some doctors. A monster that is my constant companion, and a companion to millions of others who live with chronic illness.

It is a pain I wish no one knew. It is debilitating and life changing in a way I wish none of us had to go through. Still six years later, some days I grieve for my past life. But on my good days, I am so proud of how strong I have had to be.

If you are reading this and are a fellow warrior, I see you. I understand.

If you are reading this and don't know much about Lyme disease, chronic illnesses, or invisible disabilities, check out the resources below. Having compassion, empathy, and understanding goes further than you will ever know. My hope is in the future there are more treatment options and understanding with invisible disabilities within the medical field and society. Without judgment, prejudice, and assumptions.

For my fellow Canadians, these are a great starting point:
https://canlyme.com/
https://fibrocanada.ca/en/
https://arthritis.ca/about-arthritis/arthritis-types-(a-z)/types/fibromyalgia

For my American friends:
https://www.fibro.org/

In this collection, there are stories that hold a lot of my anger and even dark wishes that I would do anything to not live chronically ill. Going into these stories, heed the following trigger warnings:

Graphic violence, body horror, chronic illness, cancer, death of a parent, grief, outing of a queer person, medical gaslighting.

The Exchange

A bnormal pain perception.

I tied my running shoes, my fingers swollen, the ends still tingling from waking with them completely numb.

I can only manage my symptoms. There is no cure. No cure. No. Cure. Slowly, I stood, my hips cracking loudly, the stiffness in my body feeling like I had been ripped apart in the night, haphazardly being thrown back together.

I can sleep for ten hours each night, but I feel like I haven't slept at all.

Dragging my gaze up, I look at my reflection. My skin is translucent, the spattering of freckles over my nose just accentuating the black circles under my eyes. My auburn hair frames my gaunt face, my T-shirt and shorts breathable. This is my battle armor. This is another morning fighting to do one of the most overwhelming tasks now in my life.

Physical exercise.

I frown, and say to my reflection, "Don't let the fucking fibromyalgia win."

Fibromyalgia, the disease everyone is convinced is all in your head, but has made me feel completely dead inside. If anyone took the time to learn, they would know it stems from your nervous system, creating a complete neurochemical imbalance, and pain signals are sent down to devour you from the inside out. It's debilitating. It's real.

And has left me completely isolated within my life.

I took my rage and left my apartment, stepping into the complete silence of the hallway, to make my way to the elevator and downstairs before anyone else in the building was awake.

The predawn sky glowed. I watched the edge of the horizon start to bleed into soft pinks, oranges, and purples that promised a brilliant sunrise. In late August in Sarnia, Ontario, if you wanted to look for beach glass, it was best to rise with the sun. Come midmorning, the beach was usually speckled with families on vacation, locals enjoying the summer, or tourists. Quite frankly, I wanted to avoid them all.

I walked down the street that connected to the public beach parking lot while adjusting my backpack straps and listening to the tempo of my footfalls on the sidewalk. *Left, right, left, right.* The comfortably cool breeze teased ideas of autumn, but I knew we were in for another couple months of plus thirty with high humidity days. Thankfully, at six A.M. it was twenty degrees and the perfect temperature. I pulled back my auburn hair and allowed myself a moment, sighing into the quiet. All while I repeated my daily mantra in my head:

You are here, today, in this moment.

A year ago, I couldn't walk more than ten minutes. Being diagnosed with chronic fatigue syndrome, and then later with fibromyalgia at twenty-seven, I often thought it was like being dragged into the undertow with no immediate way back to the surface while simultaneously being set on fire. Going through months of denial, losing my friends who didn't have the space to understand invisible chronic illnesses, having to stop working at my career . . . I literally had a funeral for my past life—it was ripped away so suddenly, so irrevocably harsh. I think drowning while on fire was a pretty accurate description of the sensations rampaging through my body and within my life.

After finding a sliver of peace knowing there was no way back to that life, to *that version* of Kinsley Matthews, I started to climb the mountain. I had to find a way to coexist with the monster that had decided to live with me. I had no choice other than to fight.

For me, the first step to climbing that mountain came in the form of walking. It was methodical—the steadiness of it—and searching for beach glass had at first been a challenge. I searched for those beautiful pieces of glass as if they were a lifeline when my body screamed that I couldn't do the walk, that I had to give up, or else I would collapse or throw up. Next came the pain, the sweeping kiss of it, the overwhelming consumption until I felt delirious. It sunk its claws so firmly in me that the rest of the day would pass in flickers. But each morning, I went a little farther, a little longer. I relished the sweat and each gritting step because they meant I was alive, that I was fighting. *This tyrant of a disease wouldn't take everything.*

Three hundred sixty-five days later, I welcomed the challenge rather than how I used to dread it. The flare reaction of my body slowly started to ebb too, like I was chiseling out a form of myself, cold-pressed and molded from my experiences, but still me.

Today, I crossed the empty parking lot that led to the beach, popping my earbuds in. They connected to my phone, and I pressed shuffle on my playlist.

Brad Arnold's voice from 3 Doors Down flooded my senses. As soon as my runners hit the sand and my calves ignited, I fell into a well of blissful routine. This was predictable. Cathartic. This walk was my choice, in my control, when most things about my body were not anymore. My pain rippled, wanting to cascade down on me, but I roared back at it internally. Like hell was it going to take this from me. The endlessness of the sky brushed Lake Huron, the still turquoise waters resembling a mirror. The beach was empty, and I made my way to the shore, eager to

3

find the smooth edges of the green, white, and blue beach glass hidden within the pale golden sands.

Sweat trickled down the back of my neck, making course for my spine. My skin felt tight and swollen, and a flush swept over my cheeks.

Just one more minute. I sat in the sand with the pier behind me. The gentle ripples of the lake's waves broke on the shore and lapped at the tips of my shoes. I looked at my haul today: eight pieces of bright green glass, one clear white, and one amber. I smiled as I secured the Ziploc bag before I slipped it into my leggings pocket. It was almost seven, and the heat of the day had started to roll out. By eight, I would be sipping my coffee under blissful AC in my apartment if I got moving.

As I stood, a light glinted in my vision from within the waters, so blinding I startled. Squinting, I took a step forward, trying to locate what the hell it was. The water was relatively calm, so I could see clearly down to the bottom of the white sand. A few smooth rocks pebbled the bottom of the shore, but there, at almost arm's length away, sat probably the biggest piece of beach glass I had ever seen.

It was a deep olive-green swirled with amber, about the size of my fist and decently thick. I waded into the water, not worried about my shoes. The heat had already started, and with a twenty-minute walk back, they would be dry. The sun reflected off the glass again, and I picked it up. Droplets of water ran over my skin, plunking delicately back into the lake. Warm golden light stretched across my palm, and I couldn't easily look away. I was the moth drifting toward the light, and the glass was the burning flame. A dull ringing filled my ears as my fingers flexed more tightly around the glass's round edges.

Ta, taaa, taaa, tum. The strange rhythm filled my mind, building in my ears. It created a sense of tunnel vision, and my eyes burned. I hadn't blinked since I picked up the glass. My throat felt thick and dry, my head like it had been stuffed with cotton.

Kinnnnsley.

My head snapped up at the cool voice. The beach was empty, and I made my way back to shore, the water sloshing against my movement. Who had whispered my name?

Maybe I pushed too hard. Was I overtired? Hearing things in my exhaustion? I didn't think so. Living with fibromyalgia was a constant guessing game of not overdoing any activity, whether it was mentally or physically taxing. If you did, you would find out later when you were debilitated by the pain. And that overwhelming pain could be your companion for maybe a couple hours, but it could linger for days or even weeks. It would bury you until all you knew was the pain.

I slid the glass into my pocket and scratched my right forearm at an itch building. Starting the walk home, I constantly checked over my shoulder, making sure no one followed. But the way that voice had dripped my name . . . drawling out each sound, like hooks that had sunk into my skin, that stretched and pulled. I couldn't shake the feeling I was being watched.

I walked faster, ready to get home.

The coffee percolated in the background as I tried not to go back to the table where that piece of beach glass sat. I paced my apartment. My forearm burned where an angry red rash had started at my wrist and was slowly crawling up my flesh in welts. It had only gotten worse.

Shit.

I walked back to the bathroom and tried to remember if I had any topical allergy cream. I had scratched my skin so raw, beads of ruby blood welled.

It burned.

I clicked my vanity mirror open, and quickly dug through the chaos that lay there. Prescription bottles, scrunchies, toothpaste, and floss. Nothing that could help this massive allergic reaction.

I shut the mirror with a click and froze. Fear dripped through me, starting at the crown of my head and dousing my body so completely, my mind went blank. A scream lodged firmly in my throat—I couldn't utter a sound. Fire and ice raced through my veins, churning my stomach, and bile rose in my throat.

Fingers had appeared from thin air, and they grew and morphed into inky claws. They curled over my shoulder and gripped it hard. Then, with pallid skin, the rest of the intruder appeared.

Standing right behind me was a creature born from a nightmare. Its skin was pale, loose, and had a sheen of wetness. The creature stood at least six feet tall, and I could see most of its long, skeletal arms. Stringy hair framed the face, where no mouth or eyes could be seen. Not until it raised those arms and massive black claws wrapped around my throat. It lowered its face close to my ear, and its flesh ripped to form a mouth, reminding me of carving a pumpkin—all the stringy guts hanging behind the cut you'd made until you scraped it out. The monster's breath wafted out in a rattling exhale, and the smell of rot filled my bathroom.

"Kinnnnsleeey Matthews," the cold voice hissed into my ear. Wet dribble smeared my neck, and icy fear coursed harder through my veins, paralyzing me.

"You have choseeeen . . . the exchange."

Its hold tightened; those inky claws dug into my flesh. I choked, and black dots filled the edges of my vision. My hands scrambled as I snapped out of drowning in my fear. Panic now filled me, and the will to fight encompassed every second.

The creature's grip only hardened.

My eyes rolled back. My lungs screamed for oxygen, for release. In our reflection, which I caught in blurred moments, my face was purple, my mouth hanging open in a silent scream. The creature pulled me closer. Its other arm wrapped around my waist. Where before it had no defined eye sockets, there now sat two massive orbs.

And they burned red.

I awoke in darkness, disoriented. I barely resurfaced from the pain that coursed through me in a pulse. *How is it night?* I couldn't remember anything after the bathroom. My skin burned like I had a fever. My first rational thought was that I was being dragged through sand. Far above me, stars glimmered, worlds away—the only witnesses to what was happening to me.

But who was dragging me? Panic made my breath come quick. Someone had broken into my apartment and taken me. But why? I tried to lean forward, like I was doing a crunch, to see who held me by my ankles.

Nothing happened.

My captor adjusted its grip, and all I could see were three onyx claws gripping my bare ankles.

I screamed . . . or tried to. It bubbled in my chest without release.

Everything from earlier manifested and slammed into me like I was being buried alive by my fear. It had all been real. The monstrous creature that had materialized in my apartment had *taken* me.

The only thing I could move was my eyes, and they swiveled madly, trying to spot anything, anyone that could help me.

But the beach was deserted, and the thought settled into my chest that I was probably about to die. Alone.

The steady rhythm of the waves overlapped with the sound of my body being dragged. The itch on my arm escalated to an inferno, but I couldn't see how bad it was. On my T-shirt lay that piece of beach glass, the curse that brought all *this*.

Both arms were limp above my head. I had lost control of my body completely, like I had been paralyzed by the creature's touch, its hold. I couldn't speak. It was dragging me below, and I had no choice, no control except to watch it unfold.

Tears seeped from the corners of my eyes. Panic bloomed within my chest. Whispers erupted along the shore. They were cold, inhuman. They repeated the same sentence:

"The exchange has begun."

I couldn't see them. But my thoughts fled as my left ankle hit the warm water first, then the right. As the water lapped up to my torso, then to my shoulders, I stared up, up to the stars and galaxies. Desperation to look at something beautiful coursed through me, and I tried to soak in every detail.

The creature dragged me into Lake Huron without hesitation. Water flooded my nostrils and surged down my throat. I held my breath until I couldn't, and water burned into my lungs, filling them. There was blinding pain, and then there was nothing.

Time always moves forward, but all around me, I could *feel* the past and present at once. It wasn't linear. I blinked slowly as my focus sharpened.

Swirling darkness made it hard to see the *hundreds* of creatures like the one that had appeared in my apartment, that had taken me here, to this place of confinement. They weren't identical, though. They had various shades of stringy hair, and those burning gazes were all different hues of flames. They stood silent, their bodies angled toward me. The memory of being dragged into the depths of Lake Huron lingered in me, a ghost of an impression. But where were we now?

"Kinsley Matthews. You have found the ancient relic of the exchange tithe."

The creature who took me floated slowly into view. It glided through the dancing shadows, its long arms almost touching the floor, and those inky claws glinted.

"Now, this ritual you have a choice in. We can rid you of your illnesses. Of your pain that is your constant companion. We can give this all to you, your deepest desire. Your most desperate wish."

My heart pounded. "What's the catch?"

"When your mortal life has come to pass, you must meet us again. You must fulfill the exchange and become like us."

Was this real? Or a twisted manifestation as my soul found peace in the afterlife? I had drowned. Dragged helplessly into the lake.

And yet . . . here I was, suspended within the depths of Lake Huron. How many times had I wished to not live with fibromyalgia? To not feel like I had the flu every fucking day of my life? To have my career back? Now these creatures promised they could give me my old life again if I accepted their offer.

How many times since my diagnoses had I yearned with every fiber of my body to be free from fibromyalgia? An incurable chronic illness that many doctors still didn't believe was real. They couldn't begin to understand how debilitating it was. I wanted to live a normal twenty-seven-year-old life. I wanted to be able to drive, to not count how many activities I could do in a day. To not be bedridden or constantly go to doctor appointments. I didn't want to be incapacitated from my pain that bore down in shivering, relentless waves anymore. Pain that made me feel like my bones were rotting. That made me feel like I had been set on fire and no one could put it out. To sleep and wake up feeling like I hadn't slept at all. I didn't want to be trapped within my own fucking body.

I raised my gaze to meet those glowing red orbs. I realized in that moment how ironic it was that they drowned me. I'd been drowning for a year within my illnesses. I had accidentally found a cursed relic that would free me, and the answer bubbled on my lips before I could think. I knew what I wanted.

"Yes."

Howling filled the space that erupted from the hundreds of creatures that looked at me. I watched a gaping mouth stretch open, pieces of flesh ripping and hanging as the creature before me smiled. Black claws held the piece of beach glass I had found, and dropped it to the ground.

The creature lunged.

It was upon me now, and its black claws tore open my throat first. My vision was washed in red. I choked, tasting hot metallic blood gushing down my throat. Pain blinded me, became me. Those claws tore and gouged my body, ripping my forearms open, my chest, my stomach. Screaming surrounded every inch of space, and the warmth of my blood pooled around me.

I relented.

The last thing I saw was burning green orbs blinking open as another creature floated above me.

It grinned; no teeth showed, just an endless void of darkness within its yawning mouth. The grin split wider, showing how the shadows went on, and on. I felt like I was being sucked into it, with no way out.

I startled awake in my bed, drenched in cold sweat. My arms flew to my face, my neck, my body. I was physically here, in my apartment.

I was okay. I was *alive.*

How? Had it all been a nightmare? A hallucination? Had I blacked out?

I shook as I flung my comforter back and got out of bed. Standing, I paused. There was no stiffness, no pain. No brain fog, no exhaustion. No anything. I lifted my gaze to my body-length mirror, taking in my shaking body and the angry red scar on my pale arm, right where the rash had been.

My eyes widened in fear, in astonishment.

I ran to the living room, my breath jagged.

The beach glass piece was nowhere to be found.

Three Months Later

I finished applying my eyeliner before assessing myself in the bathroom mirror. I had pulled my hair into a high bun, and light mascara made my green eyes stand out. With black pants, a collared shirt, and my blazer, I felt more put together than I had in years.

Don't look up. The creature is not there.

Focusing on my mismatched socks, I breathed deeply.

You are going to leave the apartment, go to the interview, and ignore it.

As I dragged my eyes back up, primal fear coiled in my stomach. I couldn't stop my gaze from drifting behind me where deep emerald orb-like eyes burned in a cold fury as they stared right back at me.

You are not losing your mind.

But I wasn't so sure anymore. It had been a whirlwind couple of months since that night.

Each morning, I woke up waiting for that nauseating feeling to take over me. To be so stiff, I couldn't put my pants or socks on. To feel that bone-deep pain rip through me, making me feel like I had digested poison and was slowly rotting away. To have a headache every morning, to be so exhausted that sleep was pointless because it was unrefreshing. But each day that passed, none of my symptoms returned. In fact, I felt great. To test the legitimacy of what I thought had happened, I had started to wean off my medication the day after the exchange. After the withdrawal symptoms of the gabapentin and duloxetine subsided in a few weeks, it felt like I had been pulled up from deep underwater. I could breathe and see the world around me clearly.

A couple weeks after that, the hallucinations began. It was the same creature that had grinned down at me as I bled out, ripped apart and dying. Those fury-filled, green orb-like eyes and knurled inky claws would show up unexpectedly—to stare back at me in a reflection or to graze my hand as I fell asleep.

"No," I snarled back at that creature, flickering half formed behind me. "Leave me alone."

I turned to stalk out of the bathroom, turning down the hallway, only to freeze in my tracks. There, standing at the end, cast in the soft morning light, was the monster, towering so tall it almost touched the ceiling. The glistening sheen of lake water clutched to its pale skin, which hung off its skeletal frame. No muscle mass to keep it in place. I was facing off with it in my home, fear making my heart pound with adrenaline. I couldn't move or make a sound.

Slap. Its foot wetly sounded as it took one step toward me. Automatically, I flinched back.

Slap. Slowly, it raised its long arm, its onyx claw unfurling to motion *come here.*

Slap. Slap. SLAP.

My back rammed into the wall, the creature sprinting down the hallway unexpectedly, and—fucking hell, were those bloody footprints left in its wake?

Along its torso, the sheen I had thought to be water changed before my eyes; thick ruby blood now ran down its shoulders, its stomach, its head. Before I could process what I was seeing, the creature was face to face with me, its claws wrapping around my neck.

My air was cut off. I sputtered as the creature squeezed tightly, choking me. I kicked my legs, trying to push this nightmare off me. My arms flailed uselessly, as if my mind and body weren't one anymore. Rot and the acrid smell of blood filled my senses, tears springing to my gaze. I couldn't make a sound, couldn't scream, or fight back. All I could do was watch as the monster tilted its head before a squelch interrupted the silence of my apartment, the flesh ripping to form that mouth like the other one did.

It leaned in closer, thick saliva dribbling down its chin.

Panic made my vision tilt, darkness bleeding along the edges swiftly.

The burning green orbs seemingly grew bigger until they were all I could see.

Warm saliva hit my neck, and tears streaked down my cheeks now, as the monster squeezed tighter.

And tighter.

The pain I felt was hot, a flame licking over my neck, traveling down to my shoulders.

It was going to kill me. My lungs strained for oxygen—to take one breath, to be free—

Then I dropped.

Gasping for air, I landed on the floor on my hands and knees. Sweet, blissful oxygen rushed through me. My hands reached for my throat, tears dripping off my chin. I watched them land on the floor. I was too scared to move, to see if that monster still towered over me. I leaned into my pain, allowing it to ground me for one second.

Dragging my gaze, I looked up. The hallway was empty. Relief washed through me, and I deflated, dropping my forehead to the ground, one raging thought coursing through me.

How the hell could a hallucination hurt me?

Sitting up in the middle of the floor, I wiped my cheeks, trembling. This creature was no hallucination, and it just showed me that even if my body was free from debilitating pain, it had no problem inflicting that pain on me.

I took the steps to the funeral home two at a time, perspiration dripping down my spine.

It was mid-September, and the heat of the summer still hadn't let go. I was running at least twenty minutes late thanks to the events of that morning, sweat pouring off me from stress and nerves.

Cool air conditioning washed over me as I pulled the door open, and a woman greeted me with a kind smile. "Hello, welcome to McConnell's Funeral Home. How can I help you today?"

"I'm so sorry I'm late, but I'm Kinsley Matthews. I have an interview at ten today."

The woman looked down at her schedule before saying, "One moment, please have a seat."

My stomach filled with dread as I did exactly that, focusing on slowing my thundering heart rate. I could do this. I wanted to eventually get my funeral director schooling, but the ad was for front desk reception, and a foot in the door would be perfect. I wiped my clammy hands on my pants, taking in the front lobby. Plush navy carpeted the floor, and it smelled like lemon cleaner with an almost musk-like scent. Massive bay windows took up one wall, and a beautiful stained-glass piece of a cardinal nestled among birch trees hung in the center. Light filtered in through the art, bleeding red light stretching toward my shoes.

My breath hitched and I couldn't move, couldn't think, as the light started to thicken—blood now coating my boot.

"Miss Matthews?" The receptionist's voice snapped me out of the vision, and I tried to smile which felt more like a grimace. "If you would please follow me, Mr. McConnell will see you now."

I swallowed the bile that rose in my throat and followed her. She led me down an adjacent hallway with beautiful framed art pieces on each wall. The first couple were abstract, bold splashes of gold and silver swirled to my right.

You are not losing your mind.

But even with my inner chiding, I didn't believe myself. First was what happened this morning, and now? What if the exchange was these . . . monsters taking away my conditions but tormenting me for doing so? For having control when I wasn't meant to? The thought rooted through me.

Or maybe you are having a great month pain wise, and it was all a fucked-up dream?

With each statement, my consciousness was trying to convince me I was in denial. I knew what happened was true for the simple fact that I knew my body. A good day wasn't completely pain free. The pain was just dulled, like a tide pulling back. It never left and would always return. But this? A complete rejuvenation—no symptoms, no pain.

That piece of beach glass had summoned those monsters, had pulled me into an impossible situation. So, was it out of the question that now the possible repercussions of my freedom were being attached to those creatures until I became one?

"Miss Matthews?"

"Sorry, uh, can you repeat the question?"

Her brows furrowed, and I could tell that if she hadn't been judging me for running late, she was now.

"Just asked how your day was going," she repeated in a clipped tone. Yup, we got off on the wrong foot.

"It's been . . ." I started, wetting my lips as my mouth ran dry. I tried to usher the word *good*. A normal response for an everyday interaction.

Something moved to my left. My steps faltered, and my response faded. It was the middle of the day, but in the hallway, the shadows deepened. On the wall in front of me, the painting was of a man wearing a collared shirt and a serious expression. His gaunt cheekbones made his eyes look more sunken. The bland yellow background with nothing in it drew the viewer in, but cast a greenish hue to the whole picture. He looked sick. The whole painting did.

My bottom lip trembled and I bit it so hard, the metallic taste of blood filled my mouth.

Stepping closer to the painting, I watched as blood—real blood—poured from this man's eyes, words appearing to write themselves along his chest:

You are mine now.

I gulped without getting oxygen. Stumbling back, I tripped, landing hard on my tailbone, sharp pain shooting up my spine. Clamping my hand over my mouth, I screamed. The blood wouldn't stop, and I couldn't stop reading those words:

You.

Are.

Mine.

Now.

I had to get out of there. I couldn't breathe, and the blood was now everywhere. It dripped down the gold frame, running down the wall in thick torrents. It pooled, oozing over the carpet, trailing toward my feet. Looking at it, reflecting up at me, was an unrecognizable mass.

I felt the plush carpet underneath me, but the receptionist whose name I didn't even know was gone. The walls were closing in, I couldn't stop staring at the blood. Squinting, I tried to make out what was reflected in front of me. A curve of a head? A face. But there was no mouth, no nose.

Eyelids moved as familiar burning emerald eyes glared up at me.

Pushing hard with my boots, I staggered up. The once musky and clean lemon-scented air turned into pungent decay. Choking, with tears streaming down my cheeks, I internally screamed at myself to run. Screw the interview, I just had to make it out of here alive.

The pressure of a hand squeezed my arm. *Thank God.* Relief split me open, and I looked up, trying to find the words to explain to the nice receptionist that I was having a panic attack and needed help to go. Now.

Her head hung at a ninety-degree angle, her once-kind face deflated like a fucking balloon.

"Oh my God." Fear rooted me again for the second time in a few hours, immobilizing me.

The rest of her body held no muscle mass either, her skin resembling melted wax. Where her mouth had once been, there was nothing more than dozens upon dozens of skin folds with a pale pink stain where her lips were stretched and distorted.

Something moved inside her mouth.

My back slammed against the opposite hallway wall, pain flooding the back of my head. The receptionist tried to shuffle toward me but fell onto the carpet. I watched, horrified and rooted in my panic, as her blobs of flesh tried to find purchase. Slowly, she dragged herself forward. Her empty, unblinking gaze stared up at me, her head still resting at that unnatural angle.

Run.

I internally screamed at my body to listen to the three-letter command that seared through my mind, pounded through my heart, charged through my very fucking soul. But I was locked, completely disjointed, had seemingly lost control.

I was left to watch. Tears streamed down my face as a gurgling sound cleaved through the silence and her mouth opened, looking like a gaping, fleshy hole. The moving around her lips intensified, and I squinted.

Hundreds of white worm-looking creatures shot onto the carpet. I screamed, the sound guttural. Before I could react, they shot forward, stretching into the length of yard sticks. Slithering, they moved so fast, I could barely see them before they were all over me, wrapping around my pant legs, arms, and neck. They wrenched my arms open wide, holding them flush against the wall. Two rose to meet me at eye level, like two cobras assessing their prey before striking.

Their heads were pointed with long translucent needles protruding from them. In a wild frenzy, I thrashed, trying to kick those sickening things, to claw, to break free, but their strength was unnatural. Their roping bodies squeezed more tightly. My lip trembled, wet with tears running into my mouth as my screams climbed. Someone else had to be here— where was Mr. McConnell?

My thin hope quickly fell into hopelessness as the writhing masses of the worms held my body firm, and my gaze repeatedly fell to the receptionist. Holes riddled her . . . body. But there were no bones, nothing but folds of her skin. These things had been in her, biding their time. Did they waste her away from the outside in, slowly over time? Was it some kind of parasite that held the appearance of the person being able to function normally while inside?

While inside, this woman had been destroyed. To nothing, and no one knew.

My heart cracked; I mourned for this stranger. A cage that was not recognizable or easily understood was still a cage. How long had she been in pain? How long was her body not her own?

Pain bloomed over my forearms, hot and intense. I wrenched my focus back. The two worms that had been previously facing me had embedded their needle noses deep into each ditch of my arms, eagerly sucking my blood. Rivulets leaked from their alabaster mouths as I watched them take too much at a time. The overflow dripped down my skin, staining it in threads of scarlet.

Voices exploded within my mind.

"We will try you on antidepressants first, and see if it helps the symptoms you are describing."

"Fibromyalgia is all in your head and isn't a real disorder, so maybe you are just trying to get attention?"

"If you lost weight and controlled your diet, you wouldn't be in this position."

"You're just tired and lazy. Try getting off the couch."

"How long have you been in pain? All your blood tests came back normal. There is nothing wrong from what I can see."

There.

My eyes fluttered, my body slick with freezing cold sweat, and my stomach bucking with nausea. When had I slid down the wall? I sat on the floor, my vision swimming as I watched the worms burrow deeper into my veins, making their bodies bulge from underneath my skin. I couldn't see their heads anymore.

Is.

The pain was sudden and deep. It started along my top gums, radiating to each tooth before it began to have a pulse of its own, flaring along the gums.

Da-dum. Da-dum. Da-dum. Fuck, the sensation pulled me away from the draining sucking of these worms. Away from the fact that they were currently burrowing into me, and not just the two now. Hundreds followed them. I could feel them rip into my skin. I felt every searing pinch as their mouths found different veins. I no longer had a sense of gravity, and the hallway spun violently. The walls were nothing more than masses of neutral browns, the worms were streaks of white amid the earthy tones. Bile burned up my esophagus. Tears flooded my eyes as I fell freely in this new agony. Pain was familiar to me, almost as routine as the sun rising and setting. I knew pain.

The next wave cleaved through me, holding me hyperaware of its presence, a level of suffering I had never been acquainted with. My nerve endings were fire, and my blood was acid in my veins. It was overwhelming, ripping me apart.

Just pass out. Please, let me just pass out. I didn't know who I silently begged, but my strength surprised even me as I stayed conscious.

Nothing.

The pain had evolved into drumming now. Each deep resonating note exploded up to my temples only to shoot down my neck into my spinal cord. I panted, my breaths uneven. Reaching up to my right incisor, my trembling fingers tried to grip it.

Wrong.

When I touched my tooth, excruciating pain exploded within it. Bile spurted out of my mouth, dribbling down my chin. Even within the pain and through my fear, I found purchase. The bile coating my fingers was hot on my skin, with acid and rot being all I could smell now. A low moan escaped me as I wiggled my tooth.

From what I can see.

Frantically, my fingers moved from tooth to tooth. My front teeth, the rest of my incisors, my molars. Every single one of them was loose.

Pop.

The metallic taste of blood filled my mouth as I stared in horror at the tooth resting in my palm.

Pop.

Another followed.

I choked, my own blood pouring down my throat, dripping off my lips. There was so much of it. I felt the strange popping sensation as every single one of my teeth fell out. They scattered onto the carpet, bouncing off my palms. How were there so many of them? I sobbed again as red dots flowed into my vision, blotting out my already blurry surroundings.

I had turned into a world of blood and splitting agony.

"Please . . . make . . . it . . . stop," I spit out, pleading to the desolate hallway. No one could hear me. I was utterly alone.

I felt them as the last of my vision faded into darkness. Their cold, slimy bodies slithered under my clothes, up my torso, on my collarbones to my neck.

"Please . . ." I sobbed, begging for my body to run, to snap out of the completely frozen state I was in. Begging for these things to leave me alone.

Above all, wishing I had never come here today for this interview.

They tasted like decay as they trailed over my wobbling lips. I could do nothing but feel them slink into my mouth, reaching hungrily for my blood, my gaping wounds left by each tooth.

I felt thirty-two mouths latch on to my gums before long bodies shot up into my skin, stretching into my maxillary sinuses.

Fire exploded within my face. My vision still clouded. I felt them all

21

dive deeper into my body.

They were draining me. Becoming me. Until I was nothing but a husk.

The touch was light on my skin, but I flinched back as someone tilted my chin up.

"W—o . . . o . . ." My words were slurred and incoherent. I tried to spit out *who the fuck is there*, but blood just dribbled more over the wiggling bodies of the worms that draped out of my mouth and what was left of my body.

A thumb ran over the bottom of my chin, almost in an intimate caress, before a voice rasped, "Did you think you would be free? That we would rid you of the one thing that drew us to you? There was so much pain in you before, now there is more. Ever since you found my relic, you have been mine, and will continue to be so. For all your days, until you are this."

My vision flooded back in sharp focus. It was the same demon from the lake, the one I saw as I was being ripped apart in their space that defied time and reality. Its burning emerald eyes. Its saggy, wet gray skin and fleshy, ripped mouth. A pocket of nightmares, born from the desperate wishes of people, like me. People who were pushed to their breaking point.

I saw my mistake just as the walls in the hallway dissolved into flakes of color.

There was never a shot of freedom within my grasp.

I drew my gaze up to those eyes that haunted my every step, my every movement. The face of torment, that had untethered my sense of what was real.

I was not free of pain. I would have absolutely no control over this life. I could not fight these monsters . . . I could not fight myself.

The funeral home dissolved like sugar in water to reveal the hallway of my apartment. It hit me like a brick wall. I had never left, never had an interview. Never had a new beginning in which I thought I could make a difference in my job and community. I had wanted to provide a space for people to honor their grief, to feel safe. For me to help during the worst times life could offer.

I dragged my gaze up. The creature leaned down.

Behind the fleshy strands of its lips, I could see the mass of worms churning like a nest of snakes. It grinned wider, allowing me to see just how many there were, and the ones that were burrowed into me slithered deeper.

It reached out to me, gently turning my shoulders with its spindly fingers to prod me down the hallway. I walked, flinching as deep pain resonated through my entire body. Its fingers curled around my shoulder again to stop me in the doorway of the bathroom to stare at our reflections. I watched as it leaned down to my ear, almost not registering the words from the shock at seeing my distorted and bloodied face, my shredded clothes, and the hundreds of ends of the worms dangling off me.

"Every time you think you are free, I will be there to remind you how wrong you are. Until the day this body, your sense of self, is a distant memory. Until all that is left is your hunger to destroy."

Fifty Years Later

Addison Jones stared at her friends, their faces washed in the warm glow from their bonfire. It was past midnight, and they passed the bottle of wine around the circle. Embers crackled and popped, sparks drifting lazily toward the night sky. Addison watched the rolling waves of Lake Huron crash on the shore behind them; the moon's silver touch highlighted each wave. It was beautiful. It was home.

Addison drank deeply when the bottle came to her. The bitter red wine wasn't great, but it was all they could sneak out of her mom's place. Tomorrow was the first day of their young adult lives. College. After tomorrow, nothing would be the same.

"Hey, did you guys hear about that woman who went missing recently?" Cameron slurred, and Addison rolled her eyes.

"Cam, Sarnia is a small town. Everyone knows about Kinsley Matthews," Addison said.

"My mom told me she was . . . unstable," Luca piped in.

That caught her attention. "What do you mean?"

"My mom was her PSW. She was elderly, but before she went missing, my mom said she was talking about these monsters."

The group went quiet, and Luca went on.

"My mom told me Kinsley said that years ago, she made a deal. That she was sick, and these monsters took her. That now they were back to hurt her. That she had to pay some kind of debt."

"Luca, stop trying to freak us out." Addison laughed but a shiver ran down her spine.

"No, seriously. My mom also heard from her coworkers that the last known place Kinsley was seen was here. On the shores of Lake Huron. In the middle of the fucking night."

A quiet hush blanketed them.

"Luca, you are such a dick," Cameron snapped. Nervous giggles ran through Addison's two other friends, Mia and Claire. But Addison was silent.

She wouldn't tell her friends this, but the Kinsley Matthews case scared her. She was an aspiring horror writer, and she knew Cam and Luca would laugh, joking that this was inspirational gold for a story. But who disappears without a trace at seventy-seven? Who whispers about monsters stalking them to their personal support worker?

Why had she been down here along these shores right before she went missing?

Addison tried to focus on her friends, who talked amiably now, having moved away from the topic of Kinsley Matthews. But Addison hadn't known that Kinsley had been down on the beach, and that fact burrowed deep within her. It cast a fascination, and she looked up and down the beach. Maybe the police had missed something.

"Oh, guys, I forgot to show you this amazing piece of beach glass I found earlier," Mia said, and Addison looked to her friend.

That's when she heard whispers. Strange, cold voices drifted on the light summer breeze, but Addison couldn't quite make the words out.

"Do you guys hear that?" She realized she was whispering, her heart pounding against her ribs.

"Addi, stop," Claire said. "We know you *love* horror, but I'm not interested—"

"No. I'm serious." Addison stood, her Converse sneakers sinking into the sand.

She took a step toward the shore, and her friends' voices bled into the background. There, on top of the water, floated a tall figure. Fear laced through Addison, and every second became hyperfocused in her adrenaline. The figure glided toward her, unnaturally fast. In the silver light from the moon, Addison picked out strings of auburn hair, wet and straggly from the creature's scalp. It had no distinguishing features, no mouth or ears or nose. Just burning emerald orbs where eyes should be.

The whispers built as Addison screamed. She tried to turn to run, to warn her friends. But, impossibly, the creature towered in front of her now. A singular black claw trailed down Addison's cheek. Frozen in fear, she couldn't seem to make her limbs work. She just stared at the horrific creature born from a nightmare.

Kinsley

I stared down at the young woman who was frozen in fear before me, totally unaware of the battle raging within me. Trailing my blackened claw down her cheek, internally I roared at my body to stop. I didn't want this—I didn't want to *hurt her.* Nothing but rage pulsed through my new body. My new existence.

After the exchange, my entire life was controlled, possessed, and worn down by these parasitic creatures. The things had twisted my days, with hallucinations tormenting me. It was never wrong for me to wish, driven by the desperate attempt to hold onto what my life had been before chronic illnesses. But what I hadn't realized at the time was that it was an impossible wish. Even fibromyalgia went beyond this horrible power I had unleashed, a curse buried deep within Lake Huron that had just been *waiting for a person desperate enough.* It was nothing that they could ever rid me of, but instead I fell victim to the possibility of it.

And that simple fact was that was pure human instinct. I hadn't wanted to be in pain every single day for the rest of my life. I hadn't wanted to navigate my white blood cell count going up to a mono-level infection for absolutely no reason, or allergic reactions that no one could explain why it was happening. I hadn't wanted to feel with every movement like shrapnel was embedded between every single joint in my body. And my days? An endless Groundhog Day, waking up feeling like I hadn't slept since I first fell ill, trying to go through the once simple daily tasks but instead each felt like climbing a mountain, only to fall back asleep for most of the day. In a matter of months, I had become unemployable, had to leave my career, go on disability, which took six months of approval and that was working with a disability lawyer to convince the government I wasn't *working the system,* as people love to say. Six months without income for food, for *anything.*

I went from making a $50,000 salary a year to $14,000 a year when I did get approved.

I went from having friends, to not having any.

I went from enjoying my life, to having to dissociate *so hard* that I didn't really feel my emotions. I didn't want this as my reality, so it was easier to shove the pain in a mental box and pretend it wasn't. I went from not seeing the doctor basically at all, to seeing mine every two weeks.

But it's just fibromyalgia, right? It's just all in people's heads, right? It's a made-up illness, right?

So yeah, I was fucking mad.

But the question that haunted me ever since I said *yes* was: what would anyone else have done in my situation?

I think they might have been tempted to say yes to the exchange as well.

But I never deserved this.

Screams pitched through the night, and in this body, everything that had once been dark, swirled with brilliant clarity and undefined colors. The stars that once twinkled with silver light, or the waxing yellow of the moon, now pulsed with life, and I could see so much more. Purple, pink, and blue mist seemed to move through the galaxies, the stars an indescribable gold. All of these colors moved together, ribboning, blazing as the Northern lights would. The night moved all around me, sparkled with unearthly dust and particles, and for a moment, the scene before me of my now sisters tearing the teenagers apart limb from limb, blood spurting across the sands in gushing splatters, splintered me.

Join themmm. A familiar voice crooned in my mind. It had occupied my dreams and every waking moment, twisting my reality into a dark and horrid place. The voice that belonged to this version of me.

"No," I snarled. It came out low and raspy. Inhuman.

The girl who stood still frozen in her fear, flinched.

For every second in this body, I could feel the familiar pull of my sense of self starting to ebb again. If I was going down, if these fucking monsters had found me because of my pain, my illness, my desperate, darkest wish, then it would be my strength and rage built by being chronically ill that would be their end. These things didn't know how deep down you had to reach within yourself to find the will and strength to make it through a day. To be in a war with yourself.

But I did.

These things preyed on people like me, but no more after tonight.

I could do this one last thing. Gritting my teeth, I internally had my cognitive clarity of Kinsley in a choke hold. I locked eyes with the teen in front of me and growled, "Run."

"Wh-what?"

"Get out of here. Run!"

Finally, it seemed to register with this stranger what was happening. I watched as she sprung into action, fleeing into the night.

The coppery scent of blood rushed through me, but I was already sprinting. In this body, the strength, the sheer space of me, sent a shot of ice down my spine. It sang through every push and pull of the strong sinewy muscle. I was built to destroy.

One of the monsters had another young girl by the head, her hands pushing down on her shoulders trying to decapitate her.

I slammed into the creature that held the teen. Moving with my thoughts, so fluid and lethal, my clawed hand punched into the chest cavity, and ripped out the monster's beating heart.

There was so much blood, it filled every crevice of me.

It smells goooood.

"NO!" I roared now, completely eviscerating the monster. I was claws shredding flesh, I was ripping, destroying, killing. I was unstoppable.

What was left of it was crumpled in a heaping bloody pulp of flesh and bone in front of the blood-spattered teen.

A dark stain flooded her jean shorts as she soiled herself, eyes wide, looking up at me.

"Run!" I bellowed, my voice cracking. Hissing filled the air, as behind me the creatures realized what was happening. What I had done.

The very thing they never imagined I could be capable of.

They charged me, but I had never been more ready for anything in my entire life.

I moved lithely, screaming behind every devastating swipe I landed, every parry and blow. "You took advantage of what I was going through!"

The end of my claws shredded through the one creature's abdomen, deep enough that I ripped out the intensities, which landed on the sand with a squelching thud.

"You knew I would never say no," I spat as I slashed another's throat, burning red eyes holding nothing but hate as I ripped out its jugular.

"Maybe with time I would have found a way. Any way that would have made the days bearable."

I looked at the last one as I said this. This terrible, wretched thing that was drawn to my pain, my desperation, just so I could fulfill this role. To lose the one thing I had always been scared to lose to my chronic illnesses. My life.

It charged.

"I will never know if I would have made peace living with my monster," I said to myself, watching my end run straight toward me, regret twisting in my stomach.

It was so close, its fleshy mouth appearing, in a too long oval of a scream as it bellowed.

I braced myself.

Pain. Four words I wouldn't have guessed in my life that I would know the sensation of so intimately.

The other creatures' hands had punched through the right side of my abdomen, ripping at my spleen and liver, but I wasted no time, landing my own blow.

I went straight for its heart.

The pain unfurled everywhere within my body. I don't know if it was because the blow was fatal, but it felt strangely warm. Like laying in the sun. Comforting, almost.

I dropped to my knees beside the body of the monster, but I refused to have my last moments, the *true* last moments looking at it.

Instead, I tilted my chin to the skies, looking up.

"It's so . . ." The unfinished sentence came out in a sigh, only to fade within the sound of the gentle waves rolling onto the sands.

Below Lakeshore Lane

Graduation

I stood with my hand lingering on top of my desk. My notebooks were stacked neatly, waiting for me to grab them and go. Mr. Agan wiped the blackboard clean as chaos erupted in the hallways. The happy chatter of my fellow senior class wafted through the doorway. We had all made it, me included.

The last day of grade 12.

Creative writing was my last exam, which seemed fitting. My most loved class where my happiest moments of the year had been. Exploring the craft and discovering what kind of stories I wanted to tell were the highlights of my senior year.

I was ready to delve into what magic perhaps lay within me, within my voice. What tales I would share and create.

"Darbie? Did you have a question?" Mr. Agan asked.

"Sorry, Mr. Agan, no. I just wanted to say thanks again for writing me the recommendation letter. I just needed the rest of my things."

"Well, have a wonderful summer. And good luck with Sheridan in the fall."

Smiling my thanks, I scooped up my belongings. I sent a silent goodbye to the room before I walked out to be mindlessly swept into the current of students that flooded the hallways.

Why did new beginnings always feel this bittersweet? I had been so excited to be done with senior year, to have my future waiting for me. College in Mississauga started in the fall, and I would be doing a four-year creative writing and publishing diploma, for shit's sake. It was my *dream*. What awaited me beyond this building was summer with my best friends.

So why was I dragging my feet? Why didn't I want to rush when that was all I wanted earlier?

"Daaaaaaaaaaarbie!" A flash of blond hair was all I saw before Jake slung his arm around my shoulders, giving them a gentle squeeze. "Look, I know with life milestones you tend to get a bit introspective."

"I do not."

"Liar." He smirked. "I've known you since we were five. You can't hide what is so painstakingly obvious to me, Darbie."

"Fine. I may have been wallowing a little."

"That's my girl!"

Playfully, I smacked his arm. Jake was my best friend and his warm, upbeat presence had loosened the knot forming in my chest.

"So, what's the plan then?" I asked as we walked the hallway together, his arm still over my shoulder.

"Okay. After we get the rest of stuff out of your locker, our ride is conveniently waiting outside. Courtesy of my organizational skills and Luke."

"Awesome. And then?"

"What else? Pizza and movies until . . ." Jake trailed off and my stomach dropped. I pulled myself out of his one-armed hug, continuing my stride now with some distance between us.

"No. *No way.*"

"Come on, Darb! You know it's senior class tradition. Everyone's going."

"That's a terrible reason to do something, Jake." I felt like I had swallowed something sour. "You know I don't even drink. So, say I do go and get offered a drink, I would decline. Then people would pry instead of just leaving it alone even though it's no one's business but mine, and that would shoot my anxiety off the deep end."

My cheeks flushed. I looked up at Jake, who was grinning from ear to ear.

"Why are you smiling at me like that?"

"Because one, if anyone does that, I promise to leave with you. Secondly, I was thinking it wouldn't be so bad if we went together."

I stumbled. My face was now flaming red, heat radiating off it so potently.

"Like a date?" My voice sounded strange even to me. I had known since last year that my feelings toward Jake had changed to something more. I hadn't wanted to tell him and risk losing this. Which, even as I thought that, I knew it was ridiculous. Jake was the most understanding person I knew.

"I was hoping it could be a date. Luke even promised me if you said yes, he wouldn't badger us too much—well, only to get your most recent recommendation about what horror books you have been devouring of late." He peeked out of the corner of his eye at me. "Well, Darb? What do you say? Will you grant me the honor of fulfilling this senior class tradition with me?"

My previous argument seemed far away as I looked into Jake's cerulean-blue eyes. My gaze drifted along his square jaw and up to his lips. Heat flooded my cheeks more deeply. The words left me before I could give them a second thought.

"I would love to."

Jake raised his eyebrows as I took three pieces of Hawaiian pizza and put them on my plate.

"Have you ever tried pineapple on your pizza?"

"What, and go against every instinct I have?" Jake's hand flew to his chest, feigning offense.

I giggled. "You are so dramatic. Plus, without trying it, your opinion can't be fully formed, can it?"

"Aren't you the Watson to my Sherlock." His eyes twinkled, and I fell into the ease of it all. The Wardon's house was my second home. We had spent endless evenings here, watching movies, playing board games. The living room had deep-maroon walls adorned with family photos. Two couches framed the TV, and my favorite wall was lined with six bookcases teeming with novels. Jake's dad loved the epic and high fantasy genres, but Mrs. Wardon had several shelves filled with horror books ranging from all of Stephen King's works to indie titles.

I snuggled onto the couch, my plate in hand. Jake flopped down beside me as I took a massive bite of my pizza.

"Okay, so it's between *Carrie* and . . ." Jake trailed, smirking at me.

"*Pet Sematary*. We haven't rewatched those yet this year."

"Right. So tonight it's lady's choice, and we should be able to get through most of it before it's time to leave."

I grinned. "*Carrie* it is."

Luke walked back into the living room to grab his pizza. He pointed at me. "What do I need to be reading this month?"

I finger gunned back at him. "Try *Misery* this month."

"Thanks, boss." He went to the first bookshelf and found his mom's weathered copy before he disappeared.

"Luke would kill me if he knew I told you this, but he thinks you're wicked. And have very good taste in books."

"So do your parents. Also, why wouldn't he want me to know he is capable of complimenting another human?"

"It would tarnish his badass reputation—being the older brother and all."

I snorted and continued to eat my dinner. Jake followed suit and we ate in comfortable silence.

"Where are your folks tonight anyway?" I asked in between bites.

"They're visiting my aunt—she has that cottage up in the Kawartha Lakes. They're gone for the week."

"Nice."

Jake smiled, leaning forward to grab the remote and turn the TV on. The 1976 *Carrie* was already queued up.

"How did you know—"

"I know you, Barlowe."

I grabbed more pizza, and leaned into Jake's warmth. His hand tentatively brushed along the top of mine. The movie and room fell away at his touch.

I tied the laces of my red Converse sneakers as Jake practically bounced beside me. The credits rolled in the background, and I stood. "Okay, I'm ready. What did you think of the rewatch?"

"Sissy Spacek is a fucking legend," Jake said. "Every time I see *Carrie*, I can't imagine another actress playing that role."

"Right? Even with the remakes, in my mind the 1976 version is the closest one to the book. I love it just as much as the first time I saw it."

We stepped out into the early summer evening. Haden was twenty minutes away from Sarnia, and so far, this summer seemed to promise beautiful, non-humid temperatures. Being close to Lake Huron had massive perks, and the lake would often push the more inclement weather inland.

Lakeshore Lane was just the next block over, so maybe a fifteen-minute walk. Jake grabbed my hand effortlessly, and I smiled as heat flooded my stomach. Maple trees lined the street, the towering branches and full leaves loomed over us. Lush shrubs bordered neighboring houses and manicured lawns.

"You're quiet tonight." Jake nudged me lightly. "You know everything is going to be okay, right?"

"I do. You were right about this. I don't want to miss out on moments that could be some of the most memorable nights of my life."

The amber blinks of fireflies winked in and out from the manicured bushes of Jake's neighbors. Haden was a small town, where mostly everyone knew one another. It had been a wonderful place to grow up, but on the edge of adulthood it started to feel a lot more like a cage. I yearned for the endlessness of being close to Toronto come fall. The promise of culture and new experiences basically had me salivating. How could I be a writer without experiencing *life*? I was prepared to fight against my anxiety and panic disorder tooth and nail to not dictate my decisions. Starting tonight. Most of the time, my disorder was managed well thanks to my doctor finding me the right dosage of medication after years of trial and error.

Everything was going to be alright.

"So, tell me again about this tradition."

"Tradition, legend . . . we will find out for ourselves very soon." Jake beamed. "Every year, the senior class throws a massive party at 1729 Lakeshore Lane. It's abandoned, and the last known owner was Gregory Lamar in 1925."

I smiled at how animated Jake was telling the tale. I had heard it from my mom once. She always warned me to stay away from the house, and Lakeshore Lane in general. *There is bad energy there, my love. It's best to leave that particular stone unturned.*

But what my mom didn't know wouldn't hurt her. She was under the impression I would be at Jake's house all night.

"It is said Gregory went to the Haden police, telling them someone was stalking him, and had broken into his home. That he was in danger." Jake waggled his eyebrows. "The next day, he disappeared without a trace. The house has been on the market several times, but no one since then has lived there more than a year."

"So, it's haunted."

"Some believe it is."

"What do you believe?" I asked. We passed towering oak and maple trees, their green leaves stretched over the road in a webbing canopy.

Jake dramatically paused under the crooked sign that read Lakeshore Lane. "I believe Gregory was telling the truth. That someone . . . or some*thing* was after him."

A shiver ran up my spine at Jake's words. I laughed, pushing him slightly. "Okay, okay, you have successfully creeped me out."

His hand squeezed mine. "It's just Haden's fun ol' urban legend. You know, the senior class successfully comes out of 1729 Lakeshore Lane unscathed, and off we go into the world."

"Well, then let's go earn our rite of passage."

"First . . ." Jake took a step closer to me. He let go of my hand to cup the back of my head, his hands running through my short pink hair. His fingers grazed the edge of my jaw along the way. He pulled me close. My eyes fluttered as he whispered against my lips, "I've wanted to do this for such a long time."

Under the yellow glow of the streetlamp at the corner of Lakeshore

Lane, Jake unabashedly kissed me. I wrapped my arms around his neck, standing on my tiptoes to kiss him back. His touch ignited me, chasing away the unease and any thought of the legendary house that beckoned to us from the shadows at the end of the street.

Victorian build. Cracked, dusty glass making up the front windows. On the second floor, massive, dark, and ominous bay windows. The house had a wraparound porch, some parts of the wood rotted and caved in. The old brick had withheld the years pretty well. From the outside looking in, it was just an old house. The seventy teenagers speckling the lawn and pumping music that wove through the air changed the vibe: a clash of creepy and jubilant celebration.

Strings of fairy lights were corded around the porch railing, the amber twinkling lights showing the variety of liquor and beer being chilled in the coolers. Jake pulled me forward, but somehow my feet weren't connected to my legs anymore. In front of so many of my classmates, I was rooted in the reality of the situation. Besides Jake, my best friend Beck was out of town on family vacation in British Columbia. A pang shot through my chest. I wished she was here; we could have found a corner to watch the ridiculousness of this tradition. Likely we would talk about books, TV shows, or just life.

My throat felt hot and thick. I swallowed down the urge to text her. *You can do this.*

"Jake!" A girl with meticulously curled blonde hair bounced up to us.

"Hey, Laure. What's up?"

I stood beside Jake, waiting for him to introduce me. Laure glared at me, her gray eyes cutting.

"Not much. Come on, let's grab a drink."

Heat clawed up the back of my neck to the tips of my ears. Laure smirked. "Darcy, isn't it?"

"Darbie." God, my voice sounded small. Why the fuck did I agree to do this?

"Come on." She looked back to Jake, ignoring me completely. "Let's get you a drink, and then a group of us are hanging out upstairs."

Jake smiled. "Sure. Sounds cool."

I flushed, my heart jackhammering hard against my rib cage. I wanted to run; I could taste the bitterness of my panic.

Jake took my hand and squeezed it. "Just to make an appearance, Darb. I mean, our other option is to stay outside."

Every fiber in my body screamed at me to leave. These people . . . I was just a ghost among them. Unknown, watching.

Nodding tightly, I followed Jake. He promised to make sure that if things went south, he would support me. As my best friend, and hopefully, eventually, my boyfriend.

But he didn't even introduce me, the small voice in my head whispered, which I promptly decided to ignore. Jake was probably just excited, pulled into the aspect of partying.

Faces blurred into unidentifiable features as we walked toward the house. Jake grinned and joked as we passed them. He swiped two beers from the cooler and a water for me.

"Thanks." Unscrewing the cap, I focused on what I was doing. The cool water ran over my tongue, wetting my sticky cotton mouth. Not missing a step, I followed Jake into the house.

The music seemed louder in the main foyer, and almost every inch of space was crammed with more classmates. Conversations layered on top of one another, creating a buzzing white noise.

"Whoa."

The inside of the house wasn't what I expected. At. All. I assumed it would be rotting and smell like moth balls. But it oozed warmth. The grand staircase looked like polished oak, the deep-umber stairs contrasting with the red plush carpet that ran up them. Pictures adorned the left wall— old-school family portraits in black and white. A chandelier hung above us, casting its warm golden light.

"Jake, how is this? The house is abandoned."

I did a double take of the clean appearance again. Jake smirked. "It was part of my surprise. Kyle said it's supposedly the town council's idea to keep the inside like this."

"And the electricity turned on?" I snapped. "Just for the senior class to party? That makes no sense."

"Does it have to?" I wanted to push it, how off this felt. But Jake leaned in close, his breath tickling my ear. "Please try to have a good time."

He pulled away and I stood awkwardly. Had he meant what he said earlier?

It's Jake, I reminded myself, determined to get out of my head. He wouldn't do anything to make me uncomfortable or hurt me.

I glanced back at the door one more time and froze.

The throng of my classmates was still there, but the groups of people moved in slow motion. The music was drawled out in slurred words and pounding bass.

I saw the arm first, with its dirty hand and broken fingernails. The girl had mousy-brown hair, and looked around my age. I couldn't look away. She crawled on her hands and knees, her gaze fixed on me. Her arms looked like they had been dislocated. As she dragged her arms awkwardly, they thumped on the floor.

My heartbeat pounded in my ears. I felt hot, my blood rushing along with adrenaline.

A different song from what had been playing now floated in the air. One I immediately recognized, transporting me into memories of watching *Dirty Dancing* with my mom every first week of summer. We would always swoon over Patrick Swayze, scarf Kernels Popcorn, and gleefully cheer at the ending when he would catch Jennifer Grey in the now-iconic move. It was a comfort movie.

The scene before me changed, the lyrics to "Hungry Eyes" floating in the background.

I stood alone.

With her.

A gurgling sound came from her mouth like she was trying to say something.

You're mine tonight. You're mine tonight. You're mine tonight.

Like a record skipping, that lyric repeated through the house. Jolted, I stepped back. The girl surged toward me, scampering on all fours.

YOU'RE MINE TONIGHT.

"Hey!"

An ice-cold liquid splashed down my back and spine. I realized I had slammed backward into a guy who now was standing with a *what the hell* expression, his beer dripping down my back.

I gasped. "I'm sorry."

"Darbie, are you okay?" Jake was there. He turned to the guy, but what he said bled away. The girl had disappeared, the sounds of the party normal.

I couldn't look away from where she had been. Primal fear coursed through me. Had I just had my first supernatural experience?

"Darbie." Jake's voice yanked me from my thoughts. He took my hand and led me to the side of the room, grabbing a fistful of napkins and dabbing my back. "What happened?"

"I saw . . . a girl." I felt sick, the walls of the room closing in, panic pressing hard on my chest. I glanced up at Jake and saw his skepticism.

"A girl?"

"I know how it may sound. But I know what I saw." Anger flooded me. "Is there any more information about Gregory Lamar?" My gut twisted, this frantic feeling overcoming me. Was the girl somehow connected to Mr. Lamar's disappearance?

I had always believed and respected the supernatural, but experiencing it . . . I couldn't shake the feeling of dread that lingered. And that song . . . repeating *you're mine tonight*. I trembled.

"C'mon. Let's grab some fresh air for a second." We left the living room, and as soon as I stepped through the front door, the night air washed over me like a curtain being raised. My skin was clammy and I closed my eyes, taking deep breaths.

"Say the word, Darb, and we will go back to my place."

Loosening my breath, I looked up at him. "No, it's okay. But do you know anything else about this house?"

For a moment, he looked so annoyed that I thought he was going to walk away. "Darb, I don't know anything else. Just what I told you earlier. It's nothing more than a stupid urban legend. Teens looking for a cheap thrill. It's supposed to be lighthearted. Fun."

"I know."

"Because we are teens."

"I know. I'm sorry."

The apology felt stale on my tongue, but Jake didn't seem to notice.

"So . . . ?"

"Let's go back in."

Jake grinned, and we walked toward the front door. The ice in my veins refused to leave, and I stepped over the threshold once again. The house had gotten my attention.

Once we had gone back in, Laure spotted Jake and insisted we join them upstairs. That was two hours ago.

Now, Jake finished his fourth beer and set it down hard on the attic floor.

The part of me that wanted to go home, that rationally tried to explain what I saw, was quiet. Maybe I had imagined the girl? A stress-induced hallucination? Those doubts were eaten by my curiosity. The frantic feeling still pulled at my gut, her words cooing with each beat of my heart. *You're mine tonight.*

"Oh my God!" Laure squealed, and I wanted to flinch against the pitch of her voice.

"I found a Ouija board!"

My blood ran cold.

"We should try to see if Gregory Lamar has much to say tonight!" She giggled as she pulled the board out and laid it on the floor with the planchette. The others voiced their excitement, and Jake smiled up at Laure.

I didn't hear what he said to her, what any of them were saying. I stood rigid, my breath coming in too fast. One by one, they sat in a semicircle around the board.

No. Had none of these idiots ever watched a horror movie? It was dangerous to use this here in this house.

"What was that, Darcy?" Laure quirked an eyebrow.

Had I said *no* aloud? We weren't in control here. I looked to Jake, who glanced with wide eyes from me to Laure as the room fell quiet.

"I'll see you later, Jake." Then I looked to Laure. "I know you know my name. But have a nice time getting haunted or possessed, probably by a much more dangerous spirit."

The chorus of *ohhhs* chased at my heels as I quickly made my way down the stairs.

Desperately holding my tears back, I navigated the rickety and caved-in stairs. Jake didn't follow me, and my heart fell into the pit of my stomach. All these years, even if he didn't want to pursue a romantic relationship, he was my best friend. He wasn't an asshole, but tonight, he was proving that maybe I didn't know him like I thought I did.

Or maybe he is a fantastic liar.

My tears fell at the thought. I felt a complete fool. Pushing the door open, I just wanted to get home and talk to my mom about this entire night.

I wasn't on the third floor of the house like I thought I was.

In fact, it looked like a completely *different* house than the 1729 Lakeshore Lane I had entered.

The tiled floor was immaculate, the walls accented with bold gold and black geometric lines. A decanter with whiskey in it sat on a table with an ashtray that was still smoking. It was like I had stepped into a fucking scene from *The Great Gatsby.* A light upbeat melody filtered through the house, the trombone prominent along with an upright bass. The song had no lyrics, and it sounded like the band was downstairs. I stepped onto the pristine marble, and a man appeared in front of me. He wore a black-and-white tux with the buttons done up haphazardly, and a glass of champagne trembled in his hand. He was distraught.

"Um . . . hey? Where am I?"

He blinked, looking at me as if for the first time. "It's strange, you know. I can feel it. I'm being watched within these walls. The police think I'm mad. You don't think so, do you?"

"No . . . Are you Gregory Lamar?"

"So strange . . ." He seemed to look past me and into me at the same time. "This house holds so much more than people think." He trembled so hard, the alcohol slopped onto his wrists. "But they are all asking the wrong questions."

"Gregory, what do you mean? What happened to you?" It felt dangerous talking to him. But why did he choose to show himself to *me*?

"They aren't asking what lies *below* Lakeshore Lane."

Abruptly, he turned, and before I could think about what I was doing, I followed him. He took the stairs two at a time, and the smell of smoke, wood oil, and whiskey overcame me. I ran after him, my heart lodged firmly in my throat. All I could think about was the girl, and what I knew about Gregory's story. Were they connected, and why—decades later—was this happening?

We passed the second floor. I had envisioned a neat room given how the third floor was straight art deco style, and it took me aback when we ran through a rotting room.

The girl was there.

She peered around the hallway corner, her broken fingernails leaving trails of blood on the walls as they curled around the frame.

"Oh, fuck me." My heart jackhammered against my ribs, but I didn't stop moving.

The first floor.

Back to the Roaring Twenties and the jazz band I heard before. A crowd filled the room—it looked like a party. No one noticed me, or Gregory for that matter. It was a sea of gold and black, streamers and overflowing champagne.

"So strange," Gregory turned to whisper to me.

"What is?"

He turned and I followed, walking down another set of stairs. Suddenly, we were in the basement. None of this made sense—the transitions between times and rooms were jarring.

The basement was more of a cellar, the damp floor mostly dirt, and several cracked jars oozed gelatin on the shelf in front of me. A pile of broken wood lay in the left-hand corner, and the lack of windows made me claustrophobic. Gregory stood with his back to me. My gaze snapped to his hand where he was holding his glass. It shattered in his palm, his blood dripping with the champagne onto the floor. Shards of glass stuck out of his skin.

"Gregory, how did you die?" I asked pointedly, trying to keep the tremor out of my voice.

"Die? No, I think you misunderstand. This house . . . is *alive*. Through it, so am I."

I took a step back.

"I stepped into its vortex when I bought it. I misunderstood what it was trying to show me. I thought it was going to hurt me."

He turned to look at me, his head tilting slowly to the left. "It showed me that I was chosen to keep it alive. Now tonight, it's your turn."

I took another step back and fell, landing hard on my tailbone, pain lacing up my spine at the impact.

I looked up and froze.

From the basement ceiling, long tendrils of gray flesh uncurled and gravitated toward me and Gregory. He tipped his chin up, and a tendril lashed out and attached to his entire face. Miniature teeth latched on to his cheekbones. A sucking sound filled the basement, and I watched Gregory float up from the floor, suspended in the air.

I scrambled back, my nails digging into the dirt. The edges of my nails cracked and pulled off, and I winced.

The tendrils reminded me of tentacles slithering through the air. The end of one sucker opened, and I couldn't move fast enough.

It attached to my face, its teeth sinking in. A flash of pain mixed with my curdling screams.

You're mine tonight.

Multiple voices whispered over the tops of one another. Memories that weren't mine flashed so fast within my mind.

I saw the night Gregory disappeared. The tendril took him in the basement, but he became a part of the house then. It was a living, breathing organism. A predator. And it needed people to sustain the legend. It fed off souls, pulling them into an endless loop through time, through space.

To draw more in.

I screamed, trying to fight the tentacle.

But it was too late.

It pulled me to stand, and the girl from earlier appeared in front of me, smiling.

She had always been *me*.

I screamed, my own shrieks the last thing I heard until the blackness took me.

Twenty Years Later

Jake

"Jake, can I get you to stand a little to the left please?"

Awkwardly, I tried not to look at the house behind me, concentrating on Jules's bleached pixie cut. She was the woman behind *Between the Shadows* who was putting the documentary together for their YouTube channel.

"Perfect!" She gave me a thumbs-up from behind the massive camera set up on a tripod. Her partner, Drew, rummaged in their van, trying to find another cord or something. Truth be told, I hadn't been paying much attention. My mind was reeling.

I was back here.

The one place I promised myself I would never return to.

Jules and Drew had tracked me down through social media. There had been enough interviews following what had happened on that fateful night and after senior year. Even when I went to college, leaving Haden, it hadn't been surprising that they'd found me. They were nice people—Jules and Drew. Easygoing and . . . warm. It sounds corny, but that was the best way to describe them. It was like when life completely overwhelmed you, and you went to that one person in your life and exposed it all. The fissures no one else saw. That was probably why Jules and Drew were the best at what they did. Getting people to expose secrets willingly was—in my opinion—a goddamned gift.

What was surprising was that I agreed to do this.

"Okay, Jake. Ready?"

I nodded.

"Welcome, ghouls and gals, to this season of *Between the Shadows*. We are here with Jake Wardon, the lone survivor of the greatest mystery that has plagued a small town called Haden, Ontario."

She nodded at me. My cue. Sweat peppered my forehead, and I cleared my throat.

"Hi, I'm Jake." I smiled sheepishly. "Twenty years ago, I had just graduated grade 12 at Haden Collegiate Institute. I was welcoming the summer by inviting my best friend Dar—" My voice caught on her name. When had I last said it aloud?

"Darbie Barlowe," I finished.

"Invited to what?" Jules asked.

"The senior class had this stupid tradition. Party in an allegedly haunted house, I guess, is the best description of that." I waved to the structure behind me.

"Can you tell me what you mean by that?"

"It all started in 1925. A man named Gregory Lamar disappeared without a trace. He went to the police before and said he was in danger."

"Viewers, in the police report we obtained thanks to Haden PD, they did follow up on Gregory's complaint and even staked out the house. There was no sign of break-ins, no sign of anything," Jules added.

"Something like this happening in a town like Haden . . . it made ripples. Those ripples became our local urban legend. I thought it would be fun for Darbie and me to be part of that tradition." I looked deadpan into the lens. "I was wrong. I see that house for what it is."

A wolf in sheep's clothing.

"It's dangerous."

Jules's eyebrows shot up.

"Let me explain. Before that night, it was just a story. Just words. Darbie didn't even want to go, and I . . . I asked her on a date."

"So that she would say yes?"

"I knew she would say yes if I asked her. At that point, I had been in love with her for years. She had bad anxiety, and crowds weren't easy for her."

"When did you first notice something was wrong that night?"

"I didn't." *Here goes nothing.* "Darbie noticed."

Jules shut off the camera, and for a moment said nothing.

"This isn't what you told the press."

I barked out a laugh. "Those interviews were mainly scripted bullshit fed by my parents."

"Why come forward now?" Jules asked.

It was a great question. When I told my mom and dad what happened that night, I could tell they were empathetic because of the shock. They had driven back from the Kawarthas to find a massacre, and I was at the center of it. Months later, I was in several different therapies, and when my story didn't change, my parents sat me down. I was scaring people with the truth.

I looked Jules straight in the eyes. "For Darbie."

Drew had come to stand beside us. He clapped my shoulder. "I'm sorry, man. For your loss."

I exhaled shakily. "Ready to continue?"

Jules's eyes had locked on to the house. "Would you consider doing part of this interview in the house?"

My heart dropped into my stomach, and I wetted my dry lips. "No."

Jules didn't push it. Instead, she nodded and said to Drew, "Want to grab the handheld? We can get some different shots around the property."

Even the notion of going closer to the house put my teeth on edge. But I fell into step beside Jules while simultaneously falling into the past.

"That night, as soon as we arrived at the party and entered the house, Darbie questioned how the *inside* wasn't completely decrepit. There was decor in place and running electricity. And it was clean." I looked at the rotting Victorian house now, nestled at the end of the lane. This summer was hot, humidity making my black T-shirt stick uncomfortably to my skin. The property hadn't been taken care of in who knew how many years. The tall grass tickled my knees as we made our way to the backyard.

"You saw this too?"

"Of course. I thought it was a bit, you know, the town playing into the legend. I was a teen. I saw what I wanted to. Especially that night."

We came to the backyard, and I stopped. The letters on the first sign were blood red, reading *Welcome to Hell.* There were at least fifty more, all reading similar things.

The Devil lives in Haden.

Fuck Jake Wardon.

Justice for the Class of '24.

My blood ran cold. "You can obviously see I wasn't and still am not that popular."

"Do your parents still live in Haden?"

"It's their home, of course there were challenges that came with this." I waved to the property. "But it was their choice to stay."

"So, what happened after Darbie brought it up? She thought it was off, the state of the house."

"I was being an asshole that night. Maybe I was caught up in the spirit of tradition. Fuck, I don't know."

"You weren't acting yourself?"

"No. I had promised before the party that if Darbie even had the inkling that she wanted to leave, we would. Together. Shortly after we arrived, as I was getting drinks, there was an altercation. She said she saw something. A girl."

Jules paused, and Drew was getting different shots of the house from the backyard, but out of the corner of my eye I saw him stiffen.

"She was shaken, but she wanted to find out more about Lamar's disappearance. I have relived this moment over a thousand times. I should have left with her then." I chewed my bottom lip. As much as I tried not to look at the house, I could feel the pull of it. We were on the edge of its orbit.

I glanced at the empty window frames on the third floor. An assortment of sticks, feathers, and other things sat there making a nest. Even in the vilest of places, life could be reclaimed.

"I was drinking too much, way too fast," I continued. Looking away from the bird's nest, I noticed fireflies collecting by the shrubbery in the winking dusk. Their blinking amber was methodic, calming.

"Next thing I know, Laure—one of our classmates—finds this old Ouija board, and wants to try contacting Gregory Lamar. A bit cliché, I know." I smiled sadly. "Darbie thought so too. She got upset and left. She thought there was a possibility something dangerous could be brought forward instead. That was the last time I saw her."

Rapidly blinking against my tears, I tried to get out what had plagued me through nightmares since that night.

"I stayed in the attic instead of going after Darbie. I put my hand on that planchette." I looked up to Jules. "And played the game."

My heart was pounding, a bitter taste coating my tongue. I paused, a strange sensation pulling in my stomach.

"Nothing happened during the séance. It was after." *Keep going.* "Laure asked me to stay behind for a second. She looked . . . off. Everyone else left, going back downstairs where the main party was. She was humming a song I recognized but couldn't place. It wasn't until she was coming toward me. Her eyes had gone this weird milky white. She kept on repeating one line from the song, and that's when it clicked. It was 'Hungry Eyes' by Eric Carmen. I was terrified, but I froze. I tried to rationalize why she was acting so strange—maybe she drank too much. Had someone slipped her something in one of those drinks? But she drove her thumbs into the corner of her eyes, screaming at me the same sentence. She popped her own eyeballs out, ripped the optic nerves, and started eating them."

Bile rose in my throat, and I wiped the rogue tear that ran down my cheek. Jules and Drew had mirrored expressions of horror. I continued my recollection.

"I ran then. The party downstairs was chaotic. I tried . . . I tried to yell, to scream, to run. But the power was cut. I barely made it out of the house. The screams of my classmates . . . fuck, I can still hear them, that pealing terror. And then they were silenced, one by one. I knew it was Laure, but I also believe something else was controlling her."

"An entity?" Jules prompted.

"I think that whole house is the entity."

Jules reached over and pinched Drew's side. He shut off the video camera.

"Hooooolyshit," Jules said, drawing it out as one word.

"I should have done more." *I was a coward. Am still one.*

"No." Jules tucked a strand of bleached hair behind her ear. "I would have done the same in your position. You were just a kid who was terrified. I'm just . . . reeling."

"Yeah, trust me, I know how it all sounds."

"We are in the industry of believing," Drew piped in. "This is just a massive story."

I chewed my bottom lip, applying enough pressure that I broke skin. "There's more."

"Let's go back to the front, okay?" Jules glanced at her phone. "Then we will wrap it up for today, and get some more tomorrow, if that's okay?"

"Sounds great."

I felt drained. Giving my story up from the iron cage, and having someone not immediately dismiss it . . . It had come full circle, back to the place where the nightmare began.

All I could think about was Darbie.

You had been right about it all, Darb. I'm so sorry.

Walking back to the front of the house, I left that part of my heart behind with her spirit.

Jules

I was silently freaking the fuck out. My pulse was a live current under my skin, prickling my nerves, churning with adrenaline. Everything had a new light to it.

I tried to devour every detail about this place, this house. I knew there had been something here when I stumbled upon Haden in my research.

But this. Jake's interview. It was so much more than I could have ever imagined.

Golden hour crested over Haden, bathing 1729 Lakeshore Lane in its warm glow. The house's peaks and valleys created dimension and deep shadows that seemed to follow us along the rotted side panels. I shot Drew a grateful smile since he was already capturing the shot with his handheld camera. I guess that's what ten years of working together had done, and *Between the Shadows* had only grown in popularity. It was beautiful in a forbidding kind of way. Our viewers would dig the contrast, and they would eat it up when we stayed overnight at this place.

My tripod came back into view, and I prompted, "So, Jake. You said there is more to the story?"

What did this poor son of a bitch live through?

I turned my camera back on, my hand somehow steady, like it wasn't attached to the rest of my body.

"I went to the police after, to get help. I had to wait at the station for my parents to get back from out of town. I was in shock."

He stood in front of the house again, and I nodded, urging him to keep going.

"The cop who was on that night, Officer Barrow, came back to the station maybe an hour later. He was furious."

I zoomed in slightly on Jake's face. He chewed his lip a lot, his gaze darting around. I could tell the memory had a strong hold on him. He wasn't here.

"He was so furious. He brought me into a separate room and asked me what cruel joke I was playing." A tear slipped down his cheek. "There was no evidence of anyone being there. No bodies."

I squinted, catching movement behind Jake. Ice laced through my body.

"When the forensic tests came back, there were no fingerprints or any evidence of any kind, Jules."

My breath caught in my throat while my hand holding the camera shook. The front door of Lakeshore Lane had creaked open, revealing the inky room inside.

"There was nothing."

Dirty, swollen fingers with broken blackened nails slowly wrapped around the doorframe. I zoomed past Jake now, making sure this was actually happening.

On the whisper of wind, I heard the familiar lyrics to "Hungry Eyes."

A body came into view, a girl crawling on all fours, stringy hair hanging in front of her face. Until she raised her head.

And grinned.

Between the Shadows

The late summer heat became suffocating, and I couldn't breathe. I couldn't rationalize what I was seeing. My hand trembled so violently that the screen, focused on Jake, was a blur. At my expression, Jake turned around. The girl's grin widened, her eyes obsidian, no pupils, no definition within them. No echo of humanity.

Her hand slapped against the wood of the porch in slow motion as Jake turned back around to look at me, his face white, panic bursting through his eyes. "Run!" he screamed.

Fear. It was the foul, bitter taste flooding my mouth, the ice that rippled out of my nerve endings. It coursed through me. I knew I was in danger, but all I could focus on was the girl. Her bloodied state, her jerky movements, her grin that held no kindness but a madness so defining, it held me within its grasp.

Hands pulled at me. Drew's face was so close to mine, I could feel his breath against my cheeks.

"Run, Jules!" he screamed as the girl launched herself off the porch straight at Jake.

Stumbling, I almost dropped the camera, but Drew's hand slid into mine, then my surroundings were a blur. My legs felt like jelly, trying to find structure and sturdiness when there was none as Drew dragged me across the lawn.

We captured a full-fledged spirit. I saw a ghost. Those two thoughts were all I could focus on in my shock, before a scream split the air.

I stopped, twisting out of Drew's grip.

"Jules, fuck, we have to go—" His pleas mixed in with heaving sobs.

The girl had Jake by the fucking ankle, and my eyes locked on to his. His mouth twisted before he mouthed, *Go.*

He had been right behind me. *This can't be happening.* I reached toward him, damning my feet for not moving at all. It was all I could do to watch as she pulled him so forcibly back with unnatural strength, his fingers trying desperately to hold on to anything. He ripped at the grass, at the now-shaking ground, so hard that he left divots, *claw marks.* His screams resonated in my mind as she disappeared with him up the porch, back into that house, the door to 1729 Lakeshore Lane slamming shut.

Silence blanketed me.

It was cold. It left me empty, and I simply existed in that space, standing there, vaguely aware that behind me Drew called 911.

Go.

Jake's command cracked through my heart, through me entirely, until I wasn't sure what was left in its wake. I was certain it had been his last word.

I fell to my knees, emptying my stomach, still clutching the damn camera like it was my lifeline against the darkness that held this place.

One Year Later

From: Ray, Bryson
Sent: Thursday, August 10, 2045 9:00 AM
To: Quinn, Jules
Subject: Bryson Morning Show

Morning Jules,

Bryson Ray here, host of Sarnia Lambton's *Bryson Morning Show*. It's an absolute pleasure to meet you virtually. First off can I start by congratulating you and Drew on your recent success on getting a show with Discovery? I know a lot of the locals here are excited to watch the first episode of *Between the Shadows*. A little birdy told me that you would be returning to Lakeshore Lane to stay over in that house?

I would love to have you and Drew on the show next Monday if your schedule allows for an exclusive interview.

Looking forward to talking more,
Bryson

From: Quinn, Jules
Sent: Thursday, August 10, 2045 4:00 PM
To: Ray, Bryson
Subject: Re: Bryson Morning Show

Drew thinks it would be a great opportunity. Please forward the details to me.

Five. The woman's voice was chipper as she smiled encouragingly from behind the camera. Did I look as ragged as I felt? *Most likely.* I tried to ignore the thought as I fidgeted with my sweeping bangs. I tried to ignore the heat pouring onto me from the floodlights, tried to imagine the air was fresh and not stale studio air with the lingering smells of coffee and body odor.

Four. Drew leaned over to squeeze my hand, his touch cold and clammy over mine.

The overly happy camera woman held up three fingers.

Two. I was having trouble breathing, the image of swollen, dirty hands grasping a doorframe playing repeatedly in my mind.

One.

Oh God.

"Good morning and happy Monday, Sarnia-Lambton! Today we have two very special guests on the *Bryson Morning Show*. You know them, you have *begged* me to get them on for an interview. This will be an unforgettable show. Today marks the day we get to know what truly happened a year ago in our closest neighboring town of Haden."

Bryson was the literal definition of charisma. Wearing dress pants and a crisp white collared shirt, he beamed at me and Drew. But the glint in his eyes looked a little off, his teeth too white, his presence filling the room and not in a comforting way. At least not for me.

"First, can you tell us a little about how *Between the Shadows* started, and what exactly it means to be a paranormal investigator?" Bryson clasped his hands and looked to us.

"Jules and I have been best friends since we met in college in Toronto. We both were majoring in journalism and media communications, and once we got to know one another, we realized we had another major thing in common."

"Love of horror," I finished for Drew curtly. God, that was a lifetime ago.

Where other classmates went out clubbing, consuming alcohol, and who knew what else, Drew and I were making a tradition of trying new restaurants, and watching every horror movie we could. Eventually those movies turned into—

"I mean, within our first year we had devoured most of the well-known classics. But we fell for certain, more modern directors, like Mike Flanagan and James Wan. But it was Jules who found this team on YouTube, one of the founding ghost-hunting channels, and we both fell into an obsession."

Drew was on par with my thoughts. I smiled at him. "I mean, at the time we never thought, *that's what I want to be when I grow up*, but fate works in mysterious ways."

"What do you mean by that, Jules?" Bryson pushed. I tried not to look at him or the cameras. For someone who guided interviews and was used to being on camera, this fucking man set my teeth on edge.

"It means that our first case, so to speak, was at my roommate's childhood house, and we were the only ones who believed her. We decided we would try to collect evidence of the paranormal," I said.

Bryson grinned and it looked twisted. "Maria, bring up the first footage, please."

I sat back in the plush red chair as the screen behind us sprang to life, my own face flooding it. My old electric-blue pixie cut glowed between the shadows of the hallway, and I smiled. That's where our name had come from; Drew always joking that it never mattered if our location had electricity, he could spot my hair no matter what.

"My . . . my name is Jules Quinn. And my cameraman is Drew Nash. We are here tonight at my roommate's childhood home where her mom has experienced unusual activity."

The camera view spun, Drew's face occupying the screen now. His wide eyes and flaring nostrils were up close and personal as he whispered, "It's one in the morning, and Jules and I are staying over to collect evidence of the paranormal and see what is plaguing this suburban home. Also, to kick some ghostie ass."

"Drew!" my voice hissed from off camera.

The camera panned back to me, and I was now holding a Maglite, my backpack slung over my shoulder. "We have asked Mrs. Connors to leave for the night while we investigate, but let's start upstairs in her bedroom where she has told us that almost every night there is slamming or knocking on the closet doors, always in threes. Viewer, this is significant. This could hint there is a demonic spirit here, and the three symbolizes mocking of the Holy Trinity. In this room specifically as well, Mrs. Connors has experienced tugging on her limbs during the night, so hard she has bruised from them, as well as hearing disjointed voices."

Drew captured moving down the hallway and up the stairs; even then, his camera skills were great. He knew exactly where to pause, building tension and lingering on everyday objects that had a more ominous presence given the context.

The camera bounced slightly as we made our way up the stairs, and I watched as my past self open the mahogany door. The king-sized bed donned with an ivory comforter was still ruffled and used from the previous night. There was a dresser and a rocking chair in the corner, and several photos of Megan throughout the years hung on the buttery caramel walls.

"A little history about this room and the house. Drew and I dug into the library archives and found some unsettling patterns. It was built in the early nineteenth century. The first owner was Joseph Smith, who immigrated to Toronto from England. He lived here, alone, until 1925." The camera followed me walking around the room dramatically.

I froze as I sat in the plush chair, the gentle tug of my panic curling around my heart.

That year was the same year Gregory Lamar disappeared from Lakeshore Lane. Which of course I wouldn't find out until last year when I was prepping for Jake's interview. *Just a coincidence*, I thought, trying to school my features as I continued to watch our old clip.

"There wasn't much we could find in the archive except a clipping from his journal, the lone piece that Joseph didn't destroy." I faced the camera fiercely as I repeated the words I had read all those years ago:

"*I cannot escape it.*"

Ice shot down my spine, and I tried to catch Drew's eye. Was he picking up on these impossible parallels? Gregory Lamar had said something along the same lines to the police: that he was in danger, that he was being followed. Or was I so desperate to see a link that I was forming one regardless? Drew had his back turned to me, watching the screen.

"What Joseph Smith meant by this, we will never know. But he hung himself in this room a day after this entry. But that's not all, and what follows is even more sinister. The next homeowner murdered his wife. The following owner murdered her children. The heinous crimes and acts of violence can be traced back, with no one surviving in this home more than three years since Joseph Smith. The Connors? This year will be their third in this home."

I watched myself set the Maglite on the chair, adjusting the button to hallway between on and off, to be used as touch light that spirits could use in tandem to answer our questions. Along with the REM Pod, losing my focus as I explained how the REM Pod would pick up on energy fluctuations with its antenna, which covered a range of 360 degrees. Any disturbances within that field could be how spirits communicated with us.

Currently, I wasn't focusing on that or what Bryson was saying. I saw his mouth moving as Drew laughed, saying something probably witty in response to the video. My gaze had locked on the screen, but not on myself.

It was behind me, underneath the king bed. At first, I almost didn't see it. The smoky shadow moved along with the camera lithely.

I caught a flash of a hand, bloody and broken fingernails reaching toward me before whipping back.

Impossible. That can't be the same hand . . . the same girl.

"Thank you, Maria." Bryson's voice brought me out of my thoughts as our clip faded to black. "Now, Jules, what do you think you captured during your first-ever investigation?"

I clutched my hands together, trying to stop them from shaking. *Damn it, just make it through this interview, for Drew's sake. Later, you can work this out.*

"We searched the rest of the house while we set up cameras in the hot spots—where Mrs. Connor reported the most activity. If viewers are interested, we did capture compelling—"

"Oh, we intend to show the viewers the clip of the *most compelling evidence*," Bryson interrupted me. God, this man was a prick.

"Here I thought we were going to talk about what happened in Haden, or did I get my interviews mixed up?" I replied silkily.

Bryson smiled at me, all teeth, but not an inch of it reached his eyes. "Maria, roll the second clip, please," Bryson said, and he oozed tension. Like a snake about to strike. It was an unnerving kind of stillness. Was he still pissed that I didn't confirm we were going back to Lakeshore Lane? Discovery had made us sign contracts saying we couldn't share that information until closer to the release of the episode anyway. But I didn't have to explain that to anyone. I hadn't wanted to go back there, not after what happened last summer. But with the footage we caught, it was our massive break, and Discovery wanted to kick off our season with what we had set up to do at Lakeshore Lane: stay there overnight and investigate. I couldn't deny Drew that. Hell, I couldn't deny *myself* it. All of our hard work had led up to this moment. All those times our friends and family thought we were wasting our time, that we couldn't build a business out of ghost hunting.

I had known five years ago what I know now: the public is obsessed with the dark. The unexplainable speaks to people even if they deny it.

Deep down, they can never look away.

The screen jumped back to life.

"Drew, do you hear that?" my voice whispered from off camera, pitched with anxiety. Upstairs, the piercing beeps of the REM Pod were fast and urgent. The basement view was plucked straight out of a horror movie. Unfinished, the dirt floor was compact and the old shelving was filled with various mason jars of preserves and other odds and ends. The camera view dropped to the floor and then bounced wildly, taking in the stairs. I could be seen sprinting through the kitchen, skidding down the hallway, taking the stairs two at a time. Drew's heaving breath mixed with the screaming REM Pod as we rushed into the master bedroom. The camera view shook, but I watched my past self stand straighter, and my voice boomed through the room.

"If there is someone here who wishes to communicate, flash the Maglite once for yes."

Drew zoomed in, focusing on the black flashlight, which was now going absolutely wild, flashing on and off repeatedly on the chair where we left it.

"-*Beep*- me, Drew, I'm getting the spirit box out," I said off camera, the sounds of me digging it out of the backpack filling the room before the white noise of the box rapidly scanning radio stations. The morning show had edited out the string swearing that had flooded out from me in that moment.

The REM Pod fell dead silent, and Drew whispered, "Jules, it's three A.M."

"Joseph Smith, is that you? My name is Jules Quinn, and this is my partner, Drew. We are here. We are open to communicating."

The spirit box sputtered, disjointed voices starting to say clipped words before they fell back into the white noise. The camera zoomed in on my pinched face as I sat cross-legged in front of the box. I chewed my bottom lip before I whispered, "Or are we talking with someone else?"

"Yes." The reply snapped out of the spirit box so clearly before fading back into the clicking static. The screen shook, Drew's steady grip on his handheld video camera faltering.

Goosebumps pricked at the back on my neck as I continued to watch my past self. Honestly, up until this point I hadn't thought much about our past investigations. Between finishing school, starting our small business for *Between the Shadows*, and working part-time at Hazel's Café while living in my mom's basement, I had no extra time and energy.

Except now I was thrown back into the past as I watched my younger self lean forward.

"Who are we talking with?"

Flickering static hummed with overlapping distant voices.

"Who is here with us?" my voice boomed around the small room.

"Never," the monotone voices croaked out. "Left."

"What are your names? Who am I talking to?"

"Never left," the voices repeated out of the spirit box.

I watched as I tipped my face up to Drew, my eyes wide in question. "Never left . . . here?"

"NEVER LEFT."

"Maria, please stop the clip," Bryson said, turning back to us. "It's quite impressive, what you caught here."

I stared back at Bryson like he was standing at the end of a long tunnel. The clip hadn't faded to black and remained frozen on my face as I crouched in front of Drew. But behind me . . . holy hell, behind me . . .

"Now, when we were reviewing this clip, Maria and I noticed this, and we wanted to ask you and Drew if you purposefully left out going over this evidence . . ."

Drew shot me a quick *what in the actual fuck* look before I coldly cut in, "We never leave anything out purposefully."

"Then you missed catching this?" Bryson asked.

Yes, but I don't know how, I thought before saying, "Yes."

I didn't need the red outline that popped up, and Bryson's voice turned to a whine as he asked Drew questions. Because on the frozen screen, standing behind me in the corner of the room, was a looming shadowy figure.

The only clear feature was its razor-sharp grin.

I'd always read in stories or watched in movies about *the moment.* The moment that leaves you breathless, that clicks everything into place. That spins your world on its axis from the sheer momentum of it. My moment crashed into me, staring at this footage. My reality bent against the figure shrouded in darkness. Neither Drew nor I would have missed this in our edits. Yet, clear as day was the outline of a human body.

"Now, Ms. Quinn, let's talk." Bryson moved in his seat to cross his legs, and the atmosphere of the interview shifted. He motioned to the frozen screen, and fucking Maria dragged the frozen image of *that house* onto it. With Jake standing in the frame, and the girl crouched on the porch behind him.

"After the clip of Lakeshore Lane went viral, it was a high discussion within our viewer Discord group. Some of those viewers have questions they would like answered. I have the first one here."

"I'm sorry—what?" *An online group?* My stomach churned.

"Her question is, 'Why didn't you go after Jake Wardon after you caught this footage? Or was it all just staged?'"

"We called the authorities. I'm not here to rehash what we did or didn't do in that moment. Of course it wasn't staged, a person went missing that day." My anger was slipping, bile burning in the back of my throat at the mention of Jake.

Bryson barreled on, "The next is from user @ghosthunterjunkie. 'There are similarities of the specters caught between your first investigation and Lakeshore Lane. Can you speak to that?'"

Drew jumped in, sensing my patience wearing. "We hadn't connected those dots yet, but after seeing this, I can promise you we will investigate the possibility of a connection between the hauntings."

"In your professional opinion, could that happen? A haunting being connected yet the houses being in different cities?"

"It's not something we have run into before, but when it comes to the paranormal, nothing is off the table. It's our job to keep an open mind and find the facts," Drew said professionally.

"The next is from user @Jasontheghostboy. 'What was your conclusion with your first investigation?'"

"After showing Mrs. Connors the responses of the REM Pod and spirit box, which were our big activities of the night, she ended up listing the house, and moving out a couple of months later when her experiences intensified. It's not our job to advise residents what to do, or even to conclude that their home is haunted. Our job always is to collect evidence, to provide as much information to *help* our clients make an informed decision about why they wanted our help in the first place."

My heart swelled at Drew's response. This interview was turning into a goddamned witch hunt, but he always remained calm when he could sense my fissures.

"Well, I'll ask you this, Drew, since your partner ignored the question. But it's the one thing everyone wants to know."

No.

"With the compelling case of Mr. Wardon's disappearance, and since you didn't fulfill your prior investigation, will you kick off your first episode of *Between the Shadows* by going back to Lakeshore Lane? Even though at the time you couldn't find the will to enter the house when Jake . . . went in."

I snapped.

Standing, visibly trembling from silent rage, I said, "Thank you for your time, and the interview. But it's done now." I walked off the set, ignoring the wide-eyed looks from the crew. But before I could leave the room, Drew's answer chased at my heels.

"Yes. We are going back."

DrewCrew 14/08/2045 1:00 PM: Jules, talk to me. Please.

Jules 14/08/2045 1:30 PM: What you had to resort to Discord to speak to me Drew? How high school.

DrewCrew 14/08/2045 1:32 PM: I knew you would have your phone shut off. I know you.

Jules 14/08/2045 1:35 PM: You have me there. I figured Carol from Discovery was going to see the interview and take a strip off me.

DrewCrew 14/08/2045 1:37 PM: That and you don't want to talk to me.

Jules 14/08/2045 1:40 PM: You have me there.

DrewCrew 14/08/2045 1:43 PM: I'm sorry, Jules. For even wanting to do the interview in the first place. But

Jules: 14/08/2045 1:44 PM: But what, Drew? That wasn't an interview conducted from genuine interest. It was to rake us over the fucking coals. To allow viewers to say what the internet is saying, hell what the *Haden media is saying.* That it was staged to get a nice fat paid contract with a show. Did you hear Bryson say when Jake *went in?* Like no, when Jake was dragged in that goddamned house by a ghost, but we can't prove that because we didn't catch that part on film. But sure asshole, he just walked in and was never seen again. Totally normal circumstances.

DrewCrew 14/08/2045 1:50 PM: I know, he was a proper ass. But don't you still think that's exactly why we have to go back? Because we know the truth, and we want to uncover that truth for Jake. For Darbie. For Gregory Lamar. For everyone that place has taken.

DrewCrew 14/08/2045 2:15 PM: Are you still here?

Jules 14/08/2045 2:30 PM: Yeah I'm still here. Before I answer that can we talk about how we "missed" that evidence from the Connors's haunt? I mean Drew, we both had eyes on those edits. We both worked on it. The only evidence we got that night was never left from the spirit box. And . . .

DrewCrew 14/08/2045 2:33 PM: And?

Jules 14/08/2045 2:37 PM: And I thought I saw something else in that footage. I'm going to review it again tonight . . . but I have a really bad feeling about this. About going back to that house. Like should we call up a priest and get some holy water? Bring salt? Like Drew, do we know what we are up against or what to do if things go bad?

DrewCrew 14/08/2045 2:45 PM: You go back and look at the footage again and I will research what we should bring tomorrow night. Just in case. Sound good?

Jules 14/08/2045 2:54 PM: And what if it's not safe to go back? What then?

DrewCrew 14/08/2045 3:04 PM: What if I went anyway even if you thought that, Jules?

Jules 14/08/2045 3:08 PM: You can't see me but I'm flipping the screen off. You know I would never let you go back there alone.

DrewCrew 14/08/2045 3:10 PM: And you can't see my smile. I know you are scared, I am too. But it's a six-figure salary for both of us to do this Jules. It's the beginning of *everything* we have ever dreamed of.

Jules 14/08/2045 3:12 PM: Fuck . . . I know.

DrewCrew 14/08/2045 3:15 PM: So we agree then. I will still pick you up at six tomorrow? The crew will meet us there later.

Jules 14/08/2045 3:30 PM: Yeah. I will text you later? My phone is back on. I was only half joking about the salt and holy water btw.

DrewCrew 14/08/2045 3:36 PM: I know. I got you, Sam.

Jules 14/08/2045 3:40 PM: I got you, Dean.

My eyes burned against the glow of my computer screen. Rubbing them, I raised my mug to my lips, drinking more of the cold coffee. The pit in my stomach grew as I started the footage again, moving frame by frame.

It was impossible. It made absolutely no sense, but there was no denying it. The original, unedited footage from our first investigation showed the hand reaching toward me. That same slender arm, those broken nails, those knurled, swollen fingers were undeniably the ones that haunted me every day since last year. On my second screen was more unedited footage. Different locations spanning years apart, and the hard proof glared right back at me in the shrouded darkness of my room.

It was the same girl.

Quickly, I took screenshots and opened my texts with Drew.

Me: Have I completely lost my mind?
Drew: It's almost three in the morning. I love you, but get some sleep.
Me: Seriously?

I gripped the phone so hard, willing Drew through technology to wake up. To pay attention. I had gone through this footage almost twenty times, and that was just in the last hour. And each time, I expected a glitch, some footage to reflect the facts that I had in my mind, my memories. But no matter what I wanted, what my mind screamed at me, the specters didn't change from our first investigation and were as plain as day.

Me: Drew, that footage that bastard showed the world today was right, according to my unedited files of that investigation. How could we both miss something that big? That obvious?

Message seen.

I stared at that confirmation on our thread, waiting for him to reply. The seconds stretched into minutes until I wanted to break the stupid device I clutched so hard in my hands. Fine. If Drew was so hard-pressed to go back to that place, so eager to see that we had entered our own version of *The Twilight Zone*, that was on him. I put my phone on my desk, chewing my lip just as my notifications dinged.

Drew: Never.

I stared at Drew's response, ice dousing me. Never what?

"Fuck you, Drew," I growled to the screen, properly throwing it across the room onto my bed. Standing up, I paced. Was I losing my mind, my sense of reality? Since Lakeshore Lane last year, my life had been turned upside down. Sure, there were a lot of positives—growing our business to the level we always wanted: our own TV show. We had been interviewed, had an amazing advance from Discovery, were paid well to do interviews and collaborate with some of our favorite colleges, doing team investigations that our audience absolutely lost it over. But no one, including me, could ever truly move away from the footage we caught . . . and didn't catch last year.

But anxiety attacks, being plagued by insomnia every night . . . That made sense to me.

Drew and I barely escaped with our lives. Jake . . . God, Jake. He was ripped into that house right before our eyes, never to be seen again. The police took down our incident report when they had showed up, and after that, a missing person's report had been issued. It was still posted on

Haden PD's social media to this day, along with others.

There weren't enough therapy sessions in the world I could go to that would get Jake's face out of my mind. It was seared there, imbued into my essence. I sighed, clenching and unclenching my hands as I looked around at all the familiar walls. My room mostly consisted of my king bed and a large desk that held two screens and a computer desktop that was decked out with my favorite stickers from cities we had traveled to throughout the years. My favorite was the *Between the Shadows* logo, with a ghost and Maglite illuminating the bold words in lime green. To the right side of my room beside the door, my shelving unit was filled with spare camera parts, cords, and an array of outdated handheld video cameras. Old horror posters speckled the wall behind it: *It, Nope, Us, Get Out, The Haunting of Hill House,* and *Midnight Mass* were always on the frontlines of the overlapping collage my wall had become.

I walked in my favorite space, ignoring the pounding of my heart, tiredness eating away at me from the inside out. The hallway that opened up to my one-bedroom apartment was still, holding its breath as I tried to untangle it all. I would have known if we caught full-ass ghosts on our first investigation. Drew would have known. And whether I liked it or not, I was heading back to Lakeshore Lane.

Plopping back into my computer chair, I moved the frozen pictures to open the folder titled "Old ghost hunts." My fingers trembled, freezing before I could double click. How many more signs were there that something incredibly wrong was going on? If Drew wouldn't listen, I would make him see. I had to.

My screen went hazy, blinking frantically black to white as I sat before it. I froze.

"Jules," a familiar voice whispered. I felt breath against my right ear. A shiver crawled down my spine.

I looked over my shoulder, but no one was in my room. It was just me. Slowly, I looked back to my computer screens.

"Jules!" Drew's voice yelled at me now, and I jumped.

My face was pressed against a smooth surface, and I was completely disoriented.

Sunlight beamed in through the windshield as we drove past fields that stretched deep into the horizon. Gold flecked with spots of green forests blurred together. How was I in a car? Where the absolute fuck was I? I had just been in my room—it was night, for fuck's sake.

I straightened in silence, looking down to my well-loved jean shorts and *Between the Shadows* tee.

Drew arched his brows beside me, looking bemused. "Having a weird dream? You were talking a lot in your sleep . . ." I caught the worry in his gaze before he schooled his features.

My bottom lip trembled in tandem with my throat burning with reflux. Wracking my mind, I was met with an expanse of nothing. I had blacked out. Tears slid down my cheeks in silent realization of how overwhelmed I was. I had never lost something so absolutely. Just . . . gone. Time and movement and memory had been taken away.

"Hey." Drew's voice was soft with question as he gently reached over, his cold fingers around mine. "Jules, I have known you for over a decade. Talk to me. What's wrong?"

"I . . . I don't remember how I got here. I don't remember going to sleep. Nothing," I whimpered. "The last thing I remember, we were texting last night after the interview. We were trying to figure out that fucked-up footage. Also, your text last night was an asshole move."

I wiped at my face, waiting for his response.

"Jules, I didn't text you last night. And we never had an interview yesterday."

My vision spun sideways. "What are you talking about? Of course, you did. We have the show today, for God's sake. Why else would I be coming back here?"

I reached for my phone in my pocket, but my reality twisted again, and I felt like I was falling.

I was driving. Not Drew.

I had the interview alone.

Drew.

Where was Drew?

Why had I been—

Alone.

A

L

O

N

E

The grating of rubber against cement reverberated against my ear drums as my van was shoved sideways on the opposite side of the road, the screech of oncoming traffic narrowly avoiding colliding into me. I distantly recognized I was on the side of a country road, and I threw the van in park. Hyperventilating, I got my phone, opening it to my thread with Drew—

There was nothing. Nothing recent except this morning at three A.M. *Never.* Sobs racked through me, and I went to Discord.

Nothing except a full-blown conversation *with myself.*

Next, I went to email where there was correspondence with Bryson, only with me, and not Drew. But what about the interview? Hastily, I followed the links from Bryson's social media to a clip of the show.

I pressed play, tears dripping off my chin.

I felt like I was out of my body as I watched myself. For the most part, the interview was the same. But every time I thought he was talking to Drew, my spine straightened, and I got a glazed look in my eyes. Bryson was polite about it, acknowledging how hard it must have been that Drew had been missing for a year. I had nodded mutely, my body twitching like a puppet being moved by an unseen hand. There was a lot more questions that I answered in one word. The interview was terrible. But . . . there. What was real, and what I *thought* had been real, collided into me like a battering ram.

"So, the begging question is, do you think you will ever return to Lakeshore Lane?"

I turned away from Bryson to stare right at the camera, right into the present fucking moment of me sitting in my van, everything I knew falling apart around me.

My head tilted so slowly to the left, and a small smile that I couldn't even begin to recognize pulled my lips as I whispered, "Never."

As Bryson closed out the interview, my gaze blazed and remained stuck on the cameras in an uncomfortable, drawn-out stare. To the left corner in the back of the studio, a tall, shadowy figure stood, features unrecognizable, its hand reaching out for me.

"Oh hell no," I snapped, tossing my phone onto the passenger seat, throwing the van into drive, and slamming on the gas, propelling back onto the country road.

I continued to where I was heading all along.

The closer I got to Haden, the more I started feeling off. I was drenched in a cold sweat, my T-shirt clinging to my body, the cotton suffocating. My blood circulation had gone from my body, my fingers bone white against the black leather of the steering wheel. A chill had settled deep within me. I was blasting heat in August, and it did nothing to relieve how freezing I was.

Then the aches started. They were nothing like I had ever felt before. They were bone deep, but in between my joints it felt like barbed wire was ripping against the bone, the synovial fluid nonexistent against that grating. Every breath, every movement, was excruciating.

I drove faster.

The presence of that fucking house snapped into me as soon as I blasted past the *Welcome to Haden* sign. A darkness that was calling me back, taunting me. All along, since going to that place a year ago, I hadn't even realized I was the lone person to leave it. I hadn't realized I was living in my own haunting. All the while it had continued to take, exerting control over me. I didn't know exactly how all the threads connected, but in my gut, I knew the answers lay there. There had been no contract with Discovery, nothing but me deteriorating in the alternate life that had existed only in my mind. All the while, Drew . . . I couldn't even think it. I *refused* to think it.

I gripped the steering wheel harder, my rage drowning me. I wove through the quiet streets at a breakneck pace, the throbbing within my body getting worse the closer I got. How could a town that looked so normal harbor a vile place like Lakeshore Lane? I swallowed hard. It had its talons in me ever since I left, thinking I was on the biggest break of my career. Except there was no break. There was no more career even, from what I could tell of ignored potential clients on the *Between the Shadows* email. There were only texts to myself, Discord messages to myself, emails to myself. A full-fledged storyline *I* wrote in the first person, a novel of what I thought my life was, Drew alive and well in it.

How terrifying that was to try and unpack. It didn't matter because

Drew was in danger.

I traveled off muscle memory alone, and it wasn't long until my headlights streaked across the front lawn, signs still staked into the ground. The only declaration of the damning nature of this entire place. And along the posts of the *Justice of Class of '24* signs were Jake's and Drew's missing person flyers. Hundreds of them, flapping gently with the long, unkept grass.

Dust kicked up behind my vehicle as I slammed the car into park. "Alright, you fucker."

I seethed at the looming, decaying thing. "I'm here. It's what you wanted all along, and I'm back."

I strapped my GoPro to my forehead and connected my phone for the live stream to be uploaded later on the *Between the Shadows* Instagram profile. Unedited, but there. Just in case. My sneaker hit the ground as I got out of the driver's seat—and I crumpled.

Loose gravel stuck on my knees and legs from the impact. Stunned, I sat more on my hip, pain blistering now through my bones, spreading through my veins like I had ingested some kind of poison. It was weakening my muscles, weakening . . . me. Through tear-laden lashes, I ground my teeth alone in the dusk, glaring at the Victorian building.

I stood, wobbly and sucking air deeply in through my nose to try and balance the lacing pain. I didn't understand what was happening fully, but that didn't mean it *wasn't*. It wasn't all in my head, and I would not be dismissed. I had peeked at notifications and DMs on the *Between the Shadows* social media accounts, and I shouldn't have.

Jules, I'm concerned about you since Drew passed away.

Jules has gone fucking nuts.

God, these guys had such promise.

Jules, you need help.

She is just being an attention whore. Get over yourself.

These assholes hid behind their screens, safe, and unleashed their hate, not caring where or how it landed. Their confidence twined with their assumptions when they didn't even know *me*. They only knew what I carved myself to be on social media, but it wasn't real. It had been a mask too, a business front. A job.

The subdivision at the end of the street was too still, too quiet. Like the simple act of being on the property at Lakeshore Lane was the dividing line between the real world and here. It sucked all sounds of civilization with it. I swallowed hard, finding my resolve.

I took a slow, agonizing step, and 1729 Lakeshore Lane shed its skin right in front of me.

The porch bled into the ground, melting on impact as if it were nothing more than ice in warm water. The decaying wood and rotting shingles fell gently from the structure like crisp autumn leaves making their final descent. The dirty windows shimmered and cracked like they were imbued with starlight itself, flaring before they burst into a thousand particles that hung in the sky like winking fireflies. The sky, which seconds ago had been painted with lush bold strokes of pink and orange, was now completely black. No clouds, no moon, nothing to indicate I was still on earth at all.

A long, drawn-out creak cut across the lawn to me, beckoning as the door—which was still intact—opened by itself. My mouth hung open at what I was seeing.

Instead of the structure made of brick, wood, concrete, and dry wall, a clean white light glowed incandescently and contained what looked like a thin skin. It showed images flashing like a silent film, faces and memories swirling together. Voices overlapped with music that ranged from instrumental jazz to modern synthetic bass.

That light shone so bright, I squinted, turning my face from it.

Then I was thrown into pitch black.

Jules.

Jules.

"Drew," I whimpered, looking back to the house that was never truly what it seemed. It had morphed again, and I knew this was its true face, all its claws and teeth out as plain as day. The massive dome-like organism moved as if it were breathing, alive. Its clear skin that had contained what I assumed were prior victims was now mottled, oozing green with infection and black with decay over the entire dome. The ground shuddered as giant veins of the substance shot toward me, a map of its blight across the dirt-like veins.

My entire body ignited. Flames licked over my skin, blazing through my blood vessels to my heart, incinerating me down to nothing more than pain. It drove every thought out of my mind, and I stood there, glancing down at my arms and seeing the same blackened and green decay spreading over my pale skin, my veins turned to the color of this infection.

It all clicked into place then, my memories rushing back in a tidal wave. And I fell.

Physically, I was aware and watched as my body was wrapped and consumed by those roots that had shot out from the house. I watched as I was dragged into the heart of its darkness, of this evil, vile thing. My GoPro lay left behind, broken and limp within the grass.

But my soul was pulled through time itself, and I could feel the past rushing up to the present, like it was always destined to do. I was beyond my body, falling chaotically, but I could still feel the tether to this gripping evil on my soul. It brought me to this moment, and I could sense just how far the reach of this . . . thing was. Darkness surrounded me, and I continued to fall deeper into it, deeper into time and space, or maybe I was passing through it, nothing more than a wink of awareness to this house.

I landed.

I was standing in a room, in the corner of it, to be exact. A man had his back to me. He was wearing a crisp black suit and paced. I caught a glimpse of the cigar hanging between his lips, whiskey in hand as he talked to himself.

"*Raving mad*, am I? Dolores told me the whole town thinks so. I know they are wrong. All wrong. I hear it inside these walls, a creaking, beckoning when I'm alone—"

"Um . . . hello? Where am I?"

The man froze, cigar ashes drifting onto the plush carpet, but he didn't seem to notice or care. Slowly, he turned to face me, features rigid and pupils blown wide.

All my questions died on my lips. *Holy shit.* This stranger who looked like he was plucked from the pages of *The Great Gatsby* had my eyes. Identical. Right down to the tiny gold flecks that streaked through the green. *My eyes.* I reached forward before I could think about what I was doing, lost in the extraordinary impossibility of what I was going through, what I was seeing. My veins were still streaked black and green, a shooting darkness against my pale skin. My fingers shakily brushed against his hand.

Energy exploded between us, the force of it making me stumble backward. Memories that I thought I didn't have came rushing back, filling the confusing moments of the last year.

Jake being ripped back by that girl—Darbie. His best friend. But Drew hadn't been beside me, like it had wanted me to remember. He ran straight into the depths of this place after Jake, screaming his name.

The door slammed, and the house settled, and I remembered. I didn't call the police. There were no missing person flyers all over here. I watched frozen, chest heaving, as along the bowing grass, slithering lazily like a snake, were the black-and-green veins. They looked like some kind of fungi . . . hundreds of spores woven together. The last rays of light blazed before slipping beyond the world's reach. That vein had wrapped around my legs and arms, my neck and shoulders, before reaching my lips, and like a dying star, every single one of those spores let go, getting breathed into my chest and airways.

A tear slipped down my cheek as I continued to breathe in the hundreds of spores, allowing them to become a part of me. I felt the shift, the foreign organisms overtaking my healthy body. I felt the command they took while attacking me at the same time. Weakening me into the ideal host. The pain was crippling, and my breath became labored, but I didn't move, I didn't run. It was a smart predator, these fungi immobilizing me completely.

It didn't care that internally I was screaming that I had to go after Drew, that I needed my best friend safe. It didn't care how unjust it was to take Jake, Drew, and now me. It didn't care about the lives it was currently shattering, the hopes it was uprooting, making sure that hope would wilt and die. It didn't care about age, that we all had so much more life ahead of us.

It continued to take.

And take.

And take.

It was well into the night before the last of the spores passed between my lips. Completely devoid of emotion, I turned, my body jerking in unnatural movement. I got into our van, turned on the ignition, and left my best friend in the clutches of darkness. My purpose wasn't to be Jules anymore, and I had work to do.

I had no words, no rational thoughts as the truth settled. How could I? This man, this house . . . God, I had never been haunted by it. Unknowingly, I was the victim, my body beaten down, infected and warped. I had become the infection, the haunting, all along.

Appearing now behind Gregory was Darbie. Behind them, hundreds of people flickered in and out of the room. All of them had my eyes, all of us connected. Without blinking, the strangers spoke, their voices all in sync, a monotone echo of each other.

"This power has been here long before humans. When the earth was young and wild, this darkness burrowed into the ground like a seed. Set to grow, to flourish. Except it turned hungry, needed flesh and blood to sustain itself, it thought at first. But it was wrong. It needed something much more potent. It tasted true fear and couldn't get enough of it. The years slipped away and so did its strength. With no physical body to hold it and just existing as energy, it couldn't move or hunt. Until the first human stumbled across it, and it tasted flesh, blood, and bone. Nerve endings and hundreds of memories filled with kernels of knowledge. It couldn't pass it up, and became addicted to the taste. It adapted, changed, and became more and more aware with each soul that stumbled upon it accidentally. It soon realized that it would starve again unless more people came. But to rely on luck alone? No. But what if it was being purposely sought out? Forever? To devour, consume, and destroy with no end?

"When settlers came and established Haden from Ireland, I was the first from the community it killed. My family home was built here. We had no idea the blight that laid below, that monster that we had unleashed. But unlike the rest of my family, I tended to be sensitive to the energies in this world. I could feel it in my bones that we had settled on a wicked land. No one would listen to me. Not even when I first noticed the mold growing in my room." A woman stepped forward, her vibrant red hair curling and cascading down past her shoulders. She fidgeted with her plain black dress. "But there was no peace to be found, no heaven." She uncurled her palm, and twisting there were identical black-and-green veins. An identical-looking fungus stretched and covered her exposed skin.

"What does an infection do? Its purpose—" Gregory Lamar asked at the same time Darbie whispered, "What would want to trick healthy people to become unhealthy?"

"It would want to spread into its environment. To continue to feed," I whispered, looking to all of them. "Did you all have families that would come looking for you?"

"Every single one, except me. But that didn't matter by the twenties. The established cycle of disappearances had already ensured that the urban legend was born within Haden. It continues, too. It's like a Venus flytrap, luring in the curious until it's too late and you are caught amid its jaws," Gregory answered.

The room filled and was wreathed in shadows as they all whispered to me. "This place, once it had our first life, would find our soul in the next."

"And the next."

"And the next."

They all nodded, my past lives, all connected by one thread, pumping breath into this real-life nightmare. But something didn't sit right with me, and I looked to Darbie now. "If this place has latched on to our souls to continue to kill us for all of eternity, to make sure the urban legend never dies, why don't our timelines make sense? I was alive already when you were . . . killed."

She eyed me nervously. "When I died, I felt myself become displaced until I found you. I . . . took over. I pushed out the essence that was there before."

Holy. Shit.

I was reeling. Horror wove through my climbing panic. "But why?"

"Not everything that happens can be explained or understood. Not everything that happens is fair. Sometimes it just *is*," Darbie offered. "But I have my own theory. Don't let this place fool you for a second—it's a monster. And Jake was never supposed to survive that night. I know you have experienced the power it can wield over you."

"So, this is all real then? This place is alive, and I carry its spores of infection? I've been, what, spreading it for the last *year*?" I squeaked.

All my past lives tilted their head in question. "Is this not real enough for you, Jules?"

Pressure wrapped around my ankles, and I was yanked down *hard*. I tried to find purchase, but it was no use, as if the floor had suddenly become viscous. I fell away from the room, the hundreds of faces staring down at me. Darkness spilled around me, winking them out from sight as I was back into a void, only for a second, and I landed again.

The house unspooled in detail all around me. Cobwebs swept down and dangled from the ceiling, the torn and decayed wallpaper curling toward me like beckoning fingers. The air was damp and stagnant, rot and decay and mold overwhelming my senses. I was in the hallway on the main floor, at least from what I could tell. Beyond that, I could see the outline of a broken window swathed in the cool light from the moon. My grip on real life was slipping as fast as grains of sand through an hourglass. All that time, I was never in control of my body. Pain collided with my grief, so potent it rose in my throat, choking off my breath.

My body wasn't mine anymore.

My life wasn't splayed out in front of me, full of hope and growth and change.

I would never investigate a potential haunting again, or share my passions with my best friend.

No more music, blasting my favorite metal bands with the windows down, wishing for an endless day of sunshine and the open road.

No more pleasure or disappointment.

No more dreaming.

I turned away from the hint of the world that was once mine, walking straight, deeper into the house that had claimed me.

I drifted, as if I floated more than walked down the hall. I felt the magnetic push and pull between me, the walls, and all the negative space.

Us.

Us.

Us.

A nondescript whisper curled around my core. "Yes," I agreed with it. "Us."

My hand drifted to trail along the faded, ripped wallpaper. It roughly caressed my skin. Underneath it, fungus bloomed in deep black-and-green patches. I was like Persephone in a withered garden, breathing and echoing the life all around me. I exhaled and spores drifted between my lips, returning home. Blistering pain overtook me. My joints were red and four times their original size, my body exhausted, searing heat moving through me as I watched the patches of skin that weren't covered in fungus become deep red rashes, raised and itchy. Through all that, I saw it: the endless cycle I hadn't known I was part of. The house's deep sense of victory as it counted all the people in the last year I had left trails for to make sure they'd come back here. That's why this place, in the fabrication of my reality it had spun, had broken through.

Darbie in the footage. Her broken nails and bruised hands reaching for me in my first investigation. I had almost reached the end of the hall, where a second set of stairs dipped down on the right, leading to the basement. But there, in the corner, loomed a towering shadow figure.

The skeleton was fused to the wall, held up by roping fungus.

Little clothing remained, and the bones shone white in the darkness of the house. I knew that after the body decayed and there wasn't any organic material left, calcium would fuse with it and turn it white. But standing there, looking at the cracked phone screen at the body's feet, I didn't feel a single ounce of emotion. The void yawned through me, as viable as oxygen. This was Drew. I knew his phone. He was *dead.*

"Never left." I wheezed, and a light erupted to my right, pulsing from the basement.

Pain exploded in a tidal wave and I was sucked within its undertow.

I dropped to my knees.

Internally, I was spun, drained, and battered against it. My fingers gripped the floor, or tried to, but my nails caught.

They broke off.

The invisible pull to the basement was a reckoning. There was no air movement, but a roaring filled my senses.

I crawled on all fours, no thought, just the pure driven instinct that I needed to be down there. *Had* to be.

Just a little farther.

I expected to grapple along the floor still as I wrenched forward, but instead I met air. I fell down the stairs, the steps slamming into my back, arms, and legs. Stars exploded within my vision, and I lay stunned at the bottom. The cold seeped in through the floor, and it smelled like wet dirt and mildew. In snippets, I registered the old, cracked shelving and antiquities scattered within the desolate space. I used to view basements as the belly of the beast in a way—collections of memories of the people that lived there. Years' worth of *stuff* that had been ingested by the worst thief of all: time.

But here, I was in the heart. The tendrils that hung from the ceiling curled frantically and hungrily, hypnotizing tentacles of gray flesh. I couldn't move, my internal pain reaching a blinding crescendo. An orchestra of complete destruction started by this place, by the threads of fate that had long ago claimed my soul.

The first tendril shot forward in a gray blur, punching through to my heart. I saw the red blood spatter, but within my veins, within my blood, peeked green-and-black fungus. I watched in horror as, inside me, thousands of teeth latched on.

The next tendril curled lazily down toward my face, the sucker end of the tentacle flaring as the teeth gleamed. The pain surpassed what I was capable of registering. Maybe I was in shock now. That void thundered around me. Nothing human, nothing of *Jules* left.

Darkness took over as the slimy flesh latched on to my face, and my awareness exploded. I felt them all there with me, every single soul. They were embedded within the walls, within the air and mold and rot. But I could also feel echoes of the people who had died. *Drew. Jake.*

Approval coursed through them all to me. I had spread the fungus to many others over the past year: Bryson, his team, and the *Camcorder Ghouls* most recently. The other team of ghost hunters would come. I could feel their desperation to prove this place was haunted; it was as potent as a fire growing and burning. I could feel the connection that would pull them here like flies that would get stuck in our web before they would be devoured.

My last conscious thought was the sigh of *us*.

The Bite

The embers popped and I watched the sparks float up toward the clear August sky. They flared gold and orange before they winked out of existence. My campsite was small, just enough room for my tent car and dining tent I put up just before dusk swept in. Cedarwood Park was almost fully booked, so I was lucky to get this site last minute. Being right beside Algonquin Park, it often took on the overflow.

Camping had gotten trendy over the last couple years; usually my mom would have cracked a joke. It was our tradition since I was five to come here for a girls' trip. The woods were a sanctuary, absorbing our secrets, dreams, and fears as we shared them over a campfire. Those words were held in our hearts, unless we wanted to breathe them into reality.

I poked the fire with a long stick I had found earlier, staring down at the text from my girlfriend.

Be safe. I love you, Vi, and I'm here for you when you're ready. We will get through this.

I didn't know how long I stared at it. The tiny black letters time stamped me; I received the message at two thirty. It was now almost ten.

Angrily, I swiped at the lone tear that trickled down my cheek. My throat was raw already, swollen from days of crying. Loss, grief . . . they were natural parts of life.

Cyclical, even.

But that bled away when it became your reality. I hadn't been ready to say goodbye to my mom. But that didn't matter either.

She was gone. The funeral that Monday had been a numbed-out day taking people's condolences and thanking them. I hated it. Mom would have wanted something more lighthearted. I think she would have hated how that day went, and I could hear her saying, *"Funerals are for the living, love. A formal way to process."*

She was my role model, my best friend. No one tells you when you're younger that you will always need your parents in a way. That need simply shifts as you grow up.

Cancer didn't care about that. It was a hungry beast—devourer of time and people.

I looked at the three bars on my phone and quickly typed to Laurie: *I made it safely. I love you so much. I just need time.*

I sent the message and then shut my phone off, ignoring the other texts and missed calls from work. I stared up at the sprawling expanse of stars and cracked open a beer.

I was extremely drunk. My vision swam and dipped as I tried to place another log on the fire. I hummed "Fifty-Mission Cap"—one of my favorite songs by The Tragically Hip. The heat from the flames climbed against my skin. I dropped the log, the hiss and spit cutting through my campsite. My pale arm was washed in red from the glow of the flames, and I had the sudden urge to shove my hand in. To feel the pain and the intensity as my skin blistered and bubbled.

I wrenched my hand back and went to sit in my chair. I took a long pull of my Innis & Gunn, which was warm, but I didn't care. I didn't much care about anything currently. My life, my work, even Laurie—who was my rock—had bled away to a distant tether.

I was alone, free floating in my grief.

Looking up, I assessed the empty chair I had set up on the other side of the fire, across from me. Six beers in, I figured it couldn't hurt. No one was here to tell me it was an unhealthy coping method. Everything I thought I once knew about losing a parent had been altered. I wasn't prepared for how a song would trigger a heart-wrenching reminder, or memory. I wasn't ready to move on or *get through it*. I wasn't ready for Mom's family, who were mostly strangers because they were assholes and bigots when I came out, showering me with their superficial condolences at the funeral.

"Mom, I'm sure you would agree with me on that thought," I mused. "You should have seen Aunt Mo's face when she saw Laurie. I think we almost sent her over the edge when we kissed." I smiled at the thought.

"I never asked you though, what you thought happens to us after we die. If you believed in the afterlife. Or what your favorite color was. Or your favorite anything."

The fire spat and crackled.

"I wish you were here. I miss you. I'm afraid I will forget the sound of your voice. Or how it felt to hug you. Why didn't I realize how fucking priceless time is?"

I took another long pull of my beer as the silence resonated.

"Why didn't I make the time to hang out with you more? To just really talk? Why didn't I clue in that I will never get that opportunity back now?"

The hum of cicadas and the odd rustling of unseen wildlife in the forest were my only answers. I opened another beer, setting the empty down beside my chair.

"Lucky number seven. Here's to you, Mom."

Toasting the empty chair, I emptied half the bottle in one swig.

My neck was on fire. Blinking, I groaned, not realizing at first where I was. I reached for Laurie, but she wasn't there. I wasn't in our bed. My chin slouched to my chest; I sat upright in a chair.

I was at Cedarwood.

Mom was dead.

I focused on the cool speckled light fracturing over the dirt, as well as on a pair of leather hiking boots directly in front of me.

I looked up; the woman wore jean shorts and a green Cedarwood collared shirt. A walkie talkie attached to her belt winked red methodically, and I flinched against it.

"Violet McArthur?" she asked.

My mouth was coated in a dry film that felt cottony and tasted like shit. I nodded tightly, swallowing against the contents of my stomach rising in my throat.

"There was a noise complaint last night."

"Really?" I croaked, trying to feign ignorance.

She raised her eyebrows in a *don't bullshit me* way, her long brown ponytail bobbing as she tilted her head, assessing me.

"This is an informal warning. I also brought you this—one second."

I watched in confusion as she disappeared behind the shrub line where I saw the front of her idling truck. A click of a door sounded, and she walked back into view with a tray of coffee from Tim Hortons. The heavenly smell of roasted hazelnut wafted toward me and my stomach lurched, half from desperate need and half from nausea.

"Why are you doing this?" The question cracked out of me, split between a growl and a mumble.

The woman's kind eyes crinkled at the edges as she smiled sadly. "Can I sit down?"

I nodded, thinking the bearer of the life-giving caffeine could do whatever she wanted.

"My name is Emily. I'm a—was a friend of your mom's."

My heart fell to my stomach in a dizzying drop. That was the last thing I expected her to say.

"I'm so sorry for your loss."

Mechanically, I tried to look appreciative, but my face felt like it was melting, pulling away from my skull.

Instead, I took a small sip of my coffee.

"Your mom and I . . . well, our history is complicated. We went to high school together and were best friends."

"Then why have I never met you before?"

"After you were born, we had a falling out. A massive fight, a lot to do with your father. It was stupid, and I can't get that time back. I missed your entire life." She sighed, looking worn. "My biggest regret." She gave a weak smile. "Anyway, during high school we would camp here, at this site, every year. About a year ago, after her diagnoses, she reached out to me. She wanted me to hold this site for you, and to give you this."

Emily passed me an envelope with a sticky note on the back.

"The Post-it has my number and email. I would love to remain in contact, to get to know each other more. But for your stay this week, I'm on. And I'm here if you need anything, okay?"

My hands trembled, the unexpected ties to my mom and Emily's compassion settling heavy on my chest.

Looking up, I tried to say thank you. But tears burned in my eyes as I completely broke down.

The late afternoon sun soaked into the back of my neck. Sweat coated every inch of my skin, dripping down my spine. My calves were on fire, but I relished the hike, the quiet it provided for my mind.

Inhale.

Exhale.

Repeat.

Don't stop walking.

The forest sprawled around me, sheltering me in canopies of reaching branches and emerald leaves. A kingdom of rock and weaving trails—my ultimate escape from reality for a while.

Emily had stayed for the morning, her kindness and openness about my mom an unexpected lifeline. We talked about when she was younger, in her high school years. The parallels to my own life tugged at my gut. She loved musicals and reading. Hated mornings but coffee always made it manageable. Emily's memories helped me keep together what my mom had been like: Brave. Spirited. Loving.

Not the rawest memory of gray sunken skin hanging off a skeletal frame. In her final days, my mom had been so confused, she hardly recognized who I was.

I pushed harder, walking faster. This lookout trail was three hours from start to finish. Grime coated my skin and I slightly felt like I was still going to puke. Being hungover in your thirties was an extreme sport. Not like when I was seventeen and could stay up all night partying and work the next day bushy tailed and ready.

Despite feeling like shit, I was more at peace. Emily was a person I genuinely liked and wanted to get to know better. Kindhearted people who had no ulterior motives were rare and refreshing.

I had a hard time connecting with people and making friends in general. When I was in public school, I had zero common ground with other girls my age. It only got more difficult—living in a small conservative town and coming out. But I wasn't that lonely kid anymore. I knew who I was. I was engaged to my soulmate.

Laurie was the most caring woman and loving partner. I loved my job, helping indie authors build their logos and format novels. I loved horror movies, nature, and basking in the simple beauty all around us in this world.

I was a woman who just lost my mom, and I didn't want to *get over it*. I wanted my found family around me, recognizing my grief, acknowledging it, and helping me learn to carry it.

The farther I climbed uphill, I knew that meeting Emily was the start of something positive and that I wanted her to be a part of my life. Laurie would love her, and the farther I went into the forest, the more I daydreamed—imagining hanging out with my mom's best friend.

A sea of green stretched until it kissed the horizon. Under the buttery light of the late afternoon sun, the lookout over the Hurley Forest was achingly beautiful. I sat on the edge of the rock cliff face with my feet dangling over the edge. It was a steep drop down, but heights didn't bug me too much. I was tired but not drowning in my grief, and that was something. Maybe everything.

Above me, a blue jay cawed, tucked away among the branches. The gentle rustle of the wind brushed against my sweat-coated skin. It was nothing but blue skies and late afternoon heat. Living in Ontario in the summer, you had to accept that the humidity would crash down with an intensity during July and August. But I leaned into it, closing my eyes.

For Cedarwood being fully booked, I hadn't crossed paths with anyone other than Emily and an older couple in their seventies who were camping near my site. I didn't really think about how that could be perceived as weird. But it wasn't a cause for concern.

This far north, isolation wasn't a cage—it was an exhale of relief. People who came to Northern Ontario needed that. I just didn't realize it, coming from Sarnia; it was a promise whispered between the fir trees and pines, kept safe within the sprawling boreal forest. *Up here, you are free.* I took a deep breath of the intoxicating fresh air, leaning into the soundlessness.

Resting my bag beside me, I dug around the granola bars, my dead phone, and the water bottles. The vial was zipped into a small pocket on the side. I gripped it, loosening a shaky breath. *Illegal*, a voice in my mind whispered. But it was in her will, one of her final wishes that a part of her be laid to rest here. I uncorked the vial, standing at what felt like the top of the world, and scattered my mom's ashes to the forest below, to the heart of the land. The last words she wrote in the letter that Emily gave me blazed through me.

I love you, Vi.

"I love you too, Mom," I whispered.

I slipped the empty vial back in the backpack. Then I memorized the view before me: the forest stretching for miles, the golden light, how the air smelled like honey and evergreen.

I willed the scene to sink in, branding into me before I left.

Feeling drained, I hefted my backpack onto my left shoulder, the strap grazing just below my armpit.

That's when I noticed the burning.

I twisted, pulling my loose tank top while lifting my arm. I had a massive welt, at least the size of my fingernail, if not bigger. Dark red ringed the lighter pink center. The welt was peaked, swollen to the point I could feel my heartbeat punching through it.

"Oh, what the hell bit me?"

Chortles sounded behind me. I spun to see a group of teenagers openly laughing at the scene they had walked into.

"Ew," one of the girls said to her friend. The other three boys with them snickered.

Ignore them, they are just stupid kids.

I tried to tune them out as I lowered my arm and readjusted my pack. The acrid smell of beer clung to the group. I didn't look at them as I walked past, thinking more of what I was going to do that night.

"You're a disgusting bitch."

The words slammed into me, making me stop. I spun, taking in the boy who had sneered the words. He stared back defiantly, smirking, as his friends howled in drunken laughter. My ears burned, my heart ramming against my rib cage.

You know better. You know the power of words.

Fuck off was on the tip of my tongue. But with my back ramrod straight, I left, starting my descent with the taste of anger and salt on my lips.

I swam in an endless lake of blood. It ran down my throat, hot, coppery. It splashed against my face as wave after wave rolled in, beating against my futile attempts to keep going. It was an abyss of red, no land in sight. Panic clawed viciously up my throat, cutting off my breath.

I was going to drown.

My arms burned, heavy and tired. My body was pulled down, and I strained to keep my head above the surface, to keep my control. I fought with everything I had.

And it wasn't enough.

Gasping, I shot up, drenched in a cold sweat. I blinked, trying to adjust to the velvet night and darkness of my tent. I was disoriented, but the events of the night came flooding back in. After my hike, I'd had a quick dinner and gone to bed, feeling off and trying not to think about the bite, which I had rubbed antihistamine lotion on.

I knew I'd been dreaming, but my chest constricted, my lungs screaming for air. That's when the pain on my left side hit me.

There was a moment between dream and reality of an almost displacement. Was my mind and soul with my physical body? That floating freedom aways came crashing down. The pain was deep in my bones, which felt like they were rotting. My tight skin burned, as if I had a fever. Scrambling for my phone, I pressed the left side, activating the screen. Silently praising my car phone charger, I looked at the time.

Two in the morning.

Texts from Laurie had come flooding in, her concern growing with my silence. I dismissed them and turned on my flashlight. Awkwardly, I tried to aim the light to my underarm to look at what was going on. My entire left side felt stiff and swollen, and I bit my lip from the pain.

I nearly dropped my phone.

The bite had doubled in size, and thick pus dripped from the center. Below it, down to my hipbone, were another fifty welts.

I tried to rationalize why I had so many, but my mind went blank with panic.

"Fuck, fuck, fuck!"

Did I bring allergy pills or disinfectant? Putting my phone down, I lunged to my backpack, shaking out the contents. Haphazardly, clothes flew and I clawed for anything that remotely looked like first aid. My vision tunneled as I panicked, all the while the voice of the teenager echoing in my mind.

Disgusting bitch.

Choked, hysterical laughter bubbled from my lips as I held the only thing that could help: a pack of baby wipes (and that was only thanks to Laurie, who must have slipped them in). Taking one out, I lifted my arm up again. I could clean the pus oozing out of it like thick cottage cheese. As soon as the wet wipe touched my skin, my vision dipped red. Pain unlike anything I had felt before exploded through my body. It was all I could see, all I could feel.

I whimpered, tears mixing with my snot, dripping off my chin as I pressed the wipe harder over the bite and moved it down.

I screamed.

The smell of rot filled the small space of the tent. I tried not to look at the wipe as I placed it down in front of me. It was impossible though. My gaze drifted to it.

Red streaked through the thick yellow pus, bright and mocking.

Look at what happens when you try to do something for yourself. Look how bad this is.

The whisper was cutting and ice rushed up my back to the nape of my neck, flowering there. I knew that voice. It was the haunting consciousness of my youth, my self-doubt. Anger and hate manifested.

It was back with a vengeance.

My tears flowed harder; my body shook from the force of my panic.

You're alone, pathetically so, the voice hissed. *You deserve this, Violet. Every ounce of this pain, this isolation. No one is coming, and no one will come. You're mine, you always have been.*

I choked, trying to not let myself be dragged down into that void, but all I could think was yes, that was the truth. I was alone, with my grief, with all the broken parts of myself.

Mechanically taking another wipe, I braced for the next wave of pain. But the pus piled on the first wipe moved.

I blinked. Did that just happen?

Two wriggling onyx antennae poked out from the pus, followed by a small glossy body.

My scream broke whatever sanity held me together.

As I wrenched my arm back up, my screams built in a guttural sound as hundreds of these beetles surged out of the bite, ripping my skin away from the middle of the welt. Hundreds of legs brushed down my side. Jumping up, I tried to fling them off me in a frenzy, hitting my side, trying to kill them. Pain split through me each time my hand connected with my side, but I ignored it. Panting, I stripped off my shorts and T-shirt to make sure there were none left on me.

I stilled, then started to hyperventilate.

My futile attempts had done nothing. I had dropped my phone, and the yellow glow shrouded my tent to illuminate hundreds of bugs scuttling across my legs, torso, arms. As if all of them sensed me staring, they simultaneously stopped, their antennae wriggling at me. Smelling me.

Trembling, I noticed that they had tiny pincers, the edges serrated. They clicked them once. Twice.

They plunged them deep into my skin, and an acute pain flowered all over me before I watched in horror as their shimmying bodies burrowed into me at the same time.

My screams cracked, mixing with my heaving sobs. I ripped at each moving lump so forcefully, my nails were bloodied, ribbons of skin curled under them.

Lunging out of the tent, I couldn't stop staring at the rippling wave the bugs made under my skin. I could feel them moving, digging deeper, weaving between muscle and veins to my bones. My pain reached such an intensity, I was vaguely aware that I dropped to my knees. I glimpsed snippets of silver moonlight, the yawning forest, and a dizzying kaleidoscope of my car.

Whimpers shuddered through me. My heart skipped like I was having palpitations before a blinding pain stabbed under my left breast. My breath left my lungs with a garbled whoosh. Tears streamed down my cheeks from my unblinking eyes. I couldn't move, couldn't breathe. Realizing I had lost control of my body, fear so primal rushed to the surface.

MOVE, my consciousness bellowed at me, but all I could do was feel the pain splintering through my body while my skin moved, wriggling, the bugs creating their own current. Burrowing deeper. Becoming me.

My mouth hung open. A wet gurgle climbed up my throat to burst out of me. These insects were drowning me. When the first leg skimmed over my bottom lip followed by another and another, all I could think about was my dream and that endless sea of red.

The bugs ran over my chin, cheeks, nose, and ears. They formed what felt like a hand, fingers spread wide-eagled to cover my mouth completely.

My pain reached an unfathomable level, my fear chasing it. I could barely process what was happening before an unseen force dragged me back by my feet, my fingers scrambling to find purchase in the dirt.

I couldn't scream for help.

I couldn't do anything.

Atticus

It had been Brian's idea to camp at Cedarwood. He was my best friend. Living in Haden, Ontario my entire life and having just finished my senior year, I could taste the excitement of my future truly for the first time. Especially considering that when my mom was a senior, most of her class fell victim to the Lakeshore Lane disappearance. She hadn't been there that night, since she had been vacationing in British Columbia at the time. But her best friend . . . nothing had ever been uncovered. No body, no bones, no fingerprints.

Gone without a trace.

So yeah, I felt lucky making it to this moment since our town had that dark of a history.

To my left, Bri cackled at something Cait said, and I had to suppress the urge to roll my eyes. Luke and Annie, who also joined us for this trip, had slipped into the night inconspicuously, which was likely why my mood had turned. I was sober, but Cait and Bri were fucking sloshed.

"Atticus, did I, uh, mention you're my new fucking hero?" Brian slurred toward my general direction. "The way you roasted that lady earlier, I didn't know you had it in you."

I know he meant it to be endearing, but shame tendrilled and stretched along the back of my neck to flare along my cheeks.

Cait snickered and I glared at her from across the campfire. She flipped me the bird, which I ignored.

I silently wished Luke and Annie would come back; at least we could chat about what movies were coming out or I could ask what Luke had been reading lately. I loved Brian like a brother, but when he was drunk and with Cait, all I could see was that we didn't have much in common— our parents were the ones who did.

"He's too much of a pussy." Cait's voice snapped me out of my thoughts.

"What?" I was getting tired of her constant challenges and insults.

The red glow from our fire made her grin predatory. "Let's do something better than tell ghost stories around a campfire."

I should have kept my mouth shut, but Cait smirked, watching as I pieced together that they were laughing at me.

"What do you have in mind?" I seethed.

Cait leaned over to grab a fresh bottle of whiskey. "Truth or dare."

I rolled my eyes. "Stop being so predictable. You guys play. I'm going to find Luke and Annie."

Brian tilted his head, his eyes glinting black in the night. He frowned, a hardness in his face that I didn't recognize. As if traces of my friend bled away into the darkness, leaving a stranger. I didn't say anything more, just stared back. The hairs on the back of my neck stood pin straight as goose bumps rippled over my skin. There was no reason for my gut to twist into knots, but a deep sense of foreboding rippled through me.

The night was warm, the humidity lingering from the day. A branch snapped behind me in the forest and I jumped in my chair, making Brian and Cait laugh more.

Turning around, I stared into the shadowy tree line bordering our site.

"Did I hear someone say truth or dare?" Annie singsonged as she and Luke sat back at the fire. I hadn't heard them return. I turned again to look at the forest, still feeling off, when a shadow moved behind a tree to the left, nearest to us. Slowly, bone-white fingers curled around the trunk, bloodied and cracked fingernails gripping the bark then dragging back behind the tree.

I blanched.

"Guys," I croaked. "I just saw something."

Annie snickered while Cait shot off a remark I didn't process. Luke stared back at me, brows furrowed; his hazel eyes locked with mine.

I ran a hand through my cropped blond hair, and ire coursed through me.

"You know what, Cait? Fuck you. Brian, I wish you could see what a bitch your girlfriend is being, but maybe you deserve each other."

Silence fell. Luke's eyebrows had disappeared into his curly hairline, and Annie's mouth hung open.

Cait stood, her expression hungry. "Well, dear little Atticus, it looks like you do have a spine after all."

My pulse spiked, and desperately I tried again. "I need you all to listen. Someone is out there watching us right now!"

Luke opened his mouth, "Atti—"

"I'll go first." Cait stood, cutting him off. "Truth or dare, Atti?"

My bottom lip trembled. Maybe it was fear, exhaustion, or realizing the people I thought were friends weren't friends at all.

"I'm not playing," I snarled, looking to Luke, hoping at least he was sober enough to see reason, but he was looking at the tree line, gaze searching. Annie leaned in close to whisper something in his ear.

"How about this. Answer my question, and I will go into the woods to make sure the boogeyman isn't there."

"We need—"

"Did you mean what you said earlier? To that woman on the trail? Or were you just trying to fit in?"

"No."

Cait stalked toward me, anger roiling within her gaze. Against the movement of the flames, her face looked stooped, distorted—her flesh melting like wax. Fat rivulets ran down to collect at her feet, a disgusting blend of flesh tone and blood. Her braided flaming red hair slowly slipped back, her freckled pale skin going with it to reveal flashes of skull.

Yelping, I jumped out of my chair to scramble back, watching in horror as she left a trail of bloodied puddles in her wake.

"Atti!" Luke's yell broke the vision. Cait's body returned to normal. She stood in front of me, slack jawed, staring behind me. The tension was thick, an almost electric current running through the night air.

Fingers dug into my shoulder before my mind could catch up, before I could act.

I was yanked back, Luke's expression of terror the last thing I saw before the forest swallowed me whole.

My back slammed into a tree, pushing all the air out of my lungs as I lay there, stunned.

The sickening crack of my back reverberated through me, and bright white stars flooded my vision. I blinked in rapid succession, trying to focus on the figure crouched down in front of me. This close, I could see the same bloodied and cracked filthy fingernails I saw before. The woman was naked, her skin mottled and bruised looking. She crouched over me, her ribcage bellowing in and out with heaving breaths.

My fear overrode my pain as a gurgling sound wheezed out from her mouth. Slowly, she looked up. I flinched. *I recognized her.*

It was the woman from the lookout trail.

"Are you . . . are you—" I stuttered. "Let me call for help. My phone is back at my campsite."

Her pupils dilated, her face composed of welts easily the size of baseballs. They pulsed, and the rest of my words died in my throat as I truly took in the state of her.

My mom's voice slipped into my mind.

"*Sometimes, Atti, places can contain the blackest of desires, not people. I know that sounds . . . well, absurd. But I've seen it in Haden, and the monster in that town took my best friend from me.*"

In this moment, it didn't sound impossible anymore. This entire trip, a malevolent energy had lingered over my friends, over this place. They had been acting strange, and now this woman . . . when I saw her last, after I said those ugly words, a sadness had cracked through her features, so deeply. There were so many unexplainable things on earth. People had yet to discover everything, let alone understand it all. And a lack of comprehension didn't mean something wasn't real.

This was very corporeal.

Pride swelled in my chest—even though my voice wobbled. "Please, let me help you. I'm sorry about earlier. It was such an asshole move."

I went rigid as she lunged forward, clamping her hand over my mouth. The scent of damp earth and blood flitted up my nose. I started hyperventilating. She was unnaturally strong, and under her touch, my body went limp. I couldn't control it. I tried to move my hands, to rip hers away from my face. To kick, to run, to *save* myself.

All I could do was watch as she leaned in closer.

I'm going to die.

Her breath brushed against my cheek.

I will never see my parents again. I won't be able to tell them I love them, and that they are the best role models. My favorite people.

A choked gurgling erupted from her; I could barely make out the strangled words.

"There's . . . no one . . . left . . . to help," she wheezed. "I ate her from . . . the . . . inside . . . out. Just as I will you."

I won't be able to find my nerve and tell Luke I love him. That I always have.

She moved so she was face-to-face with me now. Her face was slashed with pale moonlight, which made her grin that much more sinister. Hundreds of skittering beetles wove between her teeth, moving up to burrow into her blackened gums, or into gaping bloody holes where teeth had once been. Her eyes were dull, no flicker of human emotions within them.

I tried to scream, but the middle of her palm swelled and bulged against my lips.

The brush of something long swept over my bottom lip, followed by the feeling of hundreds of legs. The force of the bugs pushed my mouth open, and they charged over my tongue and down my throat.

Deep pain split through me entirely. My vision spun, and I dropped to my knees.

They said that in your final moments, your entire life flashed before your eyes. I called bullshit. My mind was blank with panic.

The woman stepped back, wiping a few stray bugs from her lips. They scurried over her digits to dive under what bloodied fingernails she had left.

I didn't understand what was happening. Was she possessed? What kind of insect could even do something like this?

I could feel them biting and digging deeper in my body with every passing second. My breath strained as my throat became obstructed. My heartbeat was a wild thrum, fighting to hold on to life.

Slowly, my thoughts bled away, my sense of self with them. My vision spun faster, a myriad of colors blending the physical environment around me. The trees dissolved into flecks; the ground disappeared beneath me. I gasped for breath, but the lingering shade all around me was red.

Luke

Our camp was in chaos. I looked to Annie, who was screaming my name repeatedly, but all I could hear was a high-pitched droning. A numbness so consuming, I was rooted in place.

"Luke!"

Brian and Cait were already in the Jeep, fighting so intensely I could see their hands flying animatedly. Fighting about leaving Atti behind. Fighting about what we had all seen with our own eyes. It was impossible. Nothing inhuman roamed through life. We weren't kids getting frightened by the thought of monsters.

But what the hell had taken him then? I knew I was in shock, but that fucking hand that had grasped Atti's shoulder was burned into my mind. Rotting skin, swollen knuckles.

Something moved and rippled underneath the skin.

I looked back to the woods and tree line, which had started to spin in my vision.

Why did I drink so much? Damn my nerves. I had been working up to telling Atti that I liked him. Hoping maybe we could go out sometime.

Damn my fear.

"Luke, get in the car now!" Annie had left me standing by the firepit, gray smoke curling and billowing out behind me languidly. We had dumped the water cooler on it, but all it did was plunge the site into deep shadows. Cait and Brian both rolled down their windows, looking at me.

My resolve snapped into place. I straightened and strode over to the Jeep. With my six-foot-three frame, I was over to them in a couple of strides. Brian's, Cait's, and Annie's faces were drained of color, and I realized that this group of people—besides Annie and Atti—weren't true friends. Their friendship was hollow, filled with perceptions of how to act, how to be cool.

It was a waste of time to be nothing but your true self.

"We are not leaving him behind. And none of you can drive. You are all fucking drunk!" I boomed, narrowing my eyes at the keys in Brian's hands.

"Did you see what just happened?" Cait snarled. "Get in the car or we are leaving you to die with your lover boy."

I felt like I had been slapped. The ground fell out from underneath me. Ice doused me from the top of my head to my toes. My mouth hung open slightly as I stared at Annie, tears brimming in my eyes.

"You . . . you told them?" My rage deflated and shock rushed through me in its wake. Annie was my closest friend and the only one I had trusted to come out to so far.

"Luke—"

"Fuck you, Annie. And all of you," I croaked. "I'm going to find Atti."

Annie's face contorted as if my words were a physical blow. Behind her, Brian's hands shook, hovering over the ignition.

A lone tear slipped down my cheek and dripped off my chin.

Cait snatched the keys out of Brian's grip, her face eerily calm as she started the Jeep. Giving me a final assessing look, she calmly said, "I don't give a shit about you."

Leaning forward, Cait put the keys in the ignition. There was a flash of white behind her, and the words bubbled on my lips. "*Behind you!*"

The woman appeared like a phantom beside the Jeep.

Most of her naked body was covered with grime, blood, and dirt. Her hair was long, stringy like parts of it had fallen out. Most shocking were the massive welts all over her. But as she lifted her gaze, I recognized her.

The woman from the lookout.

She grinned.

She moved lithely, a blur. Her pale, swollen arm grasped Brian's wrist and he slumped forward, convulsing. Cait's screams ripped through the night, but it sounded like I was standing at the far end of a tunnel, the sounds distant. I couldn't move. My fear rooted me in a place.

Within the shadows, the whites of Brian's eyes glinted as they rolled back in his head. The woman crawled into the Jeep—her long, swollen limbs moving disjointedly but impossibly fast—over Brian, to reach out and touch Cait's temple.

Her screams abruptly cut off.

"No one will be left," the stranger growled.

Annie turned to try and get to me, but the woman was suddenly

109

behind her, ripping at her hair, grabbing her arms.

Annie fell limp.

The woman then focused on me, repeatedly snarling, "No one left."

You're in reactive immobility. It's your fight or flight response. But you have to fucking move, Luke. To live. Move.

Brian's body stirred in time with Cait's. Streams of blackened blood ran from the corners of their eyes to mix with the blood trailing from their nostrils. As they got out of the Jeep, their eyes locked on me. They'd lost any definition, a milky-white film glossing over their pupils and irises. Silently, they shuffled to stand beside the woman and Annie.

"I will never stop," they all murmured in unison. The slow grin that peeled the woman's lips back was the only warning I got.

They all sprinted toward me.

I screamed, my body finally snapping out of its trance. I turned to run, only to come face-to-face with Atticus.

"No." I moaned. My world fell away. Atti's neck was snapped at a ninety-degree angle.

Shards of bone splintered and ripped through his skin. His once endearing eyes were now that same milky white. His clothes were ripped, and he was covered in spattered, dried blood.

Bile rose and burned in my throat at the most devastating sight: Atti's arms and exposed skin through the rips of his shirt and shorts . . . at first glance, his skin looked like inky scales. Until one of the scales wiggled to burrow deeper in his skin.

Bugs.

Hundreds of bugs.

His hand lashed out, his fingers grasping my throat and squeezing, cutting off my air.

My mouth flapped open and closed.

He squeezed tighter.

I managed to jerk my chin down to the left, trying to convey with my gaze, *Let me go, Atti. I love you.*

His breathing rattled, a long, drawn-out sound. His lungs sounded heavy. *Like something is in them.*

I was too horrified and heartbroken at first to realize that Atti held something else in his free hand.

The world slowed as if I was holding my breath under water as the sharpened end of the tree root pierced deeply into my abdomen. Warmth blossomed over my stomach, wet and hot. I looked down, the end of the branch sticking out of me. It seemed absurd—so deeply impossible that any of this was happening. Feeling out of my body, I touched the end of the stick. My vision spun against the intensity of the pain ripping through me.

I sputtered against my agony, and Atti let me go. Blissful oxygen chased away my sluggish reactions, my vision cleared.

There—to Atti's left, a small opening. The stranger was somehow controlling Brian and Cait, who had formed a circle around me, apparently confident Atti was doing a good job trying to kill me.

Taking my shot, I sprinted hard and fast, making a beeline for the forest. It was a loping run, awkward from the branch sticking out from my gut. But I couldn't pull it out or I would bleed to death; Atti had stabbed me deeply.

It wasn't long until the forest swallowed me whole. I could hear them, the shuffling footsteps behind me, the eerie clicking noise floating on the still air.

I didn't let up, scrambling until I realized my cell phone bounced against my leg in my pocket. *I can call for help.*

With blood-soaked hands, I desperately held my only lifeline, noticing the light brush of something against my fingers from within the depths of my pocket.

Feather light and searching, like a pair of antennae.

Emily

The sharp ring of my work cell made me jump. I snapped my book shut in one swoop; I had been re-reading the same line anyway, unable to concentrate.

The clock on the cabin wall read 12:03 in the morning. I couldn't sleep, my mind churning with memories of Violet and my deceased best friend, Ivy McArthur, my heart panging with a constant ache. Those kinds of memories were like ghosts, wistful and refusing to pass.

I picked up my shrill ringing cell. "Cedarwood Park, Emily speaking."

A muffled thumping sounded on the other end of the line.

"Hello?" I repeated calmly.

"Help me!" a young man yelled, his voice spiking in fear. The service in Cedarwood was spotty at best; his voice crackled in and out.

"My . . . friends"—I realized with horror that he was sobbing—"my friends are dead. I'm . . . badly hurt. Please help me."

There was a pause before he whispered, "There is someone else out here."

Ice slithered down my spine to settle firmly in the pit of my stomach.

"Name and site number?" I asked firmly while checking over my shoulder.

"Luke Smith. 4110. But I'm in the woods, hiding."

"Hang on, Luke. I'm calling for help."

I placed the cell down, running for my landline. As I punched in 911, I held my breath.

"911, what's your emergency?"

"I need police and ambulance to Cedarwood Park. A kid is badly injured. Some are . . . presumed dead."

"And what's your—"

The line went dead, the woman's voice cut off mid-sentence.

"Fuck." I looked at the bottom of the receiver like it might spell out the answers for me.

Why would my landline go dead unless it was cut? Trembling, I put the phone down in the receiver, my body acting before my mind could catch up or rationalize.

"Hang on, Luke. I called for help," I said into the cell, gripping my truck keys and holstered gun, licensed but never used. My dad had always hoped I would get into hunting moose more, but I disappointed him on that one.

Running across my cabin, still in my PJs, I flung the door open.

"Stay on the line, Luke. Can you describe your surroundings? I'm coming."

Adrenaline made my vision tunnel. I stepped out into the humid night—

"Violet?" I gasped.

I slammed to a halt, lowering my cell, but I didn't disconnect the call. Shock froze me in place.

The forest was thick around my cabin, a lot of spruce and fir trees mixed with the maple, but at night it always reminded me of a wall. The shadows bled with the clusters of pine needles and the pale reaching branches often disappearing out of sight.

It was the kind of night where the lack of city light pollution and people created an absolute darkness. One that could take on its own life, playing tricks with your eyes.

Normal scenery could warp and distort into something achingly beautiful. Or in this case, sinister.

Silence stretched between us, but my mind screamed at me. All my coworkers were gone—no one really preferred nights besides me. I was one of the main superintendents, so I lived on site. Violet *knew* that.

The kind, grief-stricken young woman I had spent the morning with had vanished.

Standing before me, Violet was covered head to toe in blood, her stark nakedness masked by a strange movement under the massive open wounds that wept with pus.

"Vi-*Violet?*" The obvious question slipped out of me. My mind tried to digest what I was seeing—what was happening in slow motion.

Her brown eyes were seared black. Her limbs were swollen to the point that her knees and elbows looked more like balloons, fluid hanging in them like separate appendages.

I tried to form a word, tried to still the itch to unholster my gun.

A low wheeze permeated the space between me and Violet. Slowly, her tongue flicked out to lick her cracked lips, a trail of blood and beetles left in its wake.

Hot bile rose in my throat, and I tried to swallow it back down. *Holy fuck.*

"Vi-Violet, come in and wait for the ambulance," I stuttered.

She took a disjointed step toward me, twitchy and inhuman. She held up her hands like she was reaching to me. Most of her fingernails were gone, ripped out, the blood clotted and congealed in their place. In the steely moonlight, I could see the bugs more clearly, half of them embedded in her skin, the other half crawling in and out of her blood.

Primal fear clutched me, and I took a step back.

Through my panic, like a pulsing ember within myself, my tether, was the thought that Luke was still on the line and he needed my help.

Now.

Jutting my chin out, I tried to sound authoritative, calm.

"Violet, you need to come inside. A kid needs my help. Badly."

That seemed to get her attention.

"Inside," she ground out in confirmation. Unblinkingly, she continued to stare at me.

I'm being paranoid. Violet is gravely hurt, and those bugs . . . same behavior as ticks, but they aren't. Step one is to get her inside, then I need to find Luke.

Trying to put on a brave face, I started back to my cabin, my mind swirling with thoughts. I didn't believe much in the supernatural, my brain too scientific for fabrications or what I couldn't see or touch. Was I known to indulge in a scary movie at Halloween? Sure. But that didn't mean I believed in ghosts. I wasn't about to jump to conclusions about Violet, about what had happened, or allow my fear to run off with *what ifs.*

My fingers trembled as I gripped the doorknob, the brass old and worn under my palm.

I pushed the door open.

The creak of the hinges that welcomed me home after a long shift now sounded ominous. My home yawned open before me, pitch black.

Ice dashed through my veins, my heartbeat pounding so hard, I could feel the drumming in my ears. Without a doubt, I had left the lights on.

Maybe the breakers had flipped? But my gut twisted. There was no reason for that to happen. Gripping my cell with white knuckles, I stepped over the threshold into my cabin. I heard Violet shuffle in over the step—she was way too close to me. I could feel her hot breath lap over the back of my neck, the smell of iron and rot floating up to me. I gagged, tears pricking at the corners of my eyes.

Panicked, I tried to get away fast without tipping Violet off that I was terrified. I walked, my body familiar with the layout even in the staggering darkness. Passing the living room and small kitchenette, I turned.

The hallway was surprisingly long; I had painted it burnt orange this summer, but I could only glimpse fragments of that within the reaching shadows.

There is no time to try to get the breakers back on. Your room is down there. Just get Violet to your room, and the washroom if she feels like she can clean up.

My footfalls echoed like thunder and a sharp ringing filled my ears as if I was about to pass out.

"Violet, at the end of the hall is the washroom, and the second doorway is my room. Just wait here until the ambulance comes and the medics can look at those bites."

And bugs, I thought, a shiver rippling through me.

I realized two things in that second.

One. Violet wasn't behind me anymore.

Two. A distant screaming erupted from my cell. *Luke.*

Flustered, I brought my phone up to my ear. "Luke, hang on, I'm coming right—"

"It's her!"

Two words can change everything. The air left my lungs. Left the cabin. Vacuum sealing me in this reality. I froze. Luke repeatedly bellowed the sentence, his voice cracking through his sobs. Every hair on my arm stood pin straight as I trembled, my consciousness struggling to digest what my body already knew. I was alone. With this woman who had allegedly killed teens. *Kids.*

Adrenaline kicked in and I dropped my cell. It landed on the floor with a hard thud, but my gun was already in my hands.

"Stop right there, Violet."

She was nothing more than an ambiguous outline at the end of the hallway. I could hear her ragged breathing, fluid popping within her lungs.

With no warning, she sprinted full force toward me.

A flash of white filled the hall as I fired wildly. The kickback was so strong, I punched myself in the face. Hot copper flooded down from my nose into my mouth.

Disoriented, I lost control, and she was everywhere. With her hands around my throat, Violet slammed me against the wall with inhuman strength. The gun skittered down the hallway. I fought with every goddamn thing I had, but somehow, I went limp, drained to the point where my inhales and exhales felt monumental. I stilled.

Violet came closer to my face, her features mostly cloaked in the night. Before, I thought her eyes had been pitiless, no definition from how dark they were. But now, her milky-white eyes seemed to glow.

"What are you?" I choked out. In response, she squeezed tighter. Under her touch, like grains of sand within an hourglass, I felt my sense of self start to be pulled into oblivion.

How can this be happening?

The thought quickly faded with my memories, feelings dissipating alongside them like smoke. I was emptied, and all the while she stared and stared.

She took everything I was.

With horrific clarity, I realized it never mattered if I understood this, or what was happening to me. My understanding wouldn't stop it from happening.

Whatever *this* was, it was starving, wanting to destroy. To devour. It wasn't personal if its nature was to wipe out, was it?

Behind Violet's head, movement caught my tear-blurred eyes. I blinked. The shadows were moving, rippling like curtains in a gentle breeze.

"No, no, no!" I moaned, but the words came out as a garbled sound. Flashes of silver flickered against patches of the wall as hundreds, if not thousands, of those bugs overtook my home.

I felt like I was in a fever dream. My gaze drifted up. Three figures with identical milky-white eyes crawled along the ceiling with ease. One man's neck was clearly broken, his bulging eyes fixated on me. Screams tore from my chest, up my throat, begging for release. These people were skittering on my walls like fucking spiders, coming straight toward me.

Violet leaned in as black stars winked into my vision, my lack of oxygen barreling me toward my end. Her breath was hot against my ear. "I am the start of this, and no one can stop us. It is in all of us now."

The last thing I comprehended was her hideous peeling smile.

The Study

The transition between summer and fall in southwestern Ontario, in Haden, was my favorite time of year. It always began slowly, with the cool nights sweeping out the humidity. Then, in a rush, the once-long nights turned into burning sunsets hours earlier than the darkness rolled in. The air had a cool, crisp edge, and all around there were signs, if you wanted to look. Tinges of amber, gold, red, and brown dipped along the edges of once-emerald leaves. Later sunrises, drifting leaves, honeysuckle dancing along the air . . . fragrant and nostalgic in the fact that every year we were reminded to let go. There was an allure to that. All around were signs that change could be meaningful. There was beauty in this, and we could only control how we reacted. The forest, the world, flared like a dying star before dissolving back into the universe, to the endlessness of winter.

Back to the beginning.

Usually, I found this time of year invigorating and recharging. I washed off the summer with the magic and promise of autumn. My soul sang if I found myself waking up to a foggy morning, if I could take the time to wander through the quiet of the forest. It rejoiced with every vibrant tree, with every temperature drop.

Halloween was like Christmas to me. I loved the day where the world unleashed its imagination. On what other holiday did people embrace the unfamiliar and make it their own? It had always been my outcast anthem, to celebrate my uniqueness—what others said made me *strange*. It was a day to respect the energy shift all around us, to accept that the veil between the living and dead was there but *especially* on that day, might have been more prominent. Might have been thin, even.

Also, who the fuck doesn't love candy?

Since it was a week away from Halloween, I should have been at home, curled up with my dachshund, Harold, rewatching some of our favorite scary movies. Likely something by Jordan Peele, and Mike Flannagan. Traditionally, my starting night usually includes *Nope* and *Oculus*. Harold and I would curl up, with an amount of Reese's pieces that would feed a small village, order delivery from our favorite restaurant, *Seekers*, for Pad Thai and to-go margaritas. It was a perfect night, leading into multiple perfect evenings.

Ritualistically, I took this week off from work, allowing myself to creatively recharge. I should have been stuffing my face with caffeine and chocolate then wandering my favorite trails, taking in the quiet of the world. Daydreaming about haunted things, places, or people.

But this year, I was the haunted one.

Today was gray, thick, heavy clouds looking laden with rain, like they were about to burst at any second. Leaves hit my windshield in a flurry, the wind shaking them off the branches in wild abandon. Haden had transformed into an endless sea of yellow, orange, red, and brown. The light at the intersection flicked red, and I slowed to a stop. "Season of the Witch" by Donovan filled my car, and I cranked it up, allowing the lyrics to fill me, pushing my mind to sway with it. I couldn't focus on what I was about to do.

What I had to do.

Green filled my vision, and I pressed my foot too hard on the gas, shooting forward. The rest of the drive wasn't long, and soon I turned left and pulled into the small parking lot. Four other vehicles were in the lot, and I parked.

I blinked once. Twice. My sense of time wasn't real anymore. Since *this* started happening. My days were now measured by either feeling grounded or being completely untethered from my body. A sour taste coated my dry mouth, acid burning in my throat. I took a long drink of water from my YETI while taking in my reflection in my rearview mirror. My cheeks were gaunt, deep blackened bags resting under my hazel eyes. My blue bangs brushed my forehead; the rest of my pixie cut stuck out haphazardly against my washed-out complexion. The spattering of freckles over my cheekbones and nose stood out unnaturally. My septum piercing was the only thing I recognized anymore in the reflection.

I sighed.

"For almost a year and a half of feeling like a zombie, I can do this," I told my reflection.

My stomach flipped; I knew that was far from my only problem. I looked at the dashboard, the clock reading 8:05 p.m. The building loomed to my left. It looked to be only two stories, but it was tall. The gray brick matched the roiling skies. There were several windows; one for each room, I assumed. Leaves were caught in the eaves, contrasting against the brown shingles of the roof. From the outside looking in, it was just a house. It was constructed of brick, drywall, and concrete. Surely it would be painted and decorated to be a warm, welcoming place. Made comfortable like a home. But everyone knew that was a mask for what clinical studies happened here.

I loosened my shaky breath, looking for any trace of what only I could see. But it was quiet.

Just a house.

I knew better than most how untrue that could be, and I hadn't slept over in another house since *that one* for the research of my newest horror book: the house on Lakeshore Lane. When my agent got my query pitch that this horror novel was based off the *Between the Shadows* cold case in *my* creepy-as-hell hometown, she had nearly lost her shit. Drew's body had been recovered, but Jules? Vanished.

It was great inspiration, and I had wanted to write a ghost hunting book anyway. But to be able to write, I needed to be able to think, to find words. And I couldn't do that in my current state. To be able to function, I needed *sleep*.

Finding my resolve, I grabbed my overnight bag, locking my car. The beep sounded like a bell tolling, and I pushed through my nerves, through the sense of unease.

I had to do this.

The cold was biting. I pulled my hands into my loose sweater. I walked by the sign saying "Haden's Sleep Disorder Clinic."

I was almost hyperventilating, a cold sweat slicking my palms, but I didn't stop. My phone buzzed in my pocket, and I shut it off. I was Alice following the rabbit down the tunnel. These people, this place, was my last desperate line for help. My family doctor had humored me, but at thirty-one had given me the side eye *its likely nothing because you are too young* look. But I knew my body, and it had been screaming for help for far too long.

So, I shut off the outside world, pushed the door open, and went inside.

The front desk was empty, the building so still. The pale green walls were lined with abstract art.

"Hello!" a kind voice rang out behind me. I clenched my teeth; he scared the absolute shit out of me. I was one of those people who instead of jumping, my body utterly froze. I turned. The man was young, maybe around early twenties. His auburn hair curled at the tops of his ears, his bright cerulean eyes crinkling at the edges as he smiled. He scanned the clipboard he was holding, his scrubs Halloween themed.

"Umm . . ." He searched through his list.

"Theo—uh Theodora Anderson."

"Perfect! Follow me, please."

Past the waiting room was a labyrinth of winding hallways and closed doors. As we walked, the sleep tech peeked over his shoulder. "Theodora is a unique name."

I shrugged. "Not really. My parents really loved *The Haunting of Hill House*. They were both horror enthusiasts."

"Movie or book?"

"Both, but I think the movie more." I picked at my nails, trying to take in this place. I loathed small talk, but I tried hard not to glare. This kid was just trying to be kind. It wasn't his fault I felt like I had been broken and sloppily put back together. We walked down the winding hallways; I had already lost track of how to get back to the front. My anxiety rose to grip my throat in a choke hold.

If the tech noticed my fear, he hid it well and continued to babble happily.

"Well, that's wicked, in my opinion. Okay, so here is the waiting room. Your tech for the night will come shortly to do your intake. Sound good?"

Nodding stiffly, I froze in the doorway.

The six other men and women in the room looked to be in their sixties, at least. Pairs of eyes locked on to me, but I couldn't focus.

A brilliant myriad of shadows exploded through the room. Perhaps it was the absence of light that made the nightmares attached to these strangers that much bolder.

Normally, I would be able to act naturally as I took in what lingered in the recesses of people's minds. They couldn't physically hurt me, they never have. The individuality of fear was haunting and beautiful, and as common as dreams.

I could see it all.

Like a movie, the nightmares would repeat above or behind the person, full manifestations framed in smoke and shadow.

Some mediums saw auras, others could see what happened to someone through touch or visions. Me? I only saw people's nightmares, attached to them like goddamn leeches.

The first time I realized I had this ability, I was six. It had been a quiet Sunday morning, and my mom had been making blueberry pancakes. The scents of vanilla, coffee, and maple syrup drifted through the kitchen. The buttery yellow walls of the kitchen glowed with the light of early morning. My mom had pranced around in her polka dot apron, nodding along to Fleetwood Mac. I had felt so safe, so loved, that to my six-year-old mind, the world outside was transported away when I was with her. That was my mom's superpower. Always had been.

I remembered how the light fractured through her strawberry-blonde hair, spilling over her shoulder. She beamed at me, and I smiled back.

A pale wet hand had appeared, gingerly tucking her hair back behind her ear. I was so confused. But I was six and I didn't know I shouldn't look up.

The man's mouth opened and closed like he was trying to say something but couldn't form words. Both of his hands left my mom and frantically clawed the air above her head, like he was trying to swim to the surface. Shadows exploded out behind him, swallowing up any light that had been in the room. Rooted in fear, I watched, trembling, unable to take in a breath.

The man's eyes rolled back. His body stilled. His lips paled and turned blue, his skin draining to a grayish hue. Strands of his hair floated up, defying any sense of gravity, any sense of reason. My mom acted like nothing was wrong, and I realized she couldn't see him. His body oozed with black smoke, and it drifted across the counter like a fog in front of me.

Tears spilled down my cheeks. Distantly, I heard my mom ask, "Honey, what's wrong?"

Behind her, the drowned man's eyes snapped back open. I screamed.

Wrenching out of the memory, I concentrated on my breaths, moving to sit down in an empty chair. I looked down at the ground, not focusing for too long on the nightmares all around me.

I'm in control. I'm in control.

I'm.

In.

Control.

Ghosts are my life. Memories, the past, aspirations, failures, accomplishments, trying to find self-love, were just some of the common nightmare fuels I see every day, contorted into metaphors or phobias. Ghosts are the loss of time, slipping away from youth. Ghosts are reliving the past, not able to see your future clearly. Ghosts are isolating, and ravenous. Greif, trauma, loss—that was just the fuel to pour onto these things before it exploded into devouring flames.

It had been a long time since I was in the path of another nightmare's destruction, another body in its calamity

Today was not the day that was about to change.

"Theo Anderson?" The tech looked around my age, her hair tied up in a messy bun, her liquid gold hair piled on top of her head. I stood and she offered a smile as I crossed the space toward her.

A hanged woman's rope creaked in unseen wind behind me.

A man who resembled a version of Slenderman followed my steps.

Another man cried at his desk, clutching a final notice within his grip.

A heart monitor beeped.

Someone screamed, trapped in a sealed casket.

A teenager stuck a needle in between his toes, pressing the syringe down. *I'm in control. They can't hurt you unless you acknowledge them. So don't, Theo.*

I tried to just focus on the tech, but my nails bit hard into my palm and my head tilted toward the chaos of the waiting room. I could feel each individual fear, the slimy icy feeling coating my exposed skin, my hairs stood pin rod straight on the back of my neck.

"My name is Mandy and I'll be your sleep technician tonight. Follow me, please."

Fucking finally.

Her brown eyes gleamed as we left the waiting room and went down another hallway. After almost a decade of being a successful author, I knew that look. It was the same one people had while clutching my books to their chest, coming up in line for me to sign. But you never know where you may meet a fan.

"Are you . . . *the* Theo Anderson?"

I smiled, which felt stiff on my face. Stretched too wide, too unnatural. "Yeah."

"Holllllly shit." She did an excited little dance as we turned down another hallway that was identical to the first.

"It is amazing to meet you. I've been a fan since I got into reading again a few years back and a friend of mine recommended your work. I think you are a total badass." She squeaked. "And local." She drew out local in a sigh. Like Haden was some mythical place, undiscovered. Before I could answer, she asked, "I'm sure you get this question a lot, but where do you get your inspiration from? Your books are the only ones that I actually can't read at night. *Lingering Screams* gave me nightmares for weeks—I mean, that ending was insane."

She led me into an exam room and gently the door shut behind us as she gushed. Usually, I was happy to talk about my work, but that changed this year. Exhaustion dragged me down into a place I never knew existed. One where my limbs feel like a hundred pounds, where if I even sat down, I would fall asleep. Nothing about this was gentle; it was being dragged down into an undertow, an abyss of nothing, a torturous cycle that no matter how much you slept, it would feel like you haven't slept at all.

To repeat day, after day, after day.

My stories, my dark passions that made me feel whole, along with the complete rush of adrenaline that coursed through me as my pen glided across my notebook, when my fingers flew across my laptop keyboard. It was a place without fear, without restraint, and to me, there was nothing like it. My characters were my safe space to explore my fear safely, my trauma safely. Every single book, I loved knowing even if my readers didn't, that pieces of my soul were imbued within those pages. Every time I finished a book, it was like smoothing a rough edge, cathartic for the horror I was exploring.

And I let it go.

To be free, was to be a writer.

My creative freedom was the first thing I lost in this bullshit.

The headaches at first I had just barreled through. But the exhaustion was another story. It wasn't just being tired. It was feeling like you were drugged, and the small amount of energy you have is taken up by the sheer iron will of trying to get up. It was staggering down the hallway to fall onto my bed to only stir when the day had bled away and the sweeping lull of night greeted me. The first month passed in a blur, each day eluding me, each night waiting for me, to embrace me in its dark arms.

And my words ceased. My past novels? Were a distant echo in my memory, as was my life I had been used to. My friends disappeared with each text I sent back, saying I didn't feel up to it, but not having anything more concrete than that. Turns out people didn't have much tolerance when you became an inconvenience to how they imagine you fit in their life.

When the cycle only intensified, my self-care slipped next, my daily routine dissipated like smoke in the mirror. In its wake, I was left a mere ghost. I would wander through my apartment, only to slip from my bed to the couch. If I had to go out for groceries, I would set out into the world for harsh judgements and assumptions. And exactly like a haunting, I was stuck, only to repeat this new hell. My new crushing reality was no matter how long I slept, I never feel rested.

After a year and a half, I was stretched thin, going through movements to keepsurviving, but never to live. I had long forgotten what it felt like to want something, or enjoy hobbies, to have a social life. My skin was an encasing, keeping my organs in place, keeping everything else structurally sound, but I had been drained. A living zombie, the term had turned into my sick new personal joke. This husk of myself was left behind, to watch all around me as life moved forward and I was unable to join. So I watched, left alone in my rage, grieving the person I had once been.

I watched Mandy now. She was seemingly being kind about my lack of enthusiasm or response to her being a fan. Briefly, I glanced up. She was collecting papers and her clipboard for my intake.

"Okay, so first let's take your weight and height."

Standing, I stared at my shoes, feeling a brush of breath against the back of my neck. Every single hair on the back of my neck stood straight, under the sudden chill that now spread across my skin. My gaze darted around the room. Mandy. The burning body. Her desk. The walls, adorned with puke-colored paint and bullshit art. This one had a young girl in a frilly yellow dress reaching down to pet a white rabbit.

But never what I knew was behind me.

A freezing cold hand slipped into my own from behind me. Bile, hot and acidic burned up my throat. I pressed my lips firmly together, swallowing frantically.

Get a grip. It's not there. Nothing. Is. There. Walk to the scale, don't acknowledge it.

"Come with me." The gravelly voice brushed against my ear lobe, and I flinched.

"Theeeeeeeo."

"Theo? Everything okay?"

I snapped my gaze up to Mandy, focusing only on her. The presence on my hand evaporated, along with *her* presence.

I'm fine. I tried to say those two words, but I couldn't. I opened and closed my mouth a couple times, watching as Mandy's eyes softened. Gently, she led me by my elbow to the scale, allowing space for the comfortable silence. The simple act made my lips wobble, tears pricking in my eyes. No one in the last year and a half had allowed space for this. The space to not have to explain, the space of empathy. I loosened the exhale that was knotting in my chest as I stepped onto the scale.

"My symptoms. They're getting worse. It's really getting to me."

Mandy recorded my weight, not giving me the usual bullshit of raised eyebrow, *if you only lost weight, you wouldn't be here you know* look that other doctors had even had the gall to say right to my face. A tear slipped down my cheek and frustrated, I swiped it away. Crying wouldn't help anything. I had trouble showing my emotions or expressing them to another person. Harold took the brunt of that, and embarrassment swept through me that my control was cracking in front of this stranger. My voice, my creative expression, had always been in my written words. If you asked me to try and say it, it usually came out a garbled mess. Now was no exception.

Following Mandy back to my seat, I chewed my lip. *Just try,* my subconscious whispered. What more did I have to lose?

"Something has been happening that pushed me to get the requisition to do this sleep study. I . . . I've been seeing things. Well, not a thing; someone. And hearing things that aren't there. I think, anyways."

Blink. Every single muscle in my body was taut with tension. Even in 2045, with mental health much more understood and treatable, it was hard for me to admit that this hallucination, or auditory hallucinations, was happening to me.

I watched Mandy write something down on her sheet before saying, "Did you know that parasomnia happens in one in ten sleep apnea patients? What this means is that you could experience hallucinations, sleepwalk or even sleep paralysis. The body—the brain needs oxygen to properly function, Theo. Untreated sleep apnea can cause some of these, or even all of them. And it's what I promise you we will find out tonight and get a diagnosis."

An overwhelming weight crushed my chest, every desperate emotion and frustration welling to a peak at this. A promise, to help, to get this resolved. To feel like myself again. My breath came in shallow gulps and a broken laugh escaped me.

"Thank you. I have been feeling like . . . I've been losing my grip on what's real and what's not. The girl I have been seeing, she is terrifying." I wiped my face again, unable to stop the tears that ran down my cheeks.

"You know most of my patients say similar things. Everything you have just told me is totally normal, and completely understandable. Sleep paralysis is terrifying to experience. The things that patients describe often come across as an aggressive presence. Not getting REM sleep is detrimental and add in a long term to this . . . well, let's just say it makes a perfect storm to breed nightmares, that feel extremely real." Mandy gave me an encouraging nod. "Now, let's dive into these symptoms with a bit more detail and finish our intake. Okay?"

"Okay."

Only after I go over my symptoms, medications and health history did Mandy and I go out into the hallway again. It was eerily quiet for people and workers I knew were in here, not to mention that from the outside looking in, this building was so deceiving. The hallways seemed endless, stretching and turning into its own complicated labyrinth. The padding of our footfalls on the linoleum created a soft echo, and the only noise. I couldn't handle it.

Feeling drained, I asked Mandy, trying to make small talk, "So, what was this place before it was Haden's sleep clinic? The building layout is unique."

There was a slight misstep as Mandy shot me a quick look. Was it in my head, or for a second did she look afraid?

"Um . . . well considering your career, I'm surprised you don't know." We came to a door with the label 'Room number six' beside the frame. Mandy opened the door with a creak and we stepped inside. The queen bed had a clinical looking pale-ivory sheet set, beside it was an empty wooden night table. The room had one window that looked out to the parking lot. Pale curtains framed it, and in the left-hand corner an empty dresser stood. At the opposite top corner, facing the bed, was a black security camera, the tiny button on it flashing red in steady beats. The hairs on the back of my neck pricked; this entire space had horror movie written all over it. I had the sudden urge to tell Mandy not to answer my question—that I didn't want to know. Being a medium had its perks and downfalls, and being sensitive to places was one of those downfalls, depending on the history. But it hadn't crossed my mind what it could mean, a place that not only saw hundreds of people that were plagued by their nightmares, but the building having a dark history on top of that? Horrific things and tragedy leave a residue, as much as the nightmarish wraiths I see attached to people.

It would be dangerous. The perfect storm for me.

"It was a girl's orphanage, before it was closed in the late 1960s. Eventually, the town bought the empty site for the clinic but it sat empty for a long time."

Mandy was scared. She wouldn't meet my gaze head on, and her index finger on her right hand picked at the edge of her thumb, the red and semi-healed skin around the nail suggesting that it could be a habit—one that is driven by anxiety or nervousness.

"Let me guess—it was run by nuns?"

Mandy nodded.

Fuck. My. Life.

Setting my overnight bag down, I sat on the edge of the bed. It creaked underneath me, old springs protesting through the thin and lumpy mattress. The silence stretched between us before I replied, "Why would you think it strange that me being a horror author but I don't know what happened here, Mandy?"

She shifted, not meeting my gaze. "My boss doesn't love us to say. I slipped up.

Between you and I though, there is a local haunting myth around here. Some of my coworkers like to talk about it on the down low, you know as fun." She paused, looking up to hold my gaze, the flickering flames of her nightmare behind her casting us in a red and orange glow.

"The last head nun, Sister Maria, it was rumored she abused the girls who were in the orphanage. One of the other nun's journals was found here, way back when it was first being turned into a sleep clinic. Or allegedly was." Mandy smirked, and the tension that had pinched her features before eased as she settled into the story. That was the magic of storytelling, truly. To transport into the heartbeat of the words, painting a scene so vivid it went past emotions. It possessed you, commanded your attention. Mandy was in the middle of that magic right now, and my heart wrenched, jealousy coating my mouth bitterly.

"Sister Maria would make up new rules daily, and anyone who made a discretion would be victim to brutal lashings, chained down in the basement here for days without food or water, or even reports of her burning an iron rod into the girls' backs. Fear gripped this orphanage. Fear of speaking out, to reaching out to the Church. Because Sister Maria had claimed *God* told her that these girls would need this abuse to be faithful Christians once again. That the abuse would wash their sins away, and when they would get adopted after enduring this orphanage, it would mark that their faith was pure." Mandy was visibly shaking now and I swallowed down my own rage.

"Then, girls reportedly started to go missing. I read one of the journal entries myself.

My friend found it online from the library archives. Apparently after it was found here it was turned into the Haden Museum and public archives. Anyways. This nun, Sister Theodora," Mandy winced slightly at the name coincidence, "I remember this one line: *there is no trace of humanity within her, let only faith. Rather an entity that thrives off being evil. None of the girls who were reported to have fallen fatally ill were showing signs before. I fear for us all, and I am going to try to gather proof to bring forth to the abbess in Rome. Even though Haden is but an afterthought to them, I must make them see that there is something horrifically wrong here.*"

My mouth went dry.

Mandy's voice dipped lower, as if the very walls and bones of this place was listening to their conversation. "October 31, 1959. Haden police responded to a call at three am from a Sister Theodora. In the police records—" She paused, taking in the smirk that was now pulling at my lips. "I know. I'm a bit of a horror and true crime buff. I looked into the records on my off time." Mandy grinned, mirroring my own now. "A Sergeant Smith said all that came through on the call was a disjointed voice, that whispered, *help me*. He traced the call back to the orphanage and was the first one to find them."

"Them?" I croak, the elation at sharing a passion with Mandy now swept away. A cool breeze brushed through the room, which was impossible with the windows shut. The bare walls feeling even more oppressive than before. *Get a grip. It's the suggestion of horror that's getting in your head. You're assuming the worst.*

"In the incident report, it was said . . . the carnage was almost indescribable. Sister

Theodora and all the girls had been brutally murdered. There was no sign of Sister Maria. In Smith's report, he said . . . that every body had been strung up, hung with their arms splayed out, nailed into the walls. To mimic the suggestion of a upside down cross." Mandy tried to steady the wobble in her voice.

Oh, what the fuck? My stomach churned. I felt the bile rise in my throat; I wanted to be sick.

"Did they find Sister Maria?" I whispered. "I mean, even if she ran . . ."

Mandy paused, her gaze narrowing. "Are you okay? I'm sorry, I assumed that—"

I offered a small smile. "I'm okay. It's not your fault for assuming. Horror is my life.

My career. A lot of the time, it's assumed for one to write horror that equals an inability to feel fear, or get scared. When the truth, I think it's really the opposite. I can't speak for all the horror authors out there, but I was originally drawn to the genre because I wanted to understand my fear, my trauma more. And writing being my creative outlet of choice, it really found me in a lot of ways. The genre." I glanced down at my clasped hands that rested in my lap, desperately hoping this was making sense.

"Writing horror drives me, excites me, to explore fear. I quickly fell in love with chasing that feeling, of what people find scary and why. But adding kernels of my own feelings into each story, each character it was so healing. There is a lot in the world that scares me, and quite often. Writing was—*is*—a safe way to explore that trauma."

"That's . . . really beautifully, actually," Mandy replied from the chair she had pulled from the corner that I didn't even notice. She sat across from me, brows furrowed, looking far away in thought for a moment. Behind her and her burning nightmare, I also failed to notice the medical looking stand. It looked like it would reach my hip if I was standing, with two black hooks on either end of the T-looking structure. Grey cords were wrapped around the top and bottom hook like a vacuum would be wrapped, except there were literally hundreds of them, with round flat head suction looking monitors on the top of the tray.

My stomach flipped nervously, tying itself in knots. I could ask to reschedule—I could not go through with this. Getting a sleep study done to begin with was creepy enough; knowing someone was watching you was unnerving. How would I fall asleep, I had no idea. But the cords . . . I had no idea what they were going to be used for, and I hoped nothing.

They wouldn't be in the room if they weren't being used.

Mandy followed my gaze before saying, "There's more to the story."

I'm in control. The thought made me clench my jaw so hard my teeth hurt. I nodded, my voice sounding strained and far away even to myself. "I would like you to finish it, please."

"Because of the nature of the murders and the journals left behind by

Sister Theodora, it was turned over to the homicide department. At the time too, the idea of serial killers was just being explored more and being such a small town . . . well, you can imagine how it rocked Haden. With further investigation that led back to the abbess at an abbey in Rome which is where Sister Theodora took her veil, and in the journals she had wrote what a coincidence that Sister Maria had originated from that same abbey." Mandy's cheeks drained of any color that had been left in them.

"There was never any record of a Sister Maria, not taking her veil, not having employment to go to Haden to run the orphanage. Nothing. Not even a nun that matched the description. After that was eventually released to the press, came the panic. People wondered: had it been premeditated? Had the killer watched the orphanage, Sister Theodora and the girls, a hunter blended into small everyday life? The time that would take to pull it off convincingly well. The thought of a predator like that cracked the community. I remember my grandma talking about it, vaguely. It was one of those things that I don't remember what was said but I remember the tension the words caused. The fear. But the flip side of the situation, people whispered about vengeful spirits. That the orphanage was cursed and haunted."

"That's not the first time that has been speculated about places in Haden. Or even people from Haden," I murmured. Internally, I ticked off the incidents I did know about.

Kinsley Matthews disappearance.

Darbie Barlowe.

Jules and Drew from Between the Shadows.

Up north at Cedarwood Park, a group of teens had gone missing under suspicious circumstances.

Even though my heart was in fiction, my very dreams built and carved from horror, I also had never first handed experience with anything paranormal.

Even when I spent a night camped out in the deprecated, rotting house on Lakeshore Lane, all I encountered was overwhelming sadness at the tragedy that had happened there. My allergies had flared due to the dust and mold, and the only thing I was promised was a terrible night's sleep, tucked in my sleeping bag, my phone recording hoping to pick up a disjointed voice or even maybe a spirit. The deep want I had to experience the paranormal—the mystery of what is beyond our physical life—had never been satisfied. The wraiths I saw, though was a gift of sight, was only that. They were like a clip being on repeat. They couldn't hurt me; they could only do damage to the person that the nightmare was plaguing.

So, I wrote about such things. Stories that held love, friendship, self-discovery, meeting head-on with unthinkable horrors or ghosts. Our real world was full of both—and that's what readers chased; what writers, at least myself, wanted to really highlight. That scary stories could be plausible. For it to feel *real*.

The silence that stretched between us at that was thick. Outside, the wind was picking up, spattering of rain tapping against the glass of the window, shadows of bare tree limbs moving against the curtains, stretching against the walls in the room, the wind moving them wildly. Images of a silhouette dressed in a black veil and robes flooded my mind, the story already running free in my imagination. Tap, tap, tap. A lone pale finger, against the slickened glass. *Let me in,* the disjointed voice would whisper . . .

No.

I slammed walls down mentally, stopping that train of thought.

"Mandy, that is all super fucked up," I said candidly.

"Trust me, I know. When I first started my position, my friend was surprised I accepted the job to work here. With the night shift and all that."

"I assume the case went cold?"

"Yupp."

"And that this building is . . ."

"Haunted? Between you and I, most definitely. I've heard things before, in person and on recordings. I also refuse to work on Halloween night. It's said that whatever took on the form of Sister Maria still wanders these halls, never sated. Always wanting more."

I exhaled, nodding slowly, any response dying on my lips, with two words repeating throughout my entirety.

Well, shit.

I stood in front of Mandy, arms stretched out to either side of me in my tank top and plaid pajama bottoms trying not to feel extremely uncomfortable about how *weird* this process was. Mandy had resorted to just talking, to letting me know what the next step were. I sensed she was lost in her own thoughts, just as I was. It helped, for now, to put my own speculation to the back of my mind. Many scooped another thick glob of the conductive paste from the small round jar, before applying it to my parted hair, onto my scalp. For the last forty minutes, after I had gone to the washroom, brushed my teeth, and got changed, I stood here, as glob after glob went on. It covered my ankles, legs, arms, chest and now scalp.

"Almost there," she murmured, attaching another wire.

There were over three hundred wires, Mandy had explained, that would collect data of brain waves, eye movements, heart rate, limb movement. I tried to take small breaths—the stretch band that we had first placed around my ribcage to measure my breathing patterns the most annoying thing.

"Oki doki," she chipperly said. "If you want to lay down now, then I will attach the pulse oximeter, and the nasal cannula, that will read your blood oxygen levels."

I nodded, and Mandy pulled back the sheets to help me out. Awkwardly, I settled in, wires literally crossing over my chest, arms, legs. Looking up at her, I blinked. Memories of my mom tucking me in when I was young flashed, how she would read me her own favorite *Goosebump* books, the covers creased, the pages yellowed with age. She would always do different voices for the different characters, and the sound of her regaling spooky story would always send me off to a dreamless deep sleep.

"Index finger, please."

I blinked back the tears that were burning in my eyes at the unexpected memory trigger, and stuck my right index finger out. Mandy clamped the monitor to the end of my finger gently before nodding. "Okay just the nasal cannula and then that's it! Next will be the audio check where I will ask you over the speaker above the bed to do some simple movement to make sure all the wires are working. If you need any help during the night, you can press this button, or even just ask for me out loud. I'm watching," Mandy pointed to the security camera, "and listening."

Creepy, I thought as I said, "Thanks."

"Of course. After we do the audio test, you can browse your phone or whatever, but try to fall asleep at your normal time, okay? It's ten-thirty right now," Mandy added, glancing down at her phone.

"Sounds good."

Mandy had put away the set-up wire stand and the supplies away already, but I watched her linger in the doorway. "And I am sorry about before. I shouldn't have made assumptions—"

"Mandy, trust me, it's all good. I get it. It is a really creepy story."

A tiny smile pulled at her lips and she nodded. "Yeah, it is. Night, Theo."

"Goodnight," I replied.

The room was plunged into darkness. My eyes took a second to adjust, but I could still see Mandy's silhouette was outlined in the doorway still, hand reaching toward the doorknob to pull it close—

I blinked.

Behind Mandy stood a tall black veiled woman, her grey hand moving to grip Mandy's shoulder.

"Mandy!" I squeaked and the entire room changed. The light hadn't been turned off yet.

And Mandy was only now standing in the doorway. Cold sweat peppered my forehead, and my heart was galloping, punching against my ribcage.

"Theo? Did you have a question before I go?"

You are beyond sleep deprived. I swallowed, my mouth dry and sticky.

"Sorry . . . I just thought I saw something."

Mandy's gaze softened. "Just remember I am a call away."

Hallucinations are normal, I thought repeatedly as I watched Mandy leave, this time for real.

She flicked off the light.

The door was pulled shut with a gentle creak, followed by a click.

I lay too still, my breath feeling hitched by the band around my ribs. The wires crossed over my neck and chest, the ones on my arms felt tangled in the sheets already. Weirdly, it felt like I had expanded into the wires and monitors on me, spread out like a web. My imagination already was spinning the story—the young woman laying in the dark, afraid, reduced to the sounds around her. Underneath the sheets, something wriggled. Horrified, she realized that from her flesh tendrils of skin were separating from her—turning her into something *else.*

Nope.

Mentally, I killed that thought, throwing up my walls again. You would think for a horror lover I would know better: don't think about these things alone in the night, in a place with a dark history. Of course I was going to freak myself out, but it was like breathing to me, my imagination running with simple situations, turning them into different horror stories.

Sighing, I tried to keep my mind empty, as I grabbed my phone. Pressing the button at the bottom, I entered my passcode before going into my texts. My best friend, James, was babysitting Harold tonight. I opened our thread.

Theo: Whelp, you will never guess what I found out tonight.
James: That your boi is the bestest, most spookiest wean bean in Haden?

An image of Harold flooded our thread, sitting beside James on our grey couch. On top of his tiny, perfect head was the top of a pumpkin, craved into a tiny Harold-size hat. Harold's wide brown eyes and long snout that had splashes of grey around his muzzle stared back at me, pleading through the phone screen, *Uncle James dressed me up and I don't know what to do.* Laughter burst from me, and I couldn't stop giggling or grinning as I typed back.

Theo: What did you do to my poor buddy? Sidenote, it's already my phone background.
James: Your balcony needed its Theo flare. I know it's been super shitty for you. This is a reminder that I love you and so does Harold.
Theo: You are the best.
James: Don't you forget it! Now, what did you find out tonight?
Theo: Haden's very own sleep clinic? Yeah, it was the scene of a fucking mass murder. Look it up.
James: Whaaaaaaat.
James: Holy shit.
Theo: Yeah so, I just got told that while I was being wired up and

tucked in. Knowing that the very room I was in . . .

James: There is likely a ghost girl hanging upside down above your head?

I rolled my eyes and waited for James to realize how bad of a joke that was. My phone dinged.

James: Okay that was in bad taste. But seriously Theo, what the fuck? How are you going to fall asleep knowing that?
Theo: Give Harold a squeeze for me, and I'm going to wish for the best.
James: I will get you a Starbs in the morning, my brave friend.
Theo: :D

I smiled before putting my phone back down on the side table, wires dangling and bumping as I did so. James and I had been friends since he moved in next door to my mom's house when I was seven. His ashen hair had been standing up wildly, like it had its own electric current, his almost grey eyes held a certain amount of mystery in them even at seven I wanted to know everything about this boy who suddenly showed up on my doorstep wanting to know if I had a bike and if so, could I show him around the neighborhood. Gangly, he stood tall, brow arched, demanding in a kind way.

Both answers had been yes, and so I had.

There was a beauty to the kinds of friendships that defied laws of time. As we had biked around Haden for that first time all those years ago, me showing James my favorite places where I could spend endless afternoons dreaming of the impossible by the Lumes creek, where I had built a forest that my most kept secrets were held within the branched walls. I could still feel how the sun had soaked warmly onto the back of my neck, how the breeze smelled of grass and different florals that danced on it. All the while he had shot questions that delighted me.

Favorite music to listen to?

Favorite shows?

What did I think of Haden? Of the schools? What was my family like?

Favorite movies? Books?

I had shot every single one back, and that first afternoon that felt endless—and yet looking back, I wished I had a thousand more like them—I knew James was a once in a lifetime friend. An *authentic* friend. A thing I had learned, that is rare in this life. We were lucky, to have a bond that is found family. With James having moved to Toronto and started the life he always wanted with his wife Mara, I looked forward to tomorrow, having the day with him. In our adulthood, having a full day was a luxury, a thing to be cherished.

I smiled up to the ceiling. Gods, it would be so good to hear about how baby Cole was doing, and Mara. If James was still enamored with Toronto as he had been six years ago. Sipping on our caramel macchiatos, I need to talk until my throat ran hoarse. Being around James, he was a person who always revitalized my soul, never draining it. I really needed that right now.

Lightening lit up the sky in white bursts. The curtains weren't very thick and I could see the shapes of cars in the parking lot, the sidewalk and streetlight beyond that dousing the cement in its yellowed light. Suburbia stretched out after the main road. The patter of rain had increasingly become heavier, the wind that had sounded like a sigh had now built into a howl. It sounded inhuman. The window shuddered against the storm that had been hanging over Haden all afternoon. *It's just a storm,* I chided myself. I needed to get out of my head. This was just an old building with a tragic history. Yes, there were a multitude of nightmares around, due to the other patients, but they were harmless. Here, in my room, I was alone.

Above my head, a soft static crackled from the hidden speaker system that was in here.

Mandy must be finally ready to start the last test, and then *sleep*. I shifted, the old fibers from the linen poking through my shirt to my back. Multiple lumps jabbed at my body at the slight movement, but I felt that familiar pull. It was the strangest fucking sensation, even for a lover of the written word, it was almost indescribable. As soon as my head hit the pillow, it felt like my center of gravity always shifted, like I was being swallowed by the bed, my body just this shell, or cage that released me.

Falling.

Falling.

Falling.

Into the endless black void, where there was no promise of dreams, there was no promise of rest. It was the very thing I feared most in life, a space of pure emptiness, that wanted to keep eating away at me.

Vigorously, I blinked against the insistent tug at the corner of my consciousness. Not yet.

Mandy hadn't done the test, I couldn't slip down into that heaviness, that I couldn't wake myself from. The back of my neck prickled as thunder boomed, followed by another bright burst of lightning.

Count the seconds.

One. My eyes watered as I continued to blink them hard.

Two. My breaths hitched; the damn measuring band so uncomfortable with expanding movement.

Three. The dresser door slowly creaked open, like someone had pushed it from the inside.

Four. Pale hands curled around the door frame before slipping back into the shadows of the room.

Boom.

Thunder cracked in tandem with Mandy's voice flitting into the room, clear as if she was standing right beside the bed. "Okay Theo, sorry about the wait."

My gaze was still frozen to the foot of the bed, where the dresser door was still open.

Ice shot down my spine, rooting and spreading throughout my core. I didn't move. Real or not? Couldn't Mandy see the room through the camera if it was real?

It's just your sleep deprivation, your mind playing tricks on you. Breathe.

"Okay, so first, can you wiggle and bend your left foot?"

"Good. Now your right."

"Then your right arm, please bend and roll your wrist. Good. Then your left."

My heart rate continued to climb as I watched the dresser door move again, being pushed wider from the outside in. A pale arm was in my eyesight now. Horrified, I felt my mouth freeze in a small "oh", hanging open. The body slipped from the closet with a thud. The sound of the dresser door being shut sent me careening into primal fear.

Oh, what the fuck, what the fuck, what the fuck?

"Now to the right."

I lifted my head, trying to sit up.

"Sorry, Theo. Just the movements I'm instructing, please."

She couldn't see her.

Laying back down, I saw a flash of a pale shape scuttling along the floor at the end of my bed. The shadows bent and distorted with the movement, my eyes straining to try and make out the person I had become so familiar with. Slowly, I saw the body crouch, facing the corner in something that looked like a yoga squat before slowly, curling to stand up still facing the corner.

Thunder boomed, followed more quickly by lightning. I had lost count of the seconds, lost track of holding onto my distraction of figuring out how many kilometers the storm was away. Snaps of the woman's features came into clarity—she always wore simple shorts and white t shirt, her blonde pixie cut was matted and bloodied.

Darkness washed the room again. Mandy's voice sounded so far away as she said,

"Now the right side."

My bottom lip trembled, but I did as I was told.

"Okay, so now open and close your eyes."

My vision shuttered. Open, closed. Open, closed.

Open. The woman stood taller still facing the corner of the room, her head bowed almost in reverence. Her low murmurs filled the room.

Closed. Her whispers became more hurried, more aggressive.

"Okay, perfect. One last thing, Theo. Open and close your mouth in a yawning motion, please."

I opened my eyes again, doing as Mandy asked, but I stared at the back of the woman.

In the months I had been seeing her, I could never make out what she was saying.

"Perfect. That's it, Theo, everything looks great. Remember, if you need to go to the washroom or anything, just call for me and I'll unhook you."

I nodded, looking at the camera. There was a soft click and I was alone. Well, besides her. A low moan escaped me, and I closed my eyes, trying to ignore the woman. Sleep paralysis. Two words that tip reality. Is that all this was?

I took a deep inhale before letting it go, opening my eyes—

The woman was standing right beside my bed.

She was still facing the wall, body angled toward the door.

"Wakeupgotherewakeupwakeupgo."

The murmurs were still slurred—mashed together in her insistence—but was she saying, *wake up*? And *go there*? I tried reaching to the button on the nightstand beside the monitor that all the wires were plugged into to call Mandy. I tried opening my mouth. I couldn't move, I couldn't speak. This had happened every single night for the last year, but it still kicked me into terror. I willed myself to roll, to scream, to thrash, to *move*. But all that seeped behind my lips, trapped behind my teeth, was another low moan.

Slowly, the woman sat on the side of the bed, still not facing me.

"Theeeeeeeo." The whisper sounded like it was simultaneously coming from under the bed and outside the door. Pressure squeezed my throat, weighed down on my chest so hard it was almost impossible to take breath. Sweat soaked my shirt, my heartbeat was a crescendo that filled my hearing, droning out the storm, making me hyper focus on the room.

Scuttling sounded along the floor again. A scraping sound like too long of nails against linoleum.

Lightning flashed, illuminating the room for a second. The woman was gone from the edge of my bed.

I exhaled sharply through my nose in short bursts, my gaze scourging the room since my eyes were the only thing I could move. Bile burned up my throat. Slowly, pale hands rose from the end of my bedframe. They curled over the sheets, the arms exposed but no other part of her. The hands fisted the sheets, and slowly they were pulled down. They rippled over my chest, over the wires, my stomach and legs bunching down. The hands froze, not moving as they clutched the sheets.

A tear slid out from the corner of my eye, hot as it landed on my pillow. I was hyperventilating, the bursts desperate. True fear, like this, electrified you. It sizzled sharp and unyielding through your veins and muscles, pushing back what your brain was trying to tell you was impossible because your body, your reaction, what you were taking in or watching or going through was happening. It was real. It had never made me feel so alive and completely bound at the same time.

I felt the presence in the room shift. The overwhelming knowledge that even though I couldn't move or see anything, I knew that someone was suddenly laying next to me in the bed.

A finger trailed down the right side of my cheek, moving slowly to caress a wisp of my hair. *It's not real even if it feels real to me.*

It's.

Not.

REAL.

Pale hands moved into my line of sight, to cup either side of my face, holding it.

The temperature in the room plummeted. The hands gripped my face tighter, slowly turning my head to the right, to face the window.

I was sobbing by this point, feeling like I was going to wet the bed at thirty-two, while my panic built. My screams bulged, stuck in my throat, wanting to shatter through me, but was stuck, bound, like the rest of me. I braced for the horrifying unveiling of this presence that has been my company for the last year, for the horror that has been playing with me like a cat baiting its prey before landing its blow.

No one was there.

I jumped when behind me, a terrible guttural voice bellowed into my left ear. The timber was inhuman, guttural, shaking with rage. The voice screamed into my left ear, "Theo!" I was helpless under this presence's thumb, squirming, being crushed by the sheer weight of it—

All at once, it disappeared, and a scream that would put my favorite fictional final girls to admiration erupted out of me. I sat up so fast, most cords ripped from the machine, but I wasn't thinking—I only needed out—to get away from whatever was in here with me—

My bedroom door exploded open, banging against the wall. Florescent light flooded the room. Mandy stood there, her eyes wide her mouth hanging open.

"Theo, what's happening?"

Before I could move, answer or continue ripping off the wires from my skin, the electricity cut, plunging the room into darkness again.

The sunrise burned in the sky as I parked and went back to gripping my steering wheel.

Sitting in silence, I didn't want to go back inside to my apartment where James and Harold were and would be ready to hear about an interesting sleep study. The clock on the dashboard read five in the morning. Orange and yellow hued clouds stretched along the horizon, where at the bottom reds and even a hint of purple made the colors above burn all the brighter, chasing away the chases of the storm. But all the way home, branches had scattered the roads, trees had been uprooted, damaged posts and houses everywhere I looked.

"Fuck," I said before grabbing my bag, getting out of the car, slamming the door a little too hard. Pressing the lock button on my key fob, it beeped in confirmation behind me. I took a deep inhale of the crisp October air, the coolness of it slightly helping refocus me, organizing my thoughts. After the hydro had gone out and I had calmed down, I had told Mandy what had happened, what I saw and felt, seated across from another with both of our cell phone lights pointed up to the ceiling on the night table in the makeshift form of a lamp.

The echo of what Mandy had said to me before sending me home followed me as I pulled the front door open to the lobby of my brick five story apartment complex.

"If the hydro doesn't come back on soon, usually it would be another wait for a reschedule, given our waitlists and how the system works, even though this is no fault of your own, or any of the other patients here. You know how our healthcare system works, since it was a six month wait for you to get the requisition going. But given the severity of your sleep paralysis, let me see what I can finalize with my boss before we send you home, okay? I am going to fight to get you back in tomorrow night, Theo."

I put the key into the front door lock, the mechanical voice droning as it clicked, "*front* door open."

"No shit," I muttered, walking to the elevator. It always grated on my nerves that the system declared that every time you used your front door key, but my two-bedroom apartment was on the top floor, the fifth. The rent was decent, the view of Haden beautiful, especially right now when the horizon was a myriad of bronze, orange, red and canary yellow. From my apartment I could see half of Haden, houses and business mapped out, the roads the concrete veins. I always thought of Haden as if it was a living organism, the people who lived here just part of the eco system, me included. It had always made me feel small, but in a humbling way. To not stress the things that don't really matter, because my life was just a streak across the cosmos in it all. A mere flash in the big picture.

All our lives were. The highs, the lows and everything in between creating this beautiful, monstrous, elated experience. I try to never forget that, the composition of it all and the connection that we share with one another, even without speaking a word. Everyone loses someone they love in their lifetime, experiencing death. We all have something that brings us joy, something that is our own personal titan to overthrow, something that brings us connection. We all have dreams and fears that we cultivate, in our differences, and that is a truly stunning thing.

Pressing the elevator button, I swallowed past my rawness that night had left with me. The elevator door opened and I whispered under my breath, "you have made it through days that you didn't think you could. This is no different."

Pressing the door closed, I sighed. It felt different. Why did I have to relive this creepy ass woman night after night? The healthcare system was strained after COVID and had a hard time bouncing back, and also never felt the same: prime example of having to wait six months to get my initial appointment. I clenched my jaw, trying to sort out if I was feeling . . . anything in my complete sleep deprived state.

Mandy had pulled some serious strings to slide my study to tonight. I knew that, that I should feel grateful.

I should be feeling grateful, but instead I am just . . . numb. Empty.

The elevator smelled of citrus with hints of floor cleaner, the smell of home since I turned twenty, twelve years ago. The only smell on this earth that could make me feel less edgy. Before I started having these sleep issues, I was a far cry from being a people person. My hold to be personable had begun slipping one week into experiencing unrefreshing sleep. But here, within these walls, it was home. A four-letter word that I always was so terrified I wouldn't find as an adult. It boggled my mind as a kid—home was with my parents. Home was where I grew up, spent all my nights. But when you get older, you must find a new one? In a different town? My mom had assured me that lots of people stayed in their hometown, but in the same breath I overheard her talking to my aunt about how so and so had finally gotten out of this place. Like she was proud of them. Like staying was a bad thing. It terrified me, to the point I cried and panicked with every birthday that passed until I was ten. I knew better than most adults I met in my youth that buildings, houses, had just as much character to them as a living person. Not in the sense that they are alive, but in the sense the all the years and years and years of energy, of nightmares and wishes, left traces just like it did with people. I knew I needed my second home to be safe, warm, a little bubble from the nightmares lurking outside, attached to everyone I met.

But as the years passed, Haden surprised me.

Rewind to the years of my public-school days.

Haden provided stretching forests that became my personal stage for James and mines imagination. Every dream, every character I would cook up and act out, or card game, or playing truth or dare was born under the branches and canopy of leaves. So many summer days or after school days were spent in our handmade fort, eating sour keys or sour patch kids that we had biked to the variety store to get first. Despite being in the 2040s, somehow our town had protected the nostalgia of how kids were depicted in the 90s, or even early 2000s. Playing outside, fireflies winking along the edge of the rolling cornfields in the dusky haze of summer. Once fall rolled in, dazzling and seemingly all at once, I had spent holidays and weekends at my grandma's house, lucky enough to have cousins that were more like siblings at that time in my life. We would all rake the crisp leaves that scattered the lawn, that smell of cloves and grass imprinting on the moment in time; I could recall it now as an adult. We would all build a floor plan layout, the leaves acting as walls, and we would play house until the burnt orange glow of the sun was setting behind the barn and we would all have to go. Winter was a shimmer of hot chocolates and playing outside, so long my snow suit would be drenched with sweat. Hours of snow forts, of the bite of cold against my cheek, the pure rush that every day was a new page, a new story to be discovered within my imagination.

Highschool brought a different haze over my life but was just as intoxicating. I was trying to find rhythm, quietly listening and finding heart-pounding, soul-untethering joy in writing. I had stacks of notebooks in my room, filled with everything from pages with one character of a story, to just a flash of description of a certain emotion. The first year of grade nine, every other class was a dull blur, leading me to fourth period, and my burning blaze that was English class. The syllabus in grade nine was a lot of classic literature and Shakespeare, but I didn't care; I ate it all up, taking notes, and looking forward to every day. But I remember when grade eleven came, and we could choose more different electives. Canadian Literature. Creative Writing. And English? I was in heaven. It was studying Margret Atwood that I realized I tended to lean more toward dystopian as far as enjoying reading. *But what about horror?*

It dawned on me then, that I needed to find out if that was the genre that made my heart soar. Romance? I enjoyed it now and then. Fantasy? Same as romance.

But I wanted the genre that sang to me, that would send me into gleeful transportation from my reality. So, while James was flirting with his latest conquest during lunch, I went to the library. At my request, the librarian Mrs. Howard smiled, leading me to a section labelled Horror, and picked out the biggest book I had ever seen. Its white cover was stained with a bright red clown smile and the title read *IT* by Stephen King.

"I wish I could experience this book again for the first time. It's timeless, a classic for the genre. I really hope you enjoy it."

I took the behemoth of a book with reverence. Gingerly flipping to the first weathered and yellowed page, I dove in. And a new routine was born for me, reading on my lunch. *IT* took me three months to finish, and that was with reading it late into the night, and so many renewals that Mrs. Howard eagerly granted. But it was a lightning bolt that shattered through me with each page I devoured. Realizing not only that a book could be that scary, but I had never read anything like it.

I needed more.

Salem's Lot came and *Misery* came immediately after. But then Mrs. Howard had made sure to have ordered a healthy stock of indie horror authors for the library, and my world exploded with new titles and authors to explore.

The days bled into months and it all passed in a blur. Classes—library—classes—home.

I would read, do my homework and repeat it all the next day. Sometimes I hung out with James and other friends from the school's jazz band (James played bass). But it always felt like people, making friends . . . it felt like this massive obstacle, and one I wasn't really interested in. I was friendly, but my walls were firmly up except for Mrs. Howard and James. During the times James and I did hang out, he gushed about girls he had crushes on, or did I know so and so *kissed* this person?! I realized something else during those times—I hadn't really felt what James was describing—this possession of wanting someone. To kiss someone, or to makeout. To have sex. I hadn't felt . . . anything for guys or girls. I realized I never really felt a sexual urge. At dinner one night I talked to my mom. I was nervous (was there something wrong with me?) but I knew I could talk to her about anything. I still can.

That night, I pushed my pork chops into my mashed potatoes and broccoli, trying to figure out how to bring it up. But I decided to just rip off the band aid and explained to her how I had been feeling.

"Honey, there are millions of people on this earth, each one beautifully diverse. There is nothing wrong with you. What you are describing to me sounds like asexuality. Love, or to feel love, doesn't have to equal sex."

She continued to explain what she knew about asexuality; one of her close friends from work was ace, and she suggested if I ever wanted to talk to her, or a therapist as I was navigating this, she would make sure my needs were met. Then she gave me the biggest hug, but I couldn't get over what she had said.

Love doesn't *have to* equal sex.

It clicked within me.

And I never looked back.

The rest of high school blurred. Bonfires and going to the movies on the weekend, James and I biking down deserted streets of Haden on our way back from a party. Homework and whispered dreams of the future. But I had never felt more sure than anything in my life before.

I would be an author.

I started talking to my favorite English teacher at the end of grade eleven, Mrs. Dershaw, about pursuing writing as a career. Sheridan had an excellent creative writing and publishing certificate, but she explained that was just one avenue.

"To be a writer," she started one October day after our last period English class, "you don't need to have a certificate unless *you* want it, Theo. You will never hear me saying that. Ever. It's bullshit. Not that learning or growing your craft is bullshit, but that you can't be a writer unless you have those things. That's bullshit."

I grinned. I had never heard a teacher swear before, and it drove what she was saying even more to me, because it felt candid. Not dressed pretty, or to deceive. What she was saying just was, and I think sometimes in life we miss those moments.

"You just have to write to be an author, and don't you ever let anyone make you feel that's not enough."

I didn't realize it at the time, but Mrs. Dershaw had just given me the best advice of my career right then. And I saw it time and time again when I first entered the industry; like you couldn't be a good writer, or that you weren't valid unless you had an agent, or traditionally published or went to school for it.

Which is bullshit, just as she had said.

I started filling notebook after notebook, with character ideas, descriptions, or just sentences of prose to describe different feelings or places. When I learned of the Kinsley Matthews disappearance in Sarnia, and then what happened more recently at Lakeshore Lane with Jules and Drew's death and disappearance, I knew Haden is where I would stay. It was my town, my safe spot, the light and the dark.

I continued to write with a fervor a possession that I had yearned to feel in other ways.

But lyrical prose, studying the depth of horror, building worlds, developing characters that felt real to me as any friend? It was so damn fulfilling.

My first book, which launched my career, *Bloodied Whispers,* I indie published before I got my agent I have now for the works that followed. Both ways were excellent options, depending on how you wanted to release your book.

My adult life had taken a structure that I had fallen in love with. Usually, I woke up early—in the summer my alarm was set for five thirty in the morning—I would make a coffee to go, and Harold and I would go for about an hour walk. Then I would come home, write for the morning which would free up the afternoon either for downtime or stuff around the house. And I would repeat, adjusting the walk time with each season. Haden encompassed my heart, these familiar roads, forests and stretching web of suburban life. It changed but never really at its core; this place that never once made me feel like I wanted to leave.

Wrenched out of nostalgia, I made my way slowly to my apartment. The interior of the building held a nineties vibe, the red carpet was edged with a flowered pattern, the walls painted a neutral ivory. For the first time since last night, I felt lighter with each step. James was waiting for me on the other side of apartment 505 with Harold. I could maybe make pancakes, and peameal bacon, and over coffee I would tell him everything.

I shifted my bag in my grip, chewing over how I would broach it.

"Well, James, yes. What would you think about me seeing people's nightmares attached to them clear as day? Yes, this is nothing new. I first found this out when I was six. I've been keeping this to myself. Why you ask?"

My steps faltered, and I stood there for a second alone in the hallway.

There was the question that burned in me, eating away. I was never quite sure why I hadn't ever tried to explain to James what I could see. He would listen, open minded, non-judgmental. It wasn't from a place of fear that I had held back. He would believe me.

I continued to make my way to my place. I unlocked my front door and slipped inside. I pulled the door shut as quietly as I could with a click. It was dark, the burnt orange paint of the front hallway always looked darker in the shadows. I felt a wet, cold nose nudge my ankle, a prominent boop. Harold was sitting in front of me, wagging his tail so hard his entire smooth haired body wiggled too. I put my bag down and scooped him up, planting multiple kisses on the top of his head. He licked my chin in quick succession and I put him back down. We walked together into the small kitchen that stemmed from the hallway on one end, and the living room at the other. I grabbed my water bottle, and made my way into the dining room, Harold eagerly awaiting what came next.

"Did you have a good night with Uncle James, buddy? I hope you weren't waiting by the door the whole time." I arched an eyebrow down at him, where he blinked up innocently at me, as if saying, *who, me? Never.*

I grabbed his dish while simultaneously opening his bag of food and scooping his breakfast. Harold rose on his back legs, wiggling his entire black and tan body even more energetically, while his front paws kind of jabbed toward me happily. Harold had done what I called his happy dance since I got him as a puppy. I grinned, setting it down for him.

Eagerly, he started eating his breakfast, and I took in the quiet of my space. I had two well-loved couches, with dog stairs leading up to both. The couches were placed so that from either way you could see the TV okay. I had huge bay windows on every wall, which was one of the first things I first fell in love with about the space. The dining room was where I had six bookcases lining the end wall, and the balcony door was behind my table to the decent sized balcony. I had painted the living room a deep maroon; I had wanted it to feel like an autumnal bookstore all year long, and with the light pouring in, basking the room in a warm glow, I smiled. Home. Taking a sip of my water, I looked down to Harold who was watching me, and I nodded. "Okay bud, let's let Uncle James sleep in. Outside first and then we can start breakfast?"

Licking his lips, I took that as Harold's resounding yes.

I flipped the two pancakes, the blueberries and golden-brown side making me smirk. I had always sucked at flipping. I turned the fan on from the overhead, the smell of sizzling bacon and the pancakes being sucked up into the vent. Coffee percolated to my right, the machine on the small, marbled countertop. My brown cabinets made up the cupboards, with the sink and dishwasher behind me. I wasn't much of a cook, so it served its purpose. The clock read almost nine, and I tried just to focus on the task at hand. Harold was sunbathing in the living room, laying on his back with all four paws in the air, sleeping in a nest of blankets. Behind the dining room table, beside the bookshelves, I tried not to focus on my desk. The cork board attached to the wall had pictures of 1729 Lakeshore

Lane from my research stay, the outside and the different floors I could get to, and the basement. There were a lot of pages covering my laptop, and my journal that I hadn't touched since all of this started happening. I had tried so many times to write, with most of each session just ending up me staring at the blank page, fighting to stay awake, thinking it was a void in its own sense. Mocking me. The emptiness consuming me.

The coffee machine beeped three times, making me jump slightly. Focusing back on what I was doing, I eyed the hallway. Should I bring James his? I flipped the other two pancakes when I noticed the tiny divots in the batter. They looked good, which I was pleasantly surprised about still. Grabbing two plates and two mugs, I lined them side by side on the counter. In my bedroom, I heard the door slowly creak open.

"Hey!" I called over my shoulder while I poured our two cups of coffee. Hazelnut and caramel notes had me salivating. I loved this blend from the local Two Beans. I carefully transitioned the pancakes onto the plates, with bacon following next. James didn't respond so I called back again, "Don't worry, I'm working on your coffee! Sorry if I woke you."

More shuffling steps mixed in with Stevie Nicks's voice that floated quietly from the google nest on my bookshelf. Shutting off the burners, I went to grab James's plate first.

Slowly a hand slid up my back to grip the top of my shoulder.

"Ouch James, stop being a weirdo," I said as his grip tightened. I piled the last of the bacon divided equally between our plates.

His other hand joined to squeeze me left shoulder, hard. Then in tandem, his hands slid up the sides of my neck.

I froze.

The fingers were long, almost unnaturally so, and freezing. Hot, rancid breath ruffles the back of my head, and all I could smell was rot.

"What the fuc—"

"Theeeeeo." That ever-familiar voice cooed in my right ear, before the hands, that were not James's hands, clamped down over my mouth hard. The intruder wrenched me back by the neck hard.

My apartment dissolved around me in a moment of transcendence. Ripples exploded all around me, like I was the stone dropped into the water, the object that didn't belong but had been thrown in despite that. Once disrupted, it destroyed my reality. I was never home, I was never really here.

I fell.

My arms windmilled, trying to find purchase, but I just fell.

Air howled around me like a baying creature.

I watched in horror as far above me, my illusion of my home shrunk, shriveled around the one lone dark figure clad in onyx robes. The darkness swallowed me whole.

I landed, completely disoriented on a familiar bed. In a familiar room, even as my vision desperately tried to adjust to the fact it was pitch black in here.

And I was hooked to the machine. The hundreds of wires feeling now more like ropes crossing over my body and arms.

I was at the sleep study. How the actual fuck was I at the sleep study?

A broken, wet giggle snapped my focus to the person sitting right on my chest.

I tried to scream.

I tried to fight, to thrash.

I could do nothing as it leaned down toward me, so, so slowly.

My stomach pitched, heaving, and I felt like I wanted to throw up, as I realized I was staring up not at a face, but the head was twisted completely around.

Like she was facing a corner.

Facing.

Away.

From.

Me.

Long black hair tickled my chin, its pale hands pressing down, down, down on my chest with so much force it felt as if my ribcage and sternum wanted to crack. Its bony shoulders were hunched inward, and I couldn't tell if it wore any clothes, or if it was *human,* or just something that imitated looking human? And could sleep paralysis demons change? Wasn't it usually the same one?

It giggled again, an eerie granulated sound before it hissed, "You aren't like the others. You didn't spread the infection like you were supposed to, so Haden could eat you up. It's a hungry place. It wants you, to eat, up

UP

UP."

It roared the last two *ups,* pressing harder down on my body. Was this it? Was I having some kind of medical emergency that I was so deep down the hallucination rabbit hole that I couldn't distinguish reality?

But what if this is real, Theo? What the fuck kind of infection were you supposed to spread? What is it talking about?

My thoughts raced, but I kept coming back to the fact it talked about my hometown like it was alive.

Before I could make sense of what was happening, somewhere deep within my body it felt like a lock was suddenly released open, and I was pulled down.

I was falling for the second time within minutes. But it wasn't with my physical body, I realized, as I could see my body still in bed, no demon-like creature crushing my chest. I was alone, looking peaceful in fact, hooked up to the monitor which was beeping contently, measuring my normal sleep.

Then a door-like shadow appeared over the scene, and slammed shut with such force I flinched.

The darkness was waiting to swallow me up, it was everywhere, and I fell faster, completely untethered.

I landed hard on my hands and knees. My teeth jarred together and pain exploded from my kneecaps and wrists. How could I feel pain? Nothing made sense, and my breath became sharp exhales, as I stared frantically at the linoleum floor I landed on. I arched my fingers, my body listening to what I willed. I could move. A broken cry ripped from my chest, in relief and fear. I lurched up to stand, still panicked as I tried to focus on my surroundings.

All around me, the air held a strange haze, like the thin sheen of a fog, all the normal sharpened edges dull and soft. I froze. Standing in horror as I realized I was in a carbon copy of the sleep study room. A darkened substance ran thickly on the wall, and my gaze wrenched up. The small body hung upside down, thin arms nailed wide, and I gagged as I realized the dark substance dripping down the walls onto the bed was blood—

I turned and was sprinting out of the room. "Oh, hell no," I repeated to myself as I skidded into the hallway.

"This veil should teach me, Lord, that I should die to the world . . ." a voice croaked behind me and I froze again, ice dousing my body, trickling down my spine into every extremity as my heart kicked into adrenaline.

" . . . and to myself so as to live no longer but for . . ."

I turned slowly, shaking.

"Thee."

I raised my gaze. At the end of the hallway, a towering figured clad in black robes blended in with the shadows. In the nun's grip was a hammer and long iron nails. Her pale fingers were drenched in blood. The nun had her head bowed but I squinted, seeing her pale grey lips peel back from her rotting teeth in a sinister grin.

I took a step back, getting ready to fucking run like I never have before—

The nun roared so loud, so inhumanly, the sound exploded like glass shattering all around me, and in tandem every single door in the hallway banged open. To the first door on my right, I stumbled back as pale hands curled around the doorframe. Instinctively, my hand went to my back pocket where I always kept my phone—but there was nothing there. It was second nature to try and capture this on video.

There it was—my mom always called it *Theo Anger* when I was little. Like I had coined this specific kind of anger, which always made me laugh. An intense flaring, crumbling down the bullshit lens the world liked to cover over it. It made me burn, but it also helped me clearly in a lot of situations. That the lonely people were the fake people pretending to have it all, like they were above feeling. Like it was a bad thing to feel, which it isn't. There is a safety in living your life so authentically, there is a braveness in it. Fiercely, unyielding, it made me want to rip apart the façade so many people had covering over themselves too. To be let in. Narrowing in my anger, I felt brave. And I whipped my head back to the nun snarling, "What the fuck is this place."

Theo Anger had also adopted in the fact James had sworn like a sailor since he was like seven.

James. Harold. My heart lurched at the thought of them. I had to figure this out, what ever was haunting me, because obviously this was more than just being sleep deprived. And no one was going to save me; hell, I had to persist and persist just to have been heard in the first place. Because I was too overweight or *carrying too much weight,* as my family doctor so lightly liked to put it. I was also too young to have anything seriously wrong with me, so obviously it was all in my head.

My anger flared higher. Good, this was good.

This I could use.

The nun paused, like it wasn't used to being addressed like this. To my right, the hand that clutched the doorframe, its fingers let go again, sliding back into the room.

"You were supposed to be infected," the nun snarled.

"So I've heard!" I screamed back, all the pent-up frustration, fear and adrenaline backing that sentence.

"Let's see how you survive now."

Chaos erupted around me. The door where the pale hands had retreated, now the Slenderman-like nightmare I had seen attached to the other patient in the living room towered over me. For a second, we assessed each other, my drumming heartbeat screaming with the thought they can't hurt me.

Right?

The Slenderman charged me, closing the space between us in one stride. He picked me up, those unnaturally long arms scooping my body effortlessly, and threw me.

My head cracked against the wall first, my breath stunned from my chest as stars winked and flooded into my vision. I dropped hard onto the floor. Laying there for a second, I picked up on familiar sounds.

A man crying, murmuring, "I can't pay this."

The creaking of a rope.

I rolled to the left, where suddenly an ax was embedded in the floor right where my head was. I glanced up and the ax wielder was drenched head to toe in blood, features unrecognizable, just long hair slicked back. Impossibly, I was being attacked by known and unknown nightmares, where in this reality, they were *real*.

"Either escape or join us," the nun hissed from behind the advancing group all fixated on me.

Finding my legs and feet, I stumbled to stand and began sprinting.

"Oh, what the fuck," I repeatedly said to myself. I pushed harder, running faster than I ever had in my life before, in my pajamas, and all I could hear behind me was pounding feet and more doors banging open, unleashing gods know what to hunt me.

I skidded hard to the left, rounding the corner. The hallway was empty. I either had to find somewhere to hide, or a weapon to fight back with. But what killed a nightmare? I highly doubted it was the same rules that applied to another human . . . I swore. Hiding, then. I looked to the doors and balked. They were moving. Stretched taller, like a fucking Salvador Dali painting coming to life, reaching and bending to become part of the ceiling.

I was out of options.

To my right, I gripped the doorknob, turned it, and slipped inside. I shut it with a click behind me.

Frantically, I blinked against florescent lights that flooded the room, followed with the overwhelming smell of medical grade disinfectant. I was in a completely different room, day, building, moment.

I was seated in a chair that was way too small, and reminded me of the ones they had in public school. My thighs spilled over the edges and I looked up, noticing the doctor with the clipboard eyeing me. I glanced back behind me where the door had been that I just entered through.

It was gone.

"So, Miss Anderson, what brings you in today?" the doctor asked without even making eye contact. It clicked into place then, possibly what was happening.

The nun had said: *escape or become like us*. So was this someone's nightmare and I was in a fucked-up version of something like the upside down from *Stranger Things*? If I could escape this moment, this nightmare that had plagued someone in Haden, perhaps that's the way I can fight my way back to my reality. And what if the woman I saw, my sleep paralysis demon . . . what if she was connected to this all, just not in the way I expected?

I pressed my lips together, swallowing, my mouth dry and replied, "Well, I've been experiencing some really intense symptoms." I needed time, and the only way I could think of finding a way out, through this nightmare, was to play along for the time being.

The doctor stepped closer and the smell of unwashed body odor flooded my space. Up closer, I could see his fingernails were cracked and yellowed, and his skin dirtied. My stomach pitched, but I held his gaze as he finally raised it, not an ounce of kindness, or any emotion I could easily recognize in them.

"Such as?" he said curtly, already looking back down at his clipboard and the patient file on there. What a fucking asshole.

I bristled. "Well for starters, unrefreshing sleep."

He sighed. "Well for starters, are you drinking any caffeine after four?"

I looked around the room, the walls behind him, looking for anything that could change. He had said his question mockingly, like he had already written me off.

"No, I actually only have one coffee in the morning."

"And lifestyle?"

"Excuse me?"

"Miss, my time is very important, and all I am hearing is that you had a bad night's sleep. I'm asking if you regularly exercise. If you eat healthy food. If you take care of yourself."

My cheeks flushed deep red, and my anger thundered through me.

Before I could ride that wave and sink my biting words into him, I felt something warm trickle down along my forehead, down my eyelids and then onto my chin. Lifting my hand, I ran it along my skin where the warm, wet substance was and took it away from my face.

Blood stained my hands.

"Well?" the doctor pushed.

I stood shakily from my chair, walking over to the small mirror beside the examination bed. I shook, but I forced myself to look. Warmth was spreading all over my body now, down my scalp, neck, back and arms.

My reflection was a myriad of red and blue. Blue strands from my pixie cut that hadn't been touched by the blood that seemingly welled from my skin for no reason, no wound. My face was slicked with blood and it continued to stream slowly like a river down my skin, dripping off my fingers now to pool around me.

I tasted bile in my mouth. I swallowed again. "You can't see this?"

"Please step on the weight scale, Miss Anderson."

Drip. Drip. Drip. My mind whirled, but I obliged, stepping on the scale.

He scribbled down my weight and sighed. "Please take a seat, Miss Anderson."

I did, and I was in full *Carrie* mode now, slickened with hot, coppery blood. It was everywhere, choking me, drowning me. Yet this doctor didn't see it. It poured harder now; it slickened over my eyelids, seeping in between my lips, coating my teeth, trickling hotly down my throat. It filled my ear canals and the doctors' words started to become muffled.

"It seems to me from what you have described—"

You haven't given me the chance to say anything!

"—that it's boiling down to a couple things—"

You haven't given me the space to go more into depth.

"First, I will write you a prescription for generalized depression—"

Depressed? I'm not fucking depressed!

"The next will be a lifestyle change. Clean eating. You are carrying too much weight."

I'm bleeding out in front of you and all you see is my weight? Curvy doesn't mean unhealthy, you—

"I will see you back in six months for a follow up. Otherwise, I can't help you, Miss Anderson."

The blood poured out of me now, openly bleeding out from every orifice of my body, slickening the floor. Desperately, I tried to reach out—

He slammed the prescription in my hand, gritting out, "Have a nice day now."

It rushed over me then, what this nightmare was. What their fear stemmed from.

Slipping in the blood, I ran across the room. There was a distant banging hollowing through the room. It sounded like a door was at the end of a long tunnel, but the knocking intensified, and the room kept on filling, filling, filling.

Choking, I swam through the blood until I bounced against the wall.

The wall with the mirror.

Gritting my teeth, I pulled my right arm back, screaming as I threw the punch. It connected with the mirror.

And shattered.

I was sucked under my blood by an unseen force drained through the mirror, which had unveiled as a doorway. I spun, being dragged down.

All I could see was red.

All I could taste was blood.

My sense of gravity tilted with my vision, falling with me on my back. I landed hard, pain lacing down my neck and back of my head making my eyes water. It was pitch black; I couldn't see an inch away from my face. I felt my clothes which were dry now, and blood free. I sighed, appearing for now at least that I had left that office far behind.

Inching my fingers down, I ran them along the floor or whatever I was now laying on. It was wood, a few splinters poking my index finger. Following the grains, I frowned in the darkness. Was I on a table? I found a corner but then felt the wood trailed up . . .

And up . . .

And the lid above me was also wood.

The lid.

Warmth flooded my cheeks in a panic as I pressed both of my hands on the wood lid, trying to press it open, but it wouldn't budge.

I lost it.

"Help!" I screamed, banging my hands on the lid of the casket, because that's what I was somehow stuck in: a fucking coffin. I banged my knees hard against it too, screaming at the top of my lungs, "Help!"

Tears streamed down from the corners of my eyes, the air was becoming thick and hot with my effort to break out. But it didn't budge.

Thud. Something landed heavy on top of the lid, and a dusting covered my face making me flinch back. It had filled my mouth, some of the particles, and the taste filled my mouth. I recognized it. The heady, earthy taste of dirt.

Thud.

Thud. Thud.

Thud. Thud. Thud.

From above, whoever was burying me alive picked the pace, each landing of dirt shuttering more on top of me as it seeped in through the cracks. I roared, screaming into the oblivion, my cries not a distinguishable word anymore, but a shaky, inhumane sound stretching into the void. A sound I didn't even know I was capable of making. I didn't stop, only taking heaving inhales and repeating the scream. They heard me, they had to of heard me, but again, the pace only picked up.

A sob wrenched from deep within my chest. I couldn't breathe, and the already close confines of the casket started to move, slowly pressing toward me. Closer.

And closer.

At my feet, a giggle sounded in the darkness.

I froze.

I still couldn't see anything—if anything, the darkness was more absolute. Every other sense was heightened. A hand wrapped around my right ankle and I screamed, unable to hold onto any rationality anymore.

I wasn't alone in here.

Another hand grabbed up the other ankle.

"*Haden is so hungry,*" the disembodied voice snarled. There was a dragging motion, and the grip on my ankles were pulled down *hard*. Like whoever was in here with me was slowly dragging their torso up in between my legs.

I whimpered; my mind having gone completely blank.

"*Its stomach is grumbling.*"

The hands regripped my upper thighs, scratching my skin and clawing at my clothes as they slid up more. I felt the weight of their body, the icy touch of their freezing skin. I blinked, expected a face to explode into my view at any second, and my mind ran ahead, imagining preemptively what horror was locked down here with me. Hyperventilating, I leaned away.

"*Its mouth has been stretched wide open.*"

Its hands slid up to my biceps, and I screamed, thrashing, but it pinned my arms down so they still stayed flushed to the wooden bottom, my efforts not doing anything.

Dammit! Think, Theo!

Nightmares are often created from another root cause, they can act as a mirror, or a metaphor for a deeper trauma. A deeper meaning. It's what made me fall in love with the genre, for christs' sakes, the artistry it took whether it be in writing or directing or literal art in the medium sense—horror was so much more than the reputation it was always trying to shake. That it was all about exploitation of gore, of cheap scares and adult content. That it was face value superficial. The genre was constantly changing, pushing boundaries, exploring what horror could be. When I was younger, it was Jordan Peele and Mike Flannagan that made an imprint on me, showing the world that horror could in fact be art. I mean, it's something the creators had always known, it was about showing viewers horror is more than fear.

It was all about connection. About emotions. Horror was so visceral, was so undefined of where it could go, and that had always felt beautiful to me. Not to mention that horror in real life was just about as natural as breathing. The light and the dark can't exist without each other, right?

Breathe, Theo. In my head, the command was my mom's voice, the soothing tone, something I wish I could hear again, one more time.

I felt the hands slinked up my torso, trying to pull my focus back to the horror that was unfolding.

Look beyond what's happening. Now the voice had turned into James's.

"It's been waiting and waiting," the voice hissed up at me.

I closed my eyes, trying to focus on settling my breath.

"To get a taste of you."

What am I feeling? Past the fear? Think.

"You just have to . . ." The voice was closer now, as its hands slinked up to my chest, reaching toward my neck. "Open wide."

I was trapped. Buried. My screams unheard.

"Out of control," I concluded.

The hands shot to my lips, prying open hard, but I didn't open my eyes, I didn't scream,

I didn't fight back.

I let go.

I took what little control I had in this situation and tried to find ease. Sometimes, life demands that we let go of situations, people, problems, when we don't want to the most.

I relax my jaw, immediately allowing the stranger's hands to go deeper. Over my teeth and tongue I could taste her dirtied skin. I fight to allow my breath to return to its natural rhythm. Relaxing my shoulders, I visualize my spine releasing each vertebrae to connect with the wooden bottom. I ignore the splitting pain of the edges of my lips, the skin now ripping there. I was here in the darkest corner, existing.

Underneath me moved, and I could feel the difference now; the wood was changing, and it felt like quicksand, slowly pulling me under. Soon, my face was the only thing still exposed. Pressing my eyes firmly shut, I thought, *don't look*. I could feel the stranger's oppressing presence, their nose was touching mine, their fingers stretched my lips wider, prying my mouth wider. Wanting, and frantically searching.

I slipped away. I could feel their fingers scrambling to find purchase, but they slipped away, over my lips—then, nothing.

This time, I wasn't falling.

Escape.

I drifted gently, and it struck me again, that there was a beauty—even here, in this nightmarish landscape—of letting go.

Or become.

I couldn't tell if I was floating up or down.

One.

I still didn't open my eyes.

Of.

Could I? Could I continue to fight? To confront every fear thrown at me? I found myself to be the protagonist, the flawed fucking heroes journey now coming to the crossroads of a decision. I either had to continue to fight or . . . And in that lingering *or,* there was so many questions that charged through me.

Would there be peace? Or would I live constantly in this void, thrown between nothingness and monsters?

In my reality . . . In life, would I just die to become part of this fever dream?

I hadn't thought much about death, what it means. What waits after.

It can't be nothing.

It can't.

Wasn't this place proof of that? If this . . . other Haden could exist with the imprints of trauma and fear breathing real life into those demons like ghosts making them real, then why couldn't something that was filled with love, with our *loved ones,* also exist? What happened to our energy? Our souls?

But I knew one thing for certain. I couldn't exist stuck between fear and what my life could have been. I had Harold. James. I wasn't done sharing my stories. I just wasn't *done.* I wanted it all: the bad days, the messy days, the ones where you are struck dumb about how stunning life can be in the simplest of moments. I wanted to feel everything.

I sighed, now past exhaustion. It would be easier to just give in, let them take me, fixated on the fact I disrupted their infection, whatever that meant. But it was never in my nature to do what's easy; I was so stubborn, and this is no different. I would see it through, until the end.

My feet touched solid ground. My eyes fluttered open, and I realized I was crying.

Fast, silent tracks streaked down my cheeks. All I could see at first was thick stretching darkness. Standing straighter, I whispered thickly, "You can't have me."

I clenched my fists, and a warm breeze burst from the still air, and the darkness started to writhe. It looked like droplets of ink spilling into water, the scene coming into focus around me, feathering out and spreading. The familiar sheen of the fog drifted in the air, brushing everything in silver. I was alone, in the middle of a forest. Towering maples, hemlocks, and birches fanned for as far as I could see. The mossy dirt had patches of lichen that covered the odd boulders, and I recognized the landscape—it was reminiscent of up north, in the sprawling Kawartha Highlands. It didn't seem like there was any indication of normal daylight or nighttime in this place; just this endless mist. It added an extra layer of a lurking menacing presence. I needed to grab something, to help protect myself. I started to walk, my crunching footsteps of my Converses way, way too loud. Constantly, I scanned the tree line, shadows playing tricks with my mind already. To my left, a shadow spread growing taller, looking like a thin figure silently watching me. I froze mid step, my breathing coming fast again, adrenaline pumping through me. I blinked and the figure was gone.

"Okay. Okay," I said aloud, my voice echoing, before the forest swallowed it up. I was just sitting prey here, the thick forest around me and deep shadows just playing into whatever nightmare was waiting for me this round, waiting for its chance to pounce.

I started walking again, faster this time, looking up for maybe a Hail Mary of some kind to descend to me.

A mythical ghost slash nightmare slaying weapon?

A doorway?

Anything.

A giggle slipped through my lips, sounding off kilter and strange to me.

A branch snapped behind me. I started to run now. The sense that I was being watched was overwhelming, and the laughter died quick in my chest.

The silence that returned in the forest was unnerving. Usually, in the shadows was when the forest was the loudest, teeming with chattering and chuffing of animals, buzzing of insects and winking of fireflies. This was the complete absence of life.

Snap.

Snap.

I sprinted. I didn't look over my shoulder, as the snapping branches sounded all around me, matching pace with my heavy footfalls. The trees blurred, and I thought I saw people standing as still as them, mouths slackened, hanging open.

But again, with a blink they were gone.

I skidded, turning sharply to the right and went behind the closest tree, slamming my back against it to hide, pressing myself flush with it. Heavy breathing sliced through the woods seconds after, branches snapping of multiple feet. I held in my breath, pressing my lips together. Frantically, I searched in front of me, I needed something—anything. I couldn't have outrun them, but hiding here wouldn't buy me much time either. My gaze snapped to a broken branch that lay a few feet away from me.

Puffing heavy breaths came closer. A shiver ran down the back of my neck. I had one chance. Lurching, I reached down to grab it, the bark smooth with peeled white edges in my grip, and it was heavy enough.

I turned to immediately duck as an ax swung at my head.

"Let's go, asshole. We aren't feeding into bury your gays trope—not today," I snarled before launching myself at the ax murderer.

I swung the branch like brandishing a sword. I imagined it on fire, I imagined this was something as natural as breathing to me. Up close now, I could tell the person was a man, his broad shoulders contracting as he prepared to swing again.

The branch connected with his knees, *hard*. The nightmare stumbled.

Chest heaving, I grinned. "Alright then."

The woods were a blur again. I launched myself bellowing a cry that tore from that deep place within me. That place where I was fighting for love, fighting for life, fighting for Harold, for James, for myself. For Haden, all the good and the bad that was woven in my little town's history. Fighting to keep going, just to *keep going*, even though all I wanted to do was to stop.

The branch connected with the ax murderer's head in a sickening crack and he stumbled back.

Before I could land, my next blow was lifted off the ground. Long arms wrapped around my midsection. I kicked my legs, gripped the branch within my grip. Glancing down, I saw the suited arm—I knew these two maybe weren't what nightmare these woods had promised, but they seemed to be following me through each phase.

"Pissed I got away?" I said. Before over-thinking what I was about to do, I sunk my teeth into the forearm of the Slenderman. Hot, acid-like rot burst into my mouth before I was sent sputtering, tears from the acrid taste now running down my cheeks.

He just squeezed tighter and tighter, cutting off my breath. I clawed at his arm—his grip. The ax murderer stood in front of us, looking at me, but I still couldn't make out his eyes; just the contour of where eyeball sockets should be, his skin still coated in thick blood. Languidly, he swung the ax side to side like a cat swishing his tail right before he pounced. He was enjoying this, I realized.

I screamed.

Black dots speckled my vision. It couldn't end like this.

Choking, my vision spun swirling from ax, trees, fog, ax, trees . . .

Fog . . .

I could feel my eyes flutter close.

A roar cleaved through the forest, and suddenly I was dropped. Pain shot through my hands, jarring up my wrists as they took most of the impact of the fall. The taste of dirt filled my mouth, mixed in still with the disgusting taste of sharp decay, and I lay there stunned for a second, gulping down oxygen. Another roar cleaved through the air and I rolled away from the noise, trying to avoid whatever was happening that made the nightmare drop me. Staggering up, I tried to make sense of what I was seeing.

The most terrifying creature was attacking both the ax murderer and the Slenderman nightmare. It had to be more than six feet tall, its loose and decaying skin hanging off its thin frame. Its mouth, which was open in a snarl, looked more like pumpkin guts hanging from the inside of a jack-o-lantern. I watched in fear-stricken awe as it reached its long arms out, hands clasping around the Slenderman, and there was a sickening crack, then in particles that reminded me of ash, the nightmare dissolved underneath this mysterious creature's grip. It turned. Where eyes should have been, emerald flame-like orbs burned. I caught strands of auburn hair, but then the ax murderer swung at its head, forcing the creature's attention back to them, fighting viciously.

I ran.

Pumping my arms, my legs were shaking, my calves and upper thighs burning, and I was pretty sure that I had a broken rib, but I was free, still gripping my branch like it was an extension of myself now, my protection between myself . . . and them.

The trees around me felt like they started to thicken, thick underbrush, thorns and thistles slicing my legs and arms, the thin whip-like lacerations burning. I didn't slow down. I gritted my teeth and pushed harder, needing to get out of this place now.

A guttural scream split through the air coming from behind me, and I scrambled.

How was I getting out of this?

I ducked under a low hand branch, lifting it above my head so I could move under it, and the tiniest whisper of a touch brushed against my hand. Pulling it back, I looked at my hand, where a tick looking bug was slowly making its way across my knuckles. I flicked it, sending it careening onto the ground. I wrinkled my nose—I hated ticks. Breaking back into a slower run, but still a run, I tried to shake the feeling like there were more ticks on me somehow, that they had gotten underneath my shirt, my shorts. Digging and burrowing into me. Not to mention the diseases they carried. My mom had a friend once who got bitten by a tick and didn't get seen or on antibiotics fast enough. Chronic Lyme disease. My mom didn't tell me much but I overheard snippets as a teen. *Make them see reason. You can't go on untreated, you need help. Bell palsy? I can come over later with dinner.*

Then scarier conversations as time went on, and I would continue to overhear my mom on the phone. *Hals, you're on bedrest, let me try and organize a worker to come in and help you, okay? You can't be left like this, to slip and waste away.*

The infection is getting worse.

Maid?

It's your choice . . .

At her funeral, I remember thinking what kind of world we live in if doctors are more focused on saying something is impossible to get, rather than learning and letting go of their pride or egos. Weren't they supposed to help their patients? None of this toxic bullshit of *have you tried yoga*, and *if you just really lost the weight,* or *have you been doing things that make you happy?* To prevent Hals's situation, she needed that. Not to have to fight to get treatment, to be believed. Not to be told that Lyme disease wasn't a silent epidemic and she had nothing to worry about. A beautiful life, dimmed. To just fade out.

All the while, the bitter coating of grief hung in my mouth, and I knew, my mom knew, that it should be prevented. She should have been saved, not shoved aside.

The memories overwhelmed me, grief slammed into my gut, cracking me. I dove deeper and deeper into the woods, swiping at my arms, my legs, my face trying to get the image of ticks biting into my skin—poisoning me.

Making sure my destiny was to fade out as well.

At that thought, fear dominated me, breaking that small bit of resolve I had been clinging to. My mind bled to a blankness, while my body moved in such a disconnected way, begging to run, to live, to fight.

I was just so tired.

My life had turned into a *Wes Craven* film, and I was supposed to be final girl, right?

To blaze a trail where others had failed, to be reborn in horror, stronger than ever. To defeat the impossible opponent. All the same rules seemed to apply. Die in this nightmare realm? I would be dead in real life. The stakes were as high as they could get.

My breath felt like it was swelling in my throat, cutting off my ability to take a deep breath. Snot dribbled down from my nostrils now, as the forest seemed to blur. The tree's edges were just getting swallowed more into shadow, the strange haze becoming more and more thick. I couldn't see what I was running into, let alone if I would crash into anything. Or anyone. Twigs snapped under my clumsy footing, lurching deeper into the dark. I felt the tiny legs of the ticks, who were definitely in my hair, falling down to my exposed skin on my forehead, onto the curve of my eyelids, of my lips. Something hooked the front of my right foot. I fell, hard, my sense of gravity tilting with the sudden displacement. Branches snapped loudly underneath my body.

Hot, stinging pain bloomed over both my kneecaps; I could feel the edges of the knurled roots sticking up out of the forest floor. Shimmying forward, I panted. My palms were hot and stinging as well, the wounds deep, gravel and dirt wedging into them with each movement. My vision blurred, heavier tears streaming down my face, falling, and falling.

A hand wrapped around my ankle, yanking me back. My chin smacked the forest floor, my teeth slicing into my tongue from the impact. Hot copper flooded my mouth, followed immediately by a mouthful of dirt. I flipped onto my back, to stare up at those deep green orbs. It was the same monster from before. Its chest was heaving, the emerald orbs this close I could see the depth of the shades of green, from slivers of pale light green like sun hitting blades of grass, to deep forest green, and even parts that were so dark they looked black. It was beautiful, the churning shades flickering like a kaleidoscope of light. Entrancing, even melded together within the terror. This creature had me pinned down, its clawed hand pressing down on my chest as it crouched over me. It was too big, too long limbed to sit on me, but I could feel its strength through its huge palm, the claws where nails should be, their points indenting my skin through my shirt.

This is it. This is how I go. I close my eyes, my lashes a feather touch against my flushed, salt-covered skin. *I love you, Harold. James, too.* A lot of the times in movies or books, it says your entire life flashes before your eyes, but I could only think of them.

I waited.

A gentle, tentative palm rested on my cheek and I flinched. Batting my eyes back open, the creature stared down at me, unblinkingly, so close it was almost nose to nose. No breath brushed my face from it, and those unblinking orbs only seemed to grow larger. Where a mouth had been, the flesh was now somehow flush, together, no nose, no mouth, nothing recognizably human. Under such intense focus, I squirmed. Like it was either loving playing its prey. Or . . . or something else.

I swallowed, heart beating out of my chest.

Frozen, I watched, feeling completely out of my body as it lifted its massive palm off my chest, its stare still locked onto me, like it was testing if I would run or attack. Furrowing my brows, I tried to figure out what was happening.

Moving so slow, it extended its hand, reaching toward my own. What happened next was a series of snapshots captured in mere seconds.

That massive hand engulfed my own, gripping it tightly, and the creature stood so lithely, it smoothly pulled me with it, so I stood too. My arm screamed from my sockets, feeling like it was about to be dislocated. The forest tilted on a ninety-degree axis, and I with it. The feeling that ticks were crawling all over me—the heaviness of that forest and the nightmares that hunted me, vanished.

Stunned in complete wonder, I watched as the webbed sky from the branches and leaves smoothly transitioned as well. It looked like someone clicked to a different backdrop, a different place, a different scene, and us with it. The strange foggy haze still carried over, as I took in the endless horizon, the rolling waves gently colliding with the shoreline, and the moon that hung above us, luminous and full. I recognized this beach, the familiar backdrop of the park behind us. Cantara park. Lake Huron, the great lake that borders Sarnia.

The hand that was holding mine now too was different. My mouth ran dry. I slowly looked up at the pale freckled, human arm. The woman looked around my age, she wore workout shorts, a loose t shirt and black running shoes. Her auburn hair was swept up, her green eyes framed by dark circles under them, a spattering of freckles running along her cheekbones and bridge of her nose.

"We have a second here, Theo." Complete and utter heartbreak lay in the corners of her slight smile. I opened and closed my mouth, unable to make a coherent sentence, to put together what I just saw, and went through, physically, no matter how much my mind was telling me it was impossible. I stood there, completely drained. My brain felt like it had resurfaced, resuscitated by an electric current, as I connected the dots.

Loosening an exhale, I looked out to the rolling waves, knowing exactly what bloodied history was here, staining these golden sands a lifetime ago. I had grown up though with the urban legend, the rhyme, like my mom had grown up with Lakeshore Lane.

Kinsley, Kinsley down in the depths,

All alone, a sunken wreck,

Better watch out or she'll want you dead,

Kinsley, Kinsley there she is.

Once you see her, you are next.

I cringed, involuntarily saying the rhyme in my head as I offered, "Kin . . . Kinsley

Matthews?"

She nodded.

"And before? That was you too?"

"Yeah."

"How?" I asked.

Grimly, she looked out to the lake, still grasping my hand. "They never anticipated that

I would be stuck like this, in this place. That I would still be . . . me. They never wanted that. Their purpose was to destroy, and then fucking recruit.

"When I was human, I lived chronically ill. With fibromyalgia, but with that came a shit ton of other symptoms and other illnesses. It's not one thing, you know? Fibro is a tentacled beast, devouring who you used to be at its very core. Western medicine doesn't have a grip on chronic illnesses yet, because it's not just, '*oh take this medication and you are cured.*' Most people don't hear the *chronic* part of chronic illness, and I can't sum into words properly how hard, how much a fucking battle it turns your life into. Who would want to feel like they had the flu every day? Who would want to be in survival mode every. Single. Day. Navigating the medical system, the disability system, the isolation, the loss of life, because that's what it is. Navigating the ignorance slamming against you, drowning you. *Oh you don't look sick. Oh if you only lost weight it will complete heal you. But have you tried yoga yet?*"

Tears streamed down her face.

"Toxic positivity was a knife sliding across my throat. Bleeding me out, and no one wanted to see that, to change their behavior. I didn't understand why. I still don't. Imagine yourself sitting in that isolation, and grief, and anger and every day I was fighting with every damn thing I had in me, just to walk, just to take care of basic needs. What would you do?"

"I wouldn't want to live with the chronic illnesses," I whispered, wiping at my own tears.

"Exactly. I saw all around me the media pushing and pushing, being disabled and over coming it in a heroic way, not letting it be you, being chronically ill and magically healing. But no one shows that it's okay to not be cured, to have the blunt honesty of not wanting any of it. To be real, in all the slivers of good that were still in my life, with a lot of bad."

"And when it comes to experiencing something supernatural . . . well, most don't believe until they are in it themselves. I don't know what they are, but you saw what they look like. This nightmare appeared at a point in my life—no, it was the exact moment when I was drowning and I needed a life boat. It was a certain thing that unlocked them into my life."

"What was it?" I asked, feeling like I was going to be sick.

"I think it appears differently to whoever they have been stalking. They are predators, masters at what they do best. Hunting. I would work on conditioning my body, trying to build up stamina after being bedridden for almost a year. While I walked, I would collect—used to collect—lake glass.

"This piece was so stunning. A mix of colors I had never seen before. I touched it. I took it home."

"Oh god."

"The rest . . . can I show you? I'll spare some of the details."

I nodded, overwhelmed, heartbroken that her story doesn't end a different way. Not the tragedy, not the haunting legend.

The shore of Lake Huron bled away. At first, all I could see was red. The color of blood. I looked to try to spot a landmark, to spot anything. A hand shot out of nowhere, grabbing the front of my shirt, dragging me down.

Down.

Down.

It was so subtle, the feeling of not being in my body anymore. Far away, there was a tether, an echo that I was somewhere else, with someone else.

"*A pain-free life . . .*" a disembodied voice echoed.

"*In exchange . . .*"

I was floating in that sea of red now, that eerie voice all around me. Images flashed in the sky, or images were behind my eyes. Who could be certain anymore? But I felt her there with me; her fear.

Powerless, she was dragged into the inky waters, the night so still and serene, down, down, down. It was into Lake Huron but wasn't. It was a place, like where I was. A place where nightmares lived, their world brushing with ours. I flinched as she was ripped apart, literally. I tasted iron, I tasted blood, but also relief.

"To become like us, when your life comes to an end . . ."
It wasn't wishing to be someone else, to be free of pain.
But they were liars.
The images spun, the red rolling waves draining slowly. The next images of memory came fast now. I was part of them . . . of it. Of everything this was, and is.
And we were out of time.
I recognized now the sprawling town, the quaint downtown streets with annual flower plants hanging in front of the shops. Haden. *Home.* The streets blurred, like I was in Google maps clicking down, down, down.
Snapping into focus, my perspective was looking at the front of the house, 1729 Lakeshore Lane. *The house.* Sometime between the 90s and now, if the town was any sign of it, but it wasn't a house, and dread curdled in me so potent it was all I could do but live through this. *You grow through what you go through.* Yeah. Right.
The house was a mask, and what was beneath was inexpiable. Like an invasive organism, a thin fleshy wall floated in a domelike structure. Floating off the dome were black tendrils, ones that buried into the ground, into Haden. Looking like it was poisoning the ground. They wriggled, different shoots imbedded into different things all around the property, like it was tethering the house into place; but also it went beyond the house, inky tentacles stretching and stretching beyond Lakeshore Lane, beyond Haden.
"Wakeupandgotothere." It was the woman I saw every night during my sleep paralysis saying this now, having appeared in front of me, her back to me. But her image looked distorted, flickering between having a pixie cut, or long auburn hair that was familiar now.
It was Kinsley. In my room every night, all this time reaching out trying desperately to reach me. I looked past her now, back at 1729

Lakeshore Lane.

"Wake up and go there," I whispered, it all clicking into place. One by one, the hauntings, the monsters, the people that I knew about, and some I didn't, flickered to life all around the pulsing orb.

The nun, pointing down at me from behind the distorted upstairs window. Tentacles erupted through where the front door would be, its flesh sagging, massive suckers with teeth snapping. On the lawn, more of those leering skeletal monsters that took Kinsley silently stare at me. A girl crawling on all fours rushed towards me—

There was a scuttling of bugs—

A multitude of different faces started layering and layering in my vision, blending into hundreds of eyes, gaping mouths and teeth.

All.

Watching.

Me.

Before they all disappeared.

All around me, drifting languidly like snowflakes, was what looked like spores. The house and details of my hometown were slowly swallowed by the growing shadows, until it was gone. Standing in the dark, I felt it. It was just a brush at first, like a finger trailing so slowly down my cheek. The otherness of it, completely unnatural.

The hunger.

A hard tug pulled back, and I with it, dragged through the pain, the hunger, the terror. All the terrible things that have happened in Haden, in Sarnia, stemmed from one web. That house was patient zero. It was a fucking growing entity that was infecting the place I loved most in this world.

In a rush, it felt like my bones were lit on fire. I dropped to my knees, back on that beach, back with Kinsley. The air carried the far away smell of autumn leaves, mixed with heady earth, brine from the lake.

"You're okay," Kinsley said, tears shining in her eyes, mirroring my own. My nails dug into the sand so hard that I could feel the granules imbedded underneath my nails.

"Now you understand. You are the first person to have ever gone into the belly of the beast and has left okay. Before I died . . . when I was one of them, I killed two of the monsters. They were hunting a group of teenagers. I saved only two. The rest of me wanted to not save them. But this? You? Us in this moment, in this *place*, we can hit back. To destroy it."

A hard glint flooded her shining gaze, her voice thick with emotion. "Those fuckers will pay for what they did to me. But it's not just for me. Think about how long this thing . . . this power has been here. You felt it through my memories. Hundreds of people have fell prey to its ghosts."

My heart pounded out of my chest, a bitter taste coating my tongue. The girls . . . they were just kids. How many more were killed simply because this power *wanted* to?

"We are both the final girls of our story," I whispered. The last to confront the true killer in a grim and bloody battle, for those innocent lives lost. I straightened.

"You didn't deserve what happened to you. I'm so sorry. That you were in so much pain. That people didn't understand or—no, fucking scratch that. That people didn't want to understand, that they didn't want to learn about what it really means to live with those conditions. That they were happier to cut you out of their life. That they saw you as disposable. The fucking toll . . . Kinsley, if that pain is your pain that I felt back there—" I motioned wildly around us with my spare hand, trailing off, biting the inside of my cheek trying to keep my tears from falling. She didn't want my pity; she didn't want my pain of how fucking heartbreaking her story is.

"I'm sorry that our world is forgetting what it means to have humanity. Forgetting what it means to have empathy. Forgetting that there is so much power in listening. I'm sorry that we are living in an age where honesty and having a person to grant you that space to talk freely about your situation is rare. It shouldn't be. Not you'll *get better soon.* I'm so sorry."

The tears I had been trying so hard to keep in streamed down my cheeks. I gripped her hand back, hard.

"Let's go save our fucking town."

The air was charged. It sparked with an invisible current that hadn't been there before.

Because they know now. That we are coming for them.

When we came back to this plain, it made me wonder where Kinsley had taken us, that had been safe enough for her to explain. I guess it didn't matter now, though. I trailed my hand slowly against the tree trunk, looking up to Kinsley in . . . this form.

Her head was tilted, her orb-like gaze fixed behind me.

I turned to look, gripping my branch over my head now ready to bring it down on—

Nothing. No one was there.

Kinsley came up beside me in one stride and touched the branch. Under my grip, it turned warm, like I was laying out in the sun in the middle of summer, and I felt it move. Startling, I looked up to Kinsley, a *what the hell* radiating from me. She just nodded back down to my hands and I followed her gaze.

The machete gleamed in the foggy half-light of the forest, the sharpened grey steel long, the mahogany handle in my hand cool against my touch now. Beside me, Kinsley lowered herself in a half crouch, her mouth ripping open, the grey flesh flapping in the new open space now.

She roared.

It was thunderous, the guttural sound rattling through my bones, into the ground, into the very marrow of this place. Kinsley nodded once, and then sprinted in lithe bounds, her long claws arched. *Let's go.*

I was supposed to be a victim, infected, and be nothing more than a tool to spread this to other people, to make sure they were stained for whatever next horror and tragedy this place wanted to unleash. Was this power, these hauntings, drawn to people in pain, or isolation?

I palmed the machete handle, smooth and sturdy in my grip.

I followed, pumping my arms, making sure the blade wasn't swung wildly. My legs burned, but I inhaled through my nose and out through my mouth. The fog thickened, but I could still see Kinsley's tall and skeletal frame in front of me. Heat flooded my chest, stitches running up my ribcage, but I pushed faster. Trees blurred around me; every time I passed one, I thought I saw the edges of different figures standing there, fingers curling around the trunks, or their leering grins focused on me.

It's just this place, trying to unravel you.

I clenched my teeth so hard, pain thudded along my jaw, trying to focus on Kinsley. I blinked.

I skidded to a halt. "Oh man, what the fu—"

The sentence died on my lips. I was suddenly alone, standing in a stretching hallway. The smell of wood oil wafted, the deep mahogany floors a deep umber. Kinsley and the forest had disappeared, and in their place was a heavy silence, the kind that drives any sense of reason away, the kind that kicks a person into fight or flight. There was some kind of light on beyond the doorframe at the end of the hallway, casting a warm glow along the floorboards and bare walls, the bland wallpaper curling in some parts.

It clicked off.

Darkness devoured any trace of light.

I stumbled back. Instantly, my heart kicked into double time as my vision adjusted to the sudden lack of light.

A hand settled on my lower back from behind before sliding up to my shoulder, gripping it hard.

"Theo," the raspy voice whispered into my ear, in the complete and total darkness. I dipped my body low, ungracefully slammed my elbow back, hard. Something crunched, and my elbow met flesh. I spun, swinging the blade furiously. The tall figure stumbled back and I blinked, trying to make out where it was, but I didn't stop swinging, the swish the only sound with my panicked breaths. Suddenly, I felt a hand wrap around my ankle, pulling me back, *hard*. I fell, my head cracking against the floorboards, and a galaxy of light winking in and out of existence flooded me. It was all I could see before the pain came roaring back.

I was dragged, splinters sliding into my face, my lips, my hands as I tried to find anything to hold onto. The machete slipped from my hand clattering behind. "No!" I screamed as my only defense—my only weapon—was left for the darkness.

The figure was still shrouded in the shadow as they dragged me by the ankle. My skin was hot, pounding like it may split apart. Taking in two sharp breaths, I didn't think about it—I contorted my body so I was laying on my back now. My foot was at a ninety-degree angle in the stranger's grasp. The pain was hot, blinding, slithering up my leg. The pressure built.

And built.

And *built*.

Snap.

I heard it before I felt it, this second of dissonance between the sound, this slip of my reality. This wasn't really happening, was it? How could it be—

Pain brought me slamming back. Hot, potent, deep pain pulsed from my ankle which was now hanging at a sickening angle, nothing more than limp pale flesh with a shoe attached. Because there was splintered bone sticking out from my calf. Bile surged up my throat, seeping out of my mouth. Tears mixed with throw up, and I was screaming—or maybe I had never stopped, I didn't know.

Bending my left knee up to my chest, I kicked it down at the massive hand gripping me.

My heel connected first, and I repeated it, until I felt the cracks. I shuddered to a stop as the figure let me go. I scrambled back, scooting on my ass, trying to ignore the fact my vision dipped from the amount of pain I was in.

"You are a sinner!" the figure screamed; I could make out the nun was leaning down toward me, her habit brushing against my shins and hanging, but she wore a sheen black veil that covered her face as well. I continued to scramble back.

Her voice was guttural now; "You were supposed to die. You were the catalyst to let me rise again, all these years later. You will not get away from me this time."

Oh, shit.

Get up, Theo, if you want to live. Get. Up.

The footsteps sounded, heading directly toward me. I lay there, stunned, my hand desperately stretching out across the floor, searching for the smooth handle of my machete. Gritting my teeth, my vision dipped harshly as I made myself move. Rolling onto my stomach, I dragged myself. My ankle bumped against the floor and I screamed, because the *pain*. My fucking god, the pain was white hot, blistering through bone and sinew, eradicating the sense that I had been anything before agony.

It wouldn't end like this—in the dark, alone, with this force continuing to prey on the innocents of Haden and beyond. This thing, this place thought it could so easily kill this version of me. In my thirties, feeling my most authentic self? It didn't know who *I was*.

I was Theo fucking Anderson.

A writer—but it wasn't an egotistical drive to want to do it. Since as early as the age of eight, writing was as essential as breathing to me. A Gemini; take what you will from that. Coffee lover. Ace. I would die for Harold, for James. I was a tattooed, alt, horror loving woman. I had social anxiety, most of the time having trouble following the social banter that seemed to come so easily to others. 80s horror made my soul sing with joy. I found peace in being alone, not loneliness. But that didn't mean I didn't hope one day I could find someone who saw me so damn clearly as I would see them, two halves becoming a whole, and that to me was love, attraction, it was everything. I try to be kind, in a world that is cruel, to find connection, though I wish it didn't feel so hard sometimes, so fake. But I would continue to try, period. To fight to keep going, to work hard, to chase my joy because no one else was responsible for that—you are. You are responsible for your own happiness, goals, life, dreams, wants.

I am. This body that had cultivated thousands of memories, and would make thousands more, sparking energy, creativity, a wink of a star in the cosmos that was so big, but wasn't it tragically beautiful that we all are? Navigating this one shot at life, energy calling to energy, all the heartbreak and happiness, success and failures, betrayal and loyalty, hurt and love that I have felt, that we all feel.

Hauntingly beautiful, we move all in our own unique perspective through like-minded situations, the variables about what could happen so different still. Going through the blows life could deal, and lets be real here, those blows can be massive, can be devastating. Can be everything that horror is described as, and it's not fair. Those moments could break you.

Or. Or you could become that else. That something you couldn't even believe you would be strong enough to live through. And *yet* . . .

This place wanted to take it all from me.

"Like hell," I growled, my voice sounding feral, hitched with pain, grief and rage.

I slid a little bit more of my stomach; bile, drool, sweat and tears running down from my lips, dripping onto the floor underneath me. Images of the girls burned in my memory, what she had done to them, and I felt myself start to transform into that *else* that is so shown in media. But in horror, it was a two word title.

Final. Girl.

I wrenched myself forward now, getting a lot more distance, roaring through the pain. I repeated the motion, making my way down the hall. The nun was screaming something at me, but the words bled to a droning whine. My hand searched the floor, until—

There.

I fumbled to grip the handle of the machete at first, but then found purchase on it, just as

I was flipped over, those massive hands around my throat squeezing hard.

"Who are you, to break decades of cycle? Who are you, but a filthy, heath—"

I slammed the blade into her neck with everything I had in me. I felt the thud, the crunch through veins and bone, the spray of that rotting blood spraying all over my face. I must have hit the carotid artery. There was a strange gurgling, choking sound and I screamed, wrenching the blade out and then cut it back down father into her neck.

Silence, before her body collapsed onto the floor, and the light at the end of the hallway flickered back on.

"And to dust we shall return," I spat at the crumbled habit, the only religious line I knew thanks to Mike Flanagan and *Midnight Mass*. The black ash scattered across the floor where her body should be. But this was a nightmare realm, and what should be didn't apply.

I let loose a string of cursing that would likely have James smacking my arm, and hard. I dropped down, feeling my heartbeat reverberate against the floor, feeling my staggered breath, but I was *still* breathing.

Sitting back up, I wiped the semi dry blood away best I could from my lips and eyes.

Then focused on my leg. I sucked at science, but *fibula* kept rotating around in my mind, as I stared at the red blood, my blood, contrasting against the spray of black on the hardwood floor.

"Okay," I said out loud to myself, shivering. I was freezing. Gripping the end of my loose shirt, I ripped most of the bottom off.

"Okay," I repeated before I took that makeshift wrapping and tied it as tightly as I could around the break. The bone that was sticking out made a sickening crunch. Sucking in a breath, it did nothing against the pain. Deep, splintering, like my bones had shattered and turned to ire, molten and bleeding all together in a viscous state. The swelling was bad, and the pressure of it a mountain crushing down on the broken bone. While blood continued to leak, congealing and pooling underneath my calve.

Quickly, I leaned over to my right side, projectile vomiting, missing most of myself. My eyes watered, the bile acidic and spurting through my sinuses and out my nose. Gasping, I tried to conjure up what saliva I had left in my mouth and spat out the remnants. Focusing back on my leg, I wrapped the shirt around the break again, screaming through the absolute agony. Panting, my vision swam; it was all just a mash of colors, spinning and spinning.

I tied the knot of my makeshift brace, my hands trembling.

"Okay, now stand. You have to get out of this place," I commanded myself, trying to compartmentalize through the shock, pain, exhaustion, adrenaline.

I had to find Kinsley. Find. Kinsley.

Drenched in a cold sweat now, my stomach felt like it was lodged in my throat, a strange hollowness churning in it. I grabbed the machete and then I scooted myself back to the wall, so my back was flush against it. I put my hands on either side of me, clenching my teeth so hard it felt like they would shatter under the pressure.

Using all my strength in my left leg, steadying with my hands, machete handle clamped in between my teeth, I pushed myself up to standing. The movement was slow. I spit and snarled against the machete. Internally, I bellowed every swearword I knew from mild, to what I thought was the worst, until I stood.

I looked down the hallway, to where the other room lay, doused in warm light. The only way through was to keep going, so I allowed the wall to bear a lot of my unsteadiness and I hopped not gracefully, and painfully slowly down the hallway. Each movement washed my vision in red. My skin was drenched in cold sweat, my muscles trembling against the effort. All the while the pain possessed me, burning me from the inside out.

Was the machete long enough to help my weight bear on my broken ankle? Taking it out of my mouth, I tried but the blade was too short. "Slow, then. It's better than nothing," I said to myself.

Time was agony, as the seconds dragged by and I heaved myself toward the doorway at the end of the hall. In waves of pain, I eventually made it, dry heaving and half conscious. But I leaned against that opening, leaving one nightmare behind.

To face the next.

Gripping the doorframe, I tried to bear most of my weight on my left leg holding my broken ankle up—I fell. I swiped at air, my body hoping for something to catch my fall. Pain flared as I braced my impact mostly with my hands, my wrists bending too far, the tendons screaming against my weight. I just stay there, my whole body trembling, spent.

Blinking, I looked up to take in the next room, assuming it was going to be like the state of the hallway I left.

I didn't have time to react. I was choking on my pain, then ... nothing. Spinning so I was sitting on my butt, I grappled at my ankle and my shitty makeshift bandage—the blood still sticky on my now healed skin. *Do my injuries not exist anymore because I got past the nun?* I thought. *Was this place some kind of fucked up levelled nightmare maze? Beat the bosses and get out?*

A body went sailing over my head, crashing into the wall of what looked like a living Room, and all my thoughts evaporated again. Fight or flight kicking in, I scrambled to stand, and froze.

"Kinsley!" I half yelled, half moaned. Blackened blood seeped down her body, the gashes along her chest and torso so deep that the flaps of loose skin looked like multiple gaping mouths, parted in a scream. She stood, slowly, pointing behind me.

I turned, trying to get my blade up just as a foot connected with my gut, making me double over in a wheeze. Straightening, black dots flooding in my vision, I swung the blade in front of me expecting to confront the assailant.

Except the room was filled with men and women who stood, frozen, their milky gazes fixed on me, all dressed in black, their mouths stretched too wide in bleeding smiles.

The patches of skin I could see rippled.

As if something *moved* underneath it.

I stood frozen, watching Kinsley as she didn't make a move from where she either. I dipped my chin though. "I'm glad I found you."

She dipped her chin back, her mouth materializing as she ground out,

"I didn't understand at first, but they are triggered by movement."

Great.

"How do we get to the heart of this place?" *How are we going to make it out alive to do it?* is what I held back.

My skin pricked, my hair standing on end as I looked more closely to these people who reminded me more of mannequins in this state. Their arms where pin-straight at either side, and I realized with horror most of them looked like teenagers. Their hair caked in matts and dried blood, old wounds looking more like cracks in porcelain than human skin. They stared unblinkingly, all their bodies aimed at me. My legs started to shake.

Kinsley, still frozen, ground out, "Use me . . ."

"No."

"As bait."

"Kinsley, I'm not leaving this room without you by my side, okay? It's noble, but I refuse to lose you."

"I'm already . . ."

"Don't. You are not lost," I hissed, coming out way more harshly than I intended. "You deserve—" *a life* "— to take back what they took from you. You think that because you wished for a life without pain or illness that you deserve what happened to you? No one deserves to live like that, always in survival mode, friends disappearing, because why? They think you don't fit into society's box anymore in their eyes? But that's a reflection on how shitty they are, how small-minded that they don't have the empathy to understand the fight you were in. Because that's what I fucking saw and felt through you, Kinsley. You were at war with your illness. It was the monster. Not you. Do you assume you were somehow destined to be cursed? The support in your life failed you. Society failed you, because people are selfish, and the world is cruel and somehow being disabled has been misconceived as being a dirty word, something to shy away from, to be left behind. I refuse to let you be failed again, least of all by me."

Tears were streaming down my face as I finished, but my eyes widened. In what felt like slow motion, I watched my hand jerk forward, holding the machete. I always talked with my hands when I was upset.

Chaos erupted.

The people dropped to all fours in perfect unison, their pale and swollen joints so juxtaposed against their torn and dark shirts and pants. I realized they were all bare footed.

Cracccccck.

The sound was more horrifying to me in unison as all their jaws dislocated in tandem, hanging loosely above the floor. They scuttled toward me on all fours, nothing human flickering within their gazes, the jerky movement reminding me of bugs. In their milky white eyes, pure hunger grew.

All aimed at me.

No, no, no! I tried to turn to run, but it was as if my legs weren't connected to the rest of my body anymore. My panic welled, crested and then dragged me down.

Out of my peripheral, I saw blurred movement. My heart plummeting into my stomach. Kinsley's massive hand connected with my chest, sending me careening back into the doorway. Pain shot up my tailbone and lower back. I landed hard. Stunned, I blinked up at Kinsley, her tall frame shielding me. Her wounds seeped, blood hitting the floor in thick droplets. She stood straight, her emerald orbs locked on me. My bottom lip trembled, but I couldn't utter the scream that pushed behind my teeth, that welled. I couldn't say what roared through me; *Please don't do this.* There was only a charged second. Kinsley mouthed one word:

Run.

They were on her, colliding with violence.

"No!" ripped from me, my hand outstretched. I was suspended in this horror. Their jaws clamped down hard on any part of Kinsley they could, clamoring over one another to get to her. I trembled as I saw the gush of black dots gush out from the *person's mouth*, the beetles instantly diving into Kinsley's exposed skin, like those beetles from *The Mummy*. She was fighting back, roaring against the onslaught. A sickening rip cut through the room, and I caught glimpses of Kinsley's shoulder being ripped off in a spray of black blood, sinew, skin and bone hanging from the joint.

Run.

Her other clawed hand rose up out of the tide of bugs, jaws and entangled limbs.

Reaching for help.

Run.

Lurching up, I sprinted across the room not knowing where I was headed, but just knowing I couldn't—wouldn't waste Kinsley's sacrifice. My stomach bucked, grief settling there, incinerating me. Tears swam in my vision as a roar cleaved the air. Then, silence.

Don't look back.

Almost across the bare room, I skidded. There wasn't another door. Frantic, I turned.

The doorway I came into this room through was blocked. A different sound was floating in the room now, a different kind of snapping, tearing, crunch, crunch, CRUNCH.

I slammed mental walls up, my entire body shaking. I could think about what those sounds meant after.

RUN.

There. Across the room to the right, was a dirty window. My muscles tensed, the crappy bandage job I did on my ankle coming undone to trail behind me. I sprinted, my breath a burning lash with each inhale. It was the only option. Pumping my arms, I was wrenched back to track memories in public school, back in the day when everyone had to participate. I was deemed the weird library helper and was in no way athletic (thanks, asthma) or hand any inclination to be. The coaches voice barked through my mind now. *Keep breathing. Keep your arms below your heart, Theodora! Come on now, you can do better than that.*

I was halfway across the room.

The crunching sounds started to subside.

Trying to get as much speed as I could, I ran as fast as my burning muscles would tolerate, sweat mixing with my tears flying off my cheekbones. The floor started to shake underneath my Converses. I caught a glimpse of the machete being kicked and stumbled over by these things on the opposite side of the room. There was no time. I had to leave it behind.

Almost there.

A whoosh and stirred wind rippled against my neck, like something was just trying to grab a hold of my shirt, to rip me back, to eat my flesh off my bones, to tear me apart inch by inch—

Squinting my eyes shut, I raised my arm for it to take most of the impact and jumped out the window. Shattering glass exploded all around me.

Copper flooded my mouth, then a sweeping stinging sensation, all over my face, arms, legs, torso. I fell, my sense of gravity twisting with my screams. I couldn't see anything. Just nothingness.

Disoriented, I braced for more pain, for breaking my bones again, for this place to batter me down. Chest heaving, my stomach flipped, feeling firmly lodged in my throat as I was impossibly *standing outside.*

"Oh what the hell—" I sobbed, patting my body, stretching my arms out in front of me. But I wasn't covered in lacerations that I had felt, the glass imbedded in my skin poking out. There was absolutely nothing there.

I crouched and emptied my stomach for the second time, the bile splattered on the packed gravel, and I sobbed. Kinsley . . . she was gone. And I had to be okay with her choice—she had been stripped of so many in her life—she had chosen to make sure I continued on, to destroy this place. For me to seek her revenge. But the loss *hurt*.

It was the deep ache in my chest, the inability to take a full breath.

It was in each tear that continued to slip down my cheeks.

It was in the cold shock, in the absence of their presence that rolled into me like waves.

"I'm so sorry, Kinsley," I said into the darkness. Shakily, I straightened, taking in where I was, what I was now facing weaponless. I wiped my tears.

The strange hazy fog rolled along in front of me, as I stood at the end of the laneway.

The house loomed from the shadows.

All along the lawn, there were signs staked into the grass, which in this realm, looked like blackened shoots. The letters were streaked, the ink long bled but I could still make out parts of what some said.

Fuc J Wardon.

Devil lives.

I looked back up to this place, that wore the mask of a house. The wrap around porch was rotted and the Victorian build was all sharp angles.

I balled my fists so hard my nails dug into my palm, my body was still trembling. It bubbled up then. The unfairness that Kinsley had died, that this place thought it was winning with its onslaught of living nightmares.

"No more," I ground out, to myself, to the too still air. I felt the presence, this place was watching me take my final stand.

"Fuck YOU!" I bellowed directly to the house, my sadness, my sleep deprivation and pain, my fear and adrenaline coursing through me like an electric current, that was bringing me back to life. I had to make it through this. There would always be darkness entangled with the light, the two couldn't exist without the other. But life, *love, fucking humanity,* had to prevail, right?

It has to.

In the second-floor bay window, a light flicked on, casting the warm glow against the cracked glass.

I walked forward, fists still balled, glaring at the illuminating window, imaging what it was saying mockingly. *I see you, down there, the one that got away. Funny to meet you here, in this plain of existence. But no matter, why don't you come on in, and let's—*

"Get this over with," I muttered to myself, like I do when I write.

I can't promise a quick end, though. I have to make an example of you. You were supposed to help spread the infection, not—

"Beat it," I snarled.

No matter, though. Because you have been since the moment you first came to the house, to now—

I hopped over the hole of caved in rotting porch, slamming the front door open so hard it shook the frame. I blinked, as my eyes adjusted to the deeper shadows in the house, the grey light spilling behind me enough to take in the rotting staircase, that back in the real world, in its prime, once would have been beautiful. The black mold stained almost every wall. Spores and dust particles drifted lazily through the speckled half light. My gaze snapped to the right, where in huge dark, dripping letters—*blood*—read:

MINE.

The door slammed behind me on its own, shutting me in absolute darkness.

The bang, so resolute, so *horror movie,* made me smirk but still jump, fear starting to flood into my veins. *Keep moving, find a weapon,* I commanded myself, even though I didn't know exactly what the heart of this place would be. Upstairs, I could see still the dim glow of the second-floor room.

I could practically hear the fourth wall breaking in my head, whoever watching this movie was screaming at what a dumb bitch I was, walking right into the trap, the maws of the killer. But I wouldn't find anything to fight back with in the dark.

I moved slowly, blinking rapidly, as if that would help me navigate better. My hands were out, hoping I would bump into a wall to follow or maybe the stair railing. Or run into the next assailant watching me from the corner of the room.

I stopped, my heartbeat slamming against my ribcage, checking over my shoulder half expecting a spectre, mouth yawning open hand outstretched—

Nothing. There was nothing behind me. *Keep it together, Theo.*

Shuffling, I found the base of the stairs, my hand clutching to the railing while testing my right foot on the bottom step. It creaked, a low moan. Holding my breath, I took the next step. *Creaaaaak.*

Trying to remember where the hole was, I took the stairs as fast as I could. Every creak sounded like a crack of thunder against the silence of the house, which was becoming more heavy, more stagnant. *Go, go, go.*

Relying on touch and memory, I navigated the stairs. I felt my Converse land on the next step.

And it met air.

The step clattered down beneath the staircase and I stumbled. My knees connected with something hard and wet, stinging instantly along my kneecaps. Awkwardly, I lifted myself up to the next step, freezing as I found solidness again under my feet. I listened, expecting something, or someone, to come barreling toward me. A lash back of some kind.

I exhaled.

Nothing.

As fast as I could, I scrambled up the remaining steps. *I had to be close to the top.* I scaled them, but I met empty air again and went flying face-first across the top hallway. Hot pain bloomed underneath the sting of my wounds. I stood up, feeling my hands were scraped, and my knees were wet with blood. *Keep going.*

I looked down the hallway; it seemed to branch off so I couldn't see the room where the light was coming from fully. The tension in my chest was becoming a massive knot, battered and bruised, I made my way toward the light. I racked my head for every fact, myth or legend in the horror trope world about beating haunted houses. *Holy water, and salt?* No, that was for ghosts. *Exorcism of the house?* That is usually a thing. But this wasn't normal reality; I was in the nightmare realm . . .

Behind me, the sound of a door creaking open echoed.

I froze, my heart instantly kicking up in double time. Slowly, I turned, squinting to try to see what had made the noise. What had been in the closet, waiting for the opportune moment . . .

I ran.

I didn't see anything, but I couldn't fight back in the dark. Skidding around the corner, I saw the room. It was like a dining room, but oozed art deco. I blinked against the change of light, the stained-glass lamp sitting so innocently there. Unlike the rest of the house, this room wasn't rotting, the walls weren't stained with mold. There was a whiskey tumbler. A cigarette smoking still in a crystal dish.

Slow footfalls echoed down the hallway; I swallowed as a high-pitched giggle floated from the inky shadows. The smell of the cigarette mixed with the moldy air, I haphazardly searched the room for something I could use to protect myself.

A creak split the air right in the doorway.

Slowly, I looked up.

The woman filled the entire doorframe, her long black hair trailing almost to her lower back. She wore a button-down burgundy dress, but it was *her face*. I recognized her. Knew her.

The nightmare from my childhood. I would hide under my bedsheets, terrified to get up and go to the washroom because Mrs. Twisty was watching me. She was *my* nightmare.

She didn't have eyes, but puckered and pinched skin where eyes should be, twisted and blood running down from them like she had two of those red and white peppermint candies plastered there. And her face was pulled into this permanent grin which always looked like a grimace, her pointed nose angled down at me.

Hyperventilating, I stepped back, and she took a step forward, her brown flat buckled shoes spattered with blood.

"Have you been a good girl, Theodora?" Her voice was raspy. A high-pitched scream reverberated through my ears, disoriented. I was shoved back to being five, alone in my room, Mrs. Twisty's hard breathing the only sound flitting in the air. My instinct screamed at me, to hide, now. Sprinting, the room luckily had a door that led to another hallway. I barrelled through.

Her hard inhales and exhales sounded behind me.

"You know what I do to naughty girls, Theodora."

I sprinted faster. The walls blurred, snapping from rotted house to sharp Gatsby-inspired decorations. But there, to my left.

An attic ladder and trap door in the ceiling. But also, at the end of the hall, a bedroom door was cracked open. Moving fast, I slammed the ladder door down, throwing the trapdoor open, before running down to the bedroom. It was dark, and I spotted the bed, slipping as quietly as I could underneath it. I covered my mouth with my hand, trying to stifle my heaving breath.

"Theodora." *Step. Step. Step.* "Where are you?"

Her footfalls were in this hallway now and I lay there, terrified. My skin rippled in goosebumps as I could see her blood-spattered shoes making their way so slowly down toward the ladder. I watched as they stopped, pointing toward the ladder.

She must be looking up.

Any plan I may have been forming was driven from me from the terrifying appearance of Mrs. Twisty. How many nights had I not been able to sleep, terrified, that she was going to get me? How many nights did I spend curled up against my mom, crying, still hearing her breathing from the corner of the room. She would just stalk me. Always there.

Watching.

Waiting.

A tear slipped from the corner of my eye, and I bit down hard on my trembling lip. I watched as her shoes pointed toward where I was hiding. She took another step forward, away from the attic.

Underneath the bed, from behind me, someone else grabbed my ankle, yanking hard. Clawing at the floor, my nails scratched against the dusty hardwood, screaming, "No!"

I kicked with my other foot, but the grip only tightened, and I was dragged out from underneath the bed, sobbing.

I was flipped onto my back, pinned there. I screamed as the man reeking of foul body odour and rot leaned down, his yellowed teeth so close to my face, and whispered, "Boo."

He wore an old school clown suit, like Tim Curry's version of Pennywise. But fat red buttons stood out against the brown stained yellow clown suit, the frilled ends of the neck and wrists ripped. I was speechless as another one of my childhood nightmares was breathed into flesh. Beau Boo the *fucking clown*. Pinned underneath him, I could still spot the massive yellow clown shoes that poked out from behind him. He had no hair, his face painted white, which only made the cracked black lipstick that was drawn to a point, that much more prominent. Black diamonds were painted shakily over his eyes, uneven, unsteady, but his harrowing gaze of yellowed coloured contacts glowed.

The first horror movie I watched at James's in public school was *Buried Under the Carnival*—a hit blockbuster featuring Beau Boo the murderous, vengeful spirit that haunts the small-town teens on the anniversary of his death in a way only slasher movies could deliver. Grotesque body horror that held scenes that drove the shock value to its viewers.

He pulled my ankle again, hard. "You shouldn't be hiding under there. We are all looking for you."

I wrenched, bucking my body, trying to get free. He frowned down at me. Suddenly, his hand was around my throat, squeezing. "You shouldn't be—"

I slammed my right fist into his jaw; he had been too busy to see his hold had shifted ever so slightly. His head snapped to the left.

I grinned; it was all fury, all teeth bared. He teetered, and it was just a second, a sliver of a moment.

It was all I was hoping for.

Using all my weight and my free right hand, I shoved him, hard. He fell with an *oompf*, pressure releasing from my throat, from my body. A clown horn went off, *honk honk*, reverberating through the room, sending shivers down my spine. *Get out of here*, was my thought as I rolled to the right, moving to stand. Out of the corner of my eye, I saw shadowy blurred movement. I turned, expecting to confront Mrs. Twisty now, to get out of this room, out of this house to regroup. The doorframe was empty. What the hell? Where had she gone?

Pain erupted along my temple, this sweep of cool air that teetered my center of gravity.

Something popped in my neck, the room was slipping sideways. I fell into nothingness.

Thwack.

I blinked. Was Harold throwing his ball against the door again to subtly let me know he wanted me to take him out?

Thwack.

Harold? I tried to say, but my mouth felt weird, like it was stuffed with cotton, and my neck was so stiff it was painful.

Thwack.

Cold air pinpricked against my legs, my arms. Where was my comforter?

Thwack.

Mrs. Twisty's face bloomed from the quiet of my mind, as I realized I tasted blood coating my tongue. I hadn't thought of my night terror from when I was younger since . . .

Since I was five?

No, that wasn't right.

I blinked again, trying to open my eyes. Why did they feel so heavy, like instead of blood running through my veins it was ore, hardening to metal within me? And oh my god, my shoulders, my arms were lifted above my head, the floor underneath hard.

I wasn't home.

I wasn't in my room.

My eyes snapped open as the last twenty-four hours slammed back into me, into reality. My gaze landed on Mrs. Twisty's grip, realizing the noise I had heard was my body slamming against each step down the stairs.

She was dragging me down into what looked like the basement. I couldn't spot Beau Boo anywhere, but I knew that didn't mean much. Engaging my core, I tried to lift my head, to start to fight again, to scream, but all that came out of my mouth was garbled salvia.

"Theodora." She said my name in tandem with turning her head, slowly, to look down at me.

"Good, your awake. This is all for you, after all. You have been very naughty, dear."

I didn't know what was worse: the chastising way she was saying my name, her jerky slow movements—she had always reminded me of Samara from *The Ring*—or the fact that I couldn't move. Had they drugged me? The memories of what had happened in this place—all of it—had the sheen of a fever dream now. Was this place just a figment born from my sleep deprivation and stress? Breathed into life from memories and fear?

No. That didn't explain everything. Didn't explain Kinsley.

My head slammed down onto the next step, and I bit my tongue again, opening the wound that was already there, deeper. But whatever they had done to make my body go limp, I couldn't react against the slicing pain. She dragged me down the rest of the stairs like this. Stars danced in my vision, the pain building, the thought twisting in my gut that this could be it. That I could die here, to become part of this horrific grasp that was over Haden and its residents.

The strong mildew scent was thick down here, condensation bubbling on my upper lip from the influx of heat. The walls were black with mold from what I could see from the cracked yellowed light bulbs. There was no wallpaper, but the ceiling *moved*, rippling like there was something in them pushing to get out.

My head hit dirt, my line of vision staring up. I flinched, blinking rapidly against what I knew I was seeing, but my brain couldn't catch up, couldn't digest the pure horror of it.

A nest of tentacles made up the ceiling, *was the heart of the house,* its grey flesh looking black in the shadows, they moved slowly over one another, languidly, like a nest of snakes would. In between them, different features flickered. I caught snippets of men, women and children. An open mouth stretched wide in a scream here. Blood trickling down a forehead there. The writhing tentacles moved faster, as if agitated.

I desperately tried to shut my eyes but couldn't. I couldn't do anything but be dragged and look up. They all had one thing in common: they had no eyes; the sockets were empty and blackened dry blood trailed down their cheeks like tears. But in was their mouths, widened in permanent screams, their cheeks having hundreds of puncture wounds in them. I knew then in my heart, in my gut, that they were the victims on display.

There was a creak from behind us on the staircase and the light was flicked off, dousing the basement in darkness. My heart rammed against my ribs, cold surging through my veins.

The sound of metal on metal from my left, and sparks flew in the corner of the room, igniting Beau Boo's grinning face before fading into complete darkness again.

In a smooth rhythm, sparks continued to fly. I saw the glint of knives, the small table littered with them, with a twist of my gut he was sharpening them.

That's when I noticed the others.

Every time the sparks ignited, it casted a tiny glow. They stood silently watching, their unblinking stares wide.

I knew them all.

The rest of my nightmares stood down here, to watch my end. This was personal, and this place wanted me to know that.

The faceless trio, which would eventually become the main ghost character in my first novel, *Beyond the Blood.* Three serial killers, they held thick ropes, always wearing suit and tie, always strangled their victims. This was my dream version, and they never had faces, the skin just pale and taut, their heads bowed in reverence.

The room faded to black.

The orange glow flared, and my gaze moved to the glowing red eyes. There was never a body ever, except its black clawed hand that started to reach toward me, the disembodied voice growling, "Let me in, Theo . . . Just say yes . . ."

The room was swallowed in darkness again.

Mrs. Twisty had dragged me into the middle of the room, and was now lifting me with inhumane strength by my ankles. Something cold was wrapped around them, and she attached me to what I was assuming was chains, like cured meat left on the hook. My vision churned, dipping, swinging gently back and forth, my fingers brushing the dirt floor. Tears streamed, running up my forehead.

Beau Boo stopped the whetstone and we all descended into darkness. I could hear the heavy breathing of Mrs. Twisty standing directly behind me, and the light giggle of Beau Boo.

Someone took a step toward me in the darkness. Then another.

Another.

The footfalls were heavy footed, but it wasn't until the yellow shoes were right in front of me that I knew that pain was about to descend on me.

He didn't say anything before I felt the massive knife slide in between my ribs, squelching as he ripped it back out. Blood fell onto my face like drops of rain—my tears mixing with it as all I could force out of my scream was garbled moan.

Thrusting the blade in, white hot agony bloomed in my upper abdomen.

Again, in my upper chest, a strange dislocating crunching sound as he ripped the blade back out.

Twice now, in my belly.

My stomach churned against the burst of white hot pain, and freezing cold that was now settling into my body. My vision swam, the sickening feeling like I was going to pass out filling me. *Please, let me just black out. I'm not strong enough for this.*

I knew the lore of Beau Boo; I knew what he held onto the last blow. The killing strike. Seven wounds, hitting all the major organs before shoving that blade through my jaw, into my brain.

When I didn't pass out, I panicked. I tried to move my locked jaw, to wriggle my body—anything. I didn't want to die like this, strung up with my worst nightmares surrounding me. To have unhinged primal fear coursing through me, bleeding out. I didn't want to lose my life, what was still to come. Harold needed me—

"Let the others have their fun," Mrs. Twisty rasped from behind me. "Let her suffer a little while longer."

There was a shuffling of feet, back. I swallowed.

"Theo . . ." the demonic voice cooed at me, its red eyes suddenly right in front of my face. Not being able to track any of their movements was terrifying.

"Just say yes. All this pain goes away."

Red filled my vision as the presence leaned in closer. Far above us, the smell of smoke drifted.

It was like an electric current suddenly ran through me, adrenaline replacing my pain. *Smoke.*

My last reoccurring nightmare that I have as an adult. *Did they not know?* I thought.

Were they so focused on the ones that had creatures that could inflict pain, did they overlook the key one that could maybe inflict pain onto them?

In my mind, I thought about those details of that dream, willing it to this place, this moment. I tried to ignore the fact that the spirit in front of me was sliding its clawed nails between my lips.

I remembered how the house started to creak. In my dream, I'm always watching from the ceiling, watching myself sleep.

I tried to ignore that this thing was eagerly chanting now, as it opened its mouth, mimicking my own.

I remembered how fast it happened. The smoke billowing from under my door, filling the room and being able to hear the crackling of flames. The groaning of the house as the fire from downstairs grew.

I tried to ignore the black liquid now spurting out from this thing's mouth, into my own, flooding my senses with decay.

I remembered the heat in the dream, nothing like I had ever felt before. So hot your skin instantly recoils from it, like layers peel off just from being in the same vicinity. I remembered how I would beg for myself to wake up; the smoke in the room now so thick I could barley see myself sleeping, but I could hear myself choking—the cough more like a hacking. I remembered the shaking of the walls, the floorboards.

This thing was clasping my face now, like we were embraced in a kiss, the acrid liquid pouring down my esophagus, drowning me, slowly. I felt it through the chains first. In my dream, I was never able to save myself, never able to wake up.

Not this time.

It all happened so fast.

The smell of smoke was the first indicator, trailing from upstairs down to the basement.

There was a shuddering, then the ceiling completely caved in on itself.

I tried to cover my head forgetting I couldn't move, my breath leaving my chest as I slammed onto the dirt floor. Coursing pain, there was so much, every inch of my body was screaming. But above me I saw the curling, roaring flames, widening in my vision before darkness swallowed the room again with debris, the screams of my monsters rising with the wrenching screaming of the tentacles. It was the worst sound I've ever heard in my life—worse than nails on chalkboard. It was so high pitched I had the urge to cover my ears, but all I could do was listen while we all got buried alive.

Pain built, and built, and built, cracking me wide open, demanding that I either submit to it, and rise to a version of myself I didn't know would exist. I tasted ash now, mixed in with the blood, decay, and dust.

Something clicked—*I could move my toes! I could move.* Shoving drywall and floorboards off me, I screamed, every inch of the movement burning. My fingers were slick, illuminated stained red and black, but it didn't matter. Above me, bathed in the red glow of the flames from my nightmare, that was overlooked, would be the downfall of this goddamn place. I could hear the sizzling pop of the flesh, and the thing was exposed. All around it the faces were incinerated. Embers floated down around me, winking gold in the depth of the shadows. I stood amongst the carnage.

The thing hissed, its attention swinging to me. All of it exposed, it was massive, the parasitic essence of it so embedded, so massive, my breath hitched. Parts of it rained down all around me hitting the basement floor in burnt chunks, its blood raining down, crackling as it hit flames. The house gave another shudder, heaving.

A massive tentacle stalked toward me, rearing up.

I lurched to my left, grabbing the still burning debris, trying to block out the sound of my own flesh sizzling, the excruciating agony that followed. It was a piece of floorboard that had been burnt and snapped off at the end, a makeshift spear. It was perfect. I turned to face the true evil head on.

Gripping the piece of wood so hard, my knuckles were blanched white,

I had clarity in that second, as it lowered it massive maws, hundreds upon hundred of teeth flaring in front of me.

Nightmares didn't understand the power of experiencing love.

Of having dreams.

Of learning strength.

Of the deep bonds of friendship.

Of learning acceptance.

Channeling the power of that, I loosened a scream that tore from the corners of my soul.

Because I had witnessed what this place had done to so many people, for so many years.

I had seen, felt and heard the stories of its victims. And that was everything. They deserved peace. I felt the shift all around me in that second.

The makeshift spear was imbedded into the roof of the thing's teeth. A coolness washed to my left and when I looked over my shoulder, I saw a man smoking a cigarette. He sighed before putting out the butt on the creature, and the spot he touched made a crater in the monster's flesh, before coming to standing along side me, helping my hand keep steady.

Next, a teenager with a pixie cut appeared, flipping the creature, the house, the bird, before coming to my side too, her hands gently on top of mine, to help shove it deeper.

More people continued to appear; ghosts unleashed in the nightmare. Tears burned in my eyes.

Ghosts wasn't right, though, I realized as blood sprayed my face, as heat licked closer from every angle of the room, of the house. All around me, these people were dreams embodied, that this place had ripped away without second thought.

I love you, Harold, was the thought I had as night tinged the edges of my vision, the heat of enormous fire devouring all of us. I felt my shins

bubble, my arms, my face—

It lunged further.

So did I.

I slammed that spear so far down its throat, the energy radiating off me, and I could feel it, as tangible as rays from the sun. The pain was slowly bleeding away, my sense of gravity dipped. But I heard them too. All around me like a shield, I felt them still. They had been trapped, just like me. There was the consecutive sigh of,

Finally. Thank you.

They were free.

I smiled as 1729 Lakeshore Lane fell in on itself in a fiery rain.

I never gave much thought to the afterlife. I've never been religious in the traditional sense, but I always believed there was something. I had always hoped it would be peaceful. Maybe an autumn's day, curled up in my favorite cozy sweatpants, a favorite t shirt. My family there, laughing, smiling. Just all happy to be together, after quite some time a part.

I never imagined there would be *beeping*.

Or pain.

The beeping was rhythmic, a steady droning beat. I cracked an eye open, completely disoriented. The white bare walls of the room were clinical, just like the bed I was in. Beside the bed was not only the heart monitor and IV bag, but a tear-stained Mandy sitting in a watching me with puffy eyes.

"Why are you here?" I croaked, incredibly confused. Being dead, Mandy was obviously a hallucination. Did those happen . . . wherever this was? Also, why a hospital? Weird.

I closed my eyes.

Cracking them open again, Mandy now stood, tears streaming down her face in rivers.

She opened her mouth, closed it and then in a garbled squeak, walked out of the room.

What the hell? My eyes traced her quick exit across the bland room, and I blinked again, feeling with more clarity as each sensation that rolled through my body. I felt like I was floating, a haziness that had coated the world around me. Sharp inhales of my lungs moving was causing a domino effect of liquid fire that was racing across my skin. Every ounce of it. I tried to move the thin and scratchy sheet to look at my arm, but I couldn't move it. I closed my eyes again, trying to remember how exactly I had gotten here. My mind was cloudy, each thought like a wisp of smoke floating in and disappearing before I could get a hold on it.

I shut my eyes again.

I had died because I was in a . . . sleep study?

Nightmare.

No, that wasn't right. I had gone to the sleep study because I was having sleep paralysis, unrefreshing sleep. I was seeing her. They were there to help . . .

Living nightmares.

I crinkled my nose, the thoughts feeling like I was having a back and forth with myself.

A creak permeated the air. I snapped my eyes back open, the sliver of what I could see of the bustling hallway with doctors and nurses before the door closed.

"Hello there, hun." A nurse was walking toward me, her navy scrubs making a *swish swish swish* sound as she walked. Her eyes crinkled as she smiled, holding her clipboard and stopped at the end of my bed. Her blonde hair was swept up in a neat bun, as she looked at me, then back down to my chart that I knew was there, but I couldn't see.

"Can you tell me your name, age and date of birth, please?" she coaxed. She seemed kind, but I was still so confused about why I was here. Why they were here with me.

"Uh, it's Theo—Theo*dora* Anderson," I added. "I'm thirty-two, and November first, 2014."

I watched the nurse nod, her gaze softening. "And it's true you were at a sleep study tonight? Before the incident?"

The taste of smoke and dried blood flooded my mouth, I croaked, "What happened? My memories . . ." *Can't be right . . .* "are confusing me."

"Hun, you underwent some extreme trauma tonight. It's a normal reaction for the body to protect you, sometimes by blacking out what happened completely. The police are outside talking to your sleep tech at the moment, but I will defer them to get your statement. Healing is your priority right now."

My vision dipped. The sensation like the room was spinning made my stomach churn, and the beeping of my heart monitor pitched. This was really happening.

"What happened?" I croaked. The taste of ash so strong along my dry tongue now, my spittle was forming at the edges of my lips. I blinked, fighting against the flickering images flooding against whatever strong drug they were pumping into my body.

It had been Haden, but not. Nightmares were real. Kinsley sacrificed herself. Everyone's nightmares were trying to kill you.

"Your tech, Mandy, described to the emergency dispatch that there had been a glitch. From a storm."

I was different.

"They hooked you back up and she went on her break. A symptom of extreme apnea can be sleepwalking. Her co-worker never showed up to cover her break, she had said."

That house was breeding nightmares for so long. Destroying lives, likes Kinsley's.

"You were found on the side of the road, bleeding out, stabbed twenty-two times, as well as third degree burns along your arms and torso. Hun, you were assaulted. Mandy called the police, who found you."

The space between those words; I heard what this nurse wasn't saying. Mandy had saved my life. Through the haze in my mind, Kinsley's face flooded me. Her emerald eyes, her auburn hair, and freckles. It faded, except for her eyes which flared out to burning green orbs, the monster that she had been forced to become. That couldn't have been all a dream. Could it?

"Where . . ." I didn't know when my tears had started again but my throat blazed with the flooding emotion and pain. "Where was I found?"

"Outside of a long-abandoned house. The police are trying to figure out with the firemen how exactly the fire started. There is nothing left of it, dear."

"What house?" I exhaled, closing my eyes as the nurse said exactly what I knew she was going to say.

"That one on Lakeshore Lane. 1729, I believe was the address."

The tears slipped down faster along my cheeks, my stomach sinking.

It had never been a dream.

It was real. Every fighting moment that was coming back in terrifying flickers. The nightmares that I clawed through, Kinsley sacrificing herself. My own nightmares trying to kill me.

The nurse kept talking about recovery, and the slow process of it, how I was lucky to be alive. Her words faded to the background as piece by piece it all came back to me. She patted the top of my head, like I was a dog, probably assuming the gesture was comforting, assuming the tears were because I was scared, that I had been attacked.

I swallowed hard against the shock of it all.

The door creaked open, and my gaze snapped back to it, my body still. Mandy poked her head in, seeming sheepish. "Is it okay if I visit for a bit?"

The nurse smiled down at me. "Just for a little bit. I will be back in a couple of minutes. Miss Anderson needs her rest."

As Mandy walked across the room, I noticed she carried my overnight bag. I tried to smile but winced. The nurse left us in privacy, while Mandy gestured awkwardly. "I brought the rest of your things from the sleep clinic."

She sat down, and I swallowed against the dryness in my mouth and throat again. "Mandy, thank you."

I watched the sadness and fear wash over her features. "Theo, I'm so sorry. I don't know why Rachel didn't cover my break—she had gone home sick after I asked her, apparently. And I don't know how any of our alarms didn't go off, except the only thing I can think of is that Rachel left the door unlocked. It's just so fucking weird because I came back and the footage—where I monitor on my end . . . well . . ."

She brought out her smartphone, unlocking it before pulling up the small video. "You were out there for hours, and whoever did this to you, it could have been prevented. I feel so messed up."

The video was grainy, since Mandy had obviously gone back to film it to show me. Room number six was labelled at the bottom of each monitor screen—there was four of them, with different angles of my room, and one had my vitals running. I noticed the time stamp of three am. I watched as I lay there asleep on my back, the webbing of wires crossing over my body.

God, this is creepy, I thought, but I watched the footage, heard the steady rhythm of my breath, the thunder booming in the distance, the lightening washing the room's empty walls in bursts. My stomach clenched, my heart rate monitor climbing again. Mandy's gaze flicked to the sound and she went to press pause.

"No." I jerked my chin in my best attempt to shake my head, which sent pain careening down my spine. "Please just show me."

She let it play.

The time stamp was 3:29 now, when all the screens went black. I heard Mandy offscreen in the video swear, the creak and swivel of her chair as she pulled closer to the desk.

"After you were found and brought here, I went back to watch the videos to see what time . . . when it happened," she said to me softly.

I kept staring at the screen until—there—the time stamp had stopped at 3:29 AM. At first it looked like headlights from outside running along the ceiling churning the shadows. I looked more closely, and my heart dropped into my stomach. My skin prickled, cold running through my veins while a hot flush erupted in tandem.

In the video, the room seemed to get darker, growing along the walls, the door, the ceiling. But there was movement along the ceiling coming toward me. Its arms were as long as its body, with ease moved slowly, its movements reminding me of a spider. It didn't wear clothes, its body was onyx like the shadows that grew around it in the room.

The video flickered and it disappeared.

My vision tunnelled. I couldn't look away, even though I was scared shitless, even though I wanted it to stop.

The video flickered again. It was back, stretching its long arms toward me. Mandy's hand started to tremble.

In the video now, along the ceiling, its body was parallel to my own, slowly, impossibly. It let go of its grip so its body folded back and down.

Exposing its face for the first time.

It had no nose, massive eyes that had no irises, just its blown out pupils. Its blanched skin stretched against the fact it was grinning, so wide, so unnervingly, looking straight at the camera.

The video flickered again.

It disappeared.

My heart was pounding, the pulse was a drumming in my ears; all the blood felt like it had drained out from my body, leaving me dizzy and breathless.

Like static running across the screen, the video came back into focus, the time stamp still frozen at 3:29, as this demonic looking thing dropped from the ceiling—its head still craned back in almost a ninety degree angle, aimed at the camera.

It landed on me, hands outstretched—

The video flickered again, and the room was empty.

I was gone, the thing with it. My gaze dropped down to the time stamp which now read—

"Five AM? Two hours later?" I croaked.

Mandy didn't say anything, just paused the video and screen locked her phone. We sat in silence, my mind reeling. I took in Mandy's hollowed out look, her tear rimmed red eyes, the exhaustion permeating from every inch of her.

"Obviously I reported it as soon as I . . ."

"Knew I was gone," I whispered. The room felt so small in that moment, the walls aged and flaking, just as weary and hurt as the people it kept within them.

"That . . . that . . ." Mandy stuttered over the impossibility, the sheer terror of what was captured.

"I saw it too."

I saw a tear slip down Mandy's cheek, which she swiped at. "None of this makes sense. And you almost died." She hiccoughed.

"But I didn't, thanks to you."

A silence pulled between us. A heaviness was starting to flow through my body, I felt weighted. *Probably morphine or some shit like that,* I thought. I was so, incredibly tired.

"Sometimes there isn't an explanation. What happened, what you captured . . . Mandy, there is no way to explain it."

"Other than the supernatural."

"Yeah," I agreed. "Other than that."

I blinked slowly, the edges of the room softening. The door creaked open again, and the nurse quietly came in, nodding to Mandy, while her gaze read, *time to go.*

"Theo, get better," Mandy said.

I tried to smile, but my cheeks were numb, my lips not complying with what I was trying to do. I watched this young woman, who had saved my life, leave, something in the back of my drug hazed mind not sitting well with me.

"Okay hun, my favorite way to look at recoveries, is day at a time. With burns like these we will likely do something called occlusive dressings. And that's not touching on the stab wounds . . ."

Her voice trailed off. I caught *antibacterial ointments* and *prevent infection* but I stared at the door, trying to pinpoint why the scratch was building in my mind. That something was off.

It wasn't the sheer weight of the truth that I had travelled *elsewhere* to confront the darkest corner of Haden. No, I believed that with all my heart, my soul. But those types of secrets, the ones that made no sense, that had no proof other than the experience of it, especially when you start with supernatural, or ghosts, well sometimes those secrets remained tucked close to your heart your entire life.

No, it wasn't that.

Nice Nurse—the nickname I had dubbed her in my mind now—was

checking my IV fluids and vitals, I watched her mouth move, the words she was saying not making sense now. The familiar sensation of being tugged under, away and into a space of sleep radiated through me. I blinked again, closing my eyes for just one second . . .

I blinked.

I was alone.

I must have fallen asleep. A curtain was drawn around my bed for privacy, the blue linen with HHS stamped all over it in faded black ink. The room was so dark, and the lights in the room were dimmed from their usual fluorescent. My body didn't feel like mine, just a pulsing mound of flesh with every pump of my heart was pain. I could still see the door that led to the hallway to the right, and I tried to moan, to get the attention of Nice Nurse, but nothing came out.

Button. There had to be a button to call for help. The pain was blistering, the next wave hit and a tear slid down my cheek. It had to be within reach, but I couldn't see anything. I needed to tell someone to call James, to arrange care for Harold until I'm out of here. But first I needed relief, I needed not to feel *this.*

A slow creak permeated the air, and I looked back up toward the door.

It was open, but no one was there.

What the hell?

On the side table, Nice Nurse had plugged my phone in, and the overnight bag Mandy had brought was beside the bed. I tried leaning forward, my breath hooked in my chest as the entire side of my back lanced with agony. But there along the side of the bed, was a control with a red button. I just needed to be able to reach a little bit forward.

Exhaling, I braced for the next wave of pain but—

I froze. On the other side of the curtain, a dark shadow in the shape of a someone standing was outlined.

"He-hello?"

Maybe the nurse did come in and I didn't catch it.

"I need some more pain meds, when you have a second," I croaked to the figure, but they didn't move. Complete silence stretched in the room, in the hospital, and the hairs on the back of my neck pricked. The hospital wasn't a quiet place, even in the middle of the night. There was no voices of nurses and doctors, no beeping of another heart monitor on the other side of the drawn curtain indicating someone else had filled the bed.

Just a deep expanse of complete and utter silence.

The light on my phone bloomed. I got a glimpse of text messages notifications. The light dimmed and I left it be, just starting at the outline on the other side of the curtain.

Slowly, the shadow figure moved, to walk around the perimeter, to the opening at my bed. I watched, still frozen, as they reached their long arm up, hands splayed to grab the curtain back—

It came to me then, what was bugging me about Mandy. I didn't see her nightmare attached to her.

I expected someone to say *boo*, to jump out from behind the room divider. But no one came into view.

The shadow figure had disappeared.

Since waking up in the hospital, I hadn't seen *anyone's* nightmare. Slowly, I laid back down, my heart jack hammering from the fear, from the fact that I have never, not once in my life, stopped *seeing*. My gift was as much part of me as my eye color, and even though I didn't ever wish to be able to see such terrifying things, it was part of me. Now in the absence of it, my breath hitched, fear settling in deeper. The overwhelming feeling that something, or someone was here with me didn't leave.

My thoughts went back to that fucking video. The demonic looking presence, that I didn't see in the nightmare realm, that I didn't kill, but had followed me in.

What if it had followed me back out?

Another tear slipped from the corner of my eye. Slowly, ignoring the pain that shot down from the base of my skull, down my spine, I tilted my head back, looking up at the ceiling.

The whites of its eyes and blown-out black pupils were locked on me. It clutched to the ceiling, its long limbs black and churning with shadows. It moved like a spider, exactly how it did in the video. The grin stretched even wider, lowering its face down, down toward mine. I was hyperventilating, the scream inside me building. The last thing I took in was how its eyes went completely milky opaque, its jaw yawning open like it was screaming down at me, except the bottom of its jaw was now almost the length of its body, and within its mouth was an expanse of nothingness.

A void.

Then it let go, taking me with it.

Acknowledgements

Hey, dear reader. Mal here. First off, I want to take the time to thank you for reading my short story collection. This project started to take shape in a creative writing class I took, and at first, I didn't know the direction I wanted to take with it, or if it would be anything I would publish. "The Exchange" was the first story to be penned, and it was tucked away in my file folder for a long time. But I'm going to be honest with you here. It's just us. I was scared to write the rest.

As writers, I think the projects that scare us most are the ones that should be shared. I was once given the advice to write what you know, and I know nothing better than the monsters I live with daily: chronic Lyme disease, fibromyalgia, chronic fatigue, and more recently, sleeping disorders such as sleep apnea and sleep paralysis.

But here's the thing. At first, I didn't want to delve into the fact that a simple tick bite completely derailed my life. I didn't want to take my anger, fear, and grief and look at it in the face fully. For six years, I have been fighting between doctors and specialists. For six years, I have been taking comments from strangers like "But you don't look sick," "Have you tried this diet?" "Have you tried losing weight?" The medical gaslighting, having to continue to fight to be heard, to document strange symptoms or new symptoms. A favorite line: "but your bloodwork is negative, so it can't be anything."

Or my personal favorite: "Lyme disease doesn't exist."

For six years, I took the broken pieces of my life and fought for them. I lost a lot of friends who I thought were true friends. I had to stop working full time at a career I really loved. My life didn't look like the one I had or wanted. I will live with these illnesses and disabilities for the rest of my life, and the best I can hope for is control over my symptoms. But here's the thing I really want to emphasize—what some doctors and even people don't realize. There is no cure. I will never have a total pain free day—I don't even remember what that feels like.

I knew I was ready to pen this collection when I wanted a space for my stories. Yes, they are fiction, but they are also my truth—my heart laid bare. A lot of what Kinsley says about fibromyalgia is what I have thought, or even what people have said to me. "Below Lakeshore Lane" and "Between the Shadows" hold metaphors what it feels like living with chronic illness. This unsuspecting monster that the house is, how it devours. I wanted to use what voice I do have to make people more aware of these conditions. "The Bite" holds every ounce of the one thing that terrifies me in this life: ticks. And "The Study"—fun fact—when I was getting my sleep apnea diagnoses and was getting set up with three hundred wires, the building had once been a girls' orphanage run by nuns. That story was born that night, and it helped distract me from how shitty I felt, how sleep deprived I was, and the sleep paralysis that I was experiencing. That building has now been sold, and the clinic relocated. So take of that what you will.

Knowledge is power. Maybe together we can change the future to be kinder. Maybe within society there will be more space for the chronically ill, more treatment options.

I have control through my stories. And I know there are millions of people who live chronically ill, just like me. Millions of people who have to fight and advocate for help.

And so, above anything else, I hope you have not only enjoyed the horror of the stories, but I hope they have made you think. I hope that maybe you have explored and learned more about different chronic illnesses and what they can look like and how they can manifest in a person.

Above all, I *hope*.

For the last six years, the hardest years of my life, there has also been an abundance of good that I need to touch on.

Matt. My fucking rock who weathered the storm with me, who walked into the scariest scenarios beside me with love and understanding, and the drive to learn what our new day to day would look like. Who drove me to every doctor appointment through COVID, and continues to do so (which was every two weeks for a year back in 2019 and 2020). Who helped me out of bed when I couldn't walk, who would help me shower, who would do anything that might bring me a smile when my life was falling apart around me—who held everything down while we fought for diagnoses. Who weathered a lot of bad days, who held me when words couldn't describe what we went through. Who never made me feel alone. *I love you* doesn't even begin to describe, but I don't know how I was so lucky to find my soulmate in this life, but I don't take it for granted.

My friends who have stayed in my life—you know who you are—and always have kindness and understanding in your hearts, I love you all. My tribe. I am so happy to have you all in my life.

To Link, Lenny, Luna, Lego, Lily, and Ivy—I know you can't read this, but you are there for me every day and bring endless joy into my life. And to Birdie, my weekday furkid, I love you, boo.

To my wonderful editors, Em, Denise, Brenna, Gabby, thank you for being amazing and pushing me to grow as a writer. Who were just as excited as I was when I said I was writing horror. To Tony, for believing in this book as much as I do, and for taking a chance on me. Thank you.

Lastly to you, reader. Without you, what are books but unopened, undiscovered dreams? Thank you for delving into mine.

Author Bio:

Mallory McCartney currently lives in Sarnia, Ontario with her husband, their dachshunds Link, and Leonard and their sphynx cats Luna, Legolas, Ivy and Lily. When she isn't working on her next novel or reading, she can be found day dreaming about fantasy worlds or bingeing her favorite horror movies.